Praise for Jeff Erno

SECOND CHANCES

"Jeff Erno is a wonderful writer .... What I find so interesting about his writing is that he takes risks and goes where some authors will not venture and in doing so he broadens the audience for his books. To me, for that alone, he should receive five stars on whatever he writes. He has written about gay romance, inter-generational relationships, mild S&M and now he tackles science fiction. I think that it is one thing to be diverse but it is something else all together to be diverse and to write with style .... There are several motifs here—romance, passion, emotions, life and death .... If you have not yet taken a chance on Erno, now is the perfect time to start."

—Amos Lassen

I0601418

TRUST ME

"Can I just say, 'Wow!' TRUST ME is one of those books that popped up on my radar, refused to leave and delivered an unexpected mind-blowing reading experience. I never thought I would be so drawn into the lives of Shawn and Bobby but right off the bat, Jeff Erno managed to give these two boys a compelling voice. It's a classic trope of 'good boy–bad boy,' but it never fails to keep me enamored .... The author takes the reader through the years where certain events occur in both Shawn and Bobby's life that would affect the young men they would become in the present storyline. Layer upon layer the author brought to life two very distinct personalities, who became fully fleshed-out characters ...."

—Leontine's Book Realm

PUPPY LOVE

5 Stars: "I would still strongly recommend this story to others and can't wait until the sequel comes out."

—Rainbow Reviews

PUPPY LOVE 2: BUILDING A FAMILY

"The writing is smooth, moving from one crisis to another with wicked fluidity. The relationship dynamic between Petey and Matt is super sexy and sweet, the urgency of their love making lava hot .... The supporting characters create a nice well rounded story that fuels the fire and makes our heroes shine .... The final pages to this book are so explosive and filled with angst, it was just brilliant. I could go on forever about how awesome this book is, I could go on about how hot and steamy the sex is (take my word, it's effing hot). I could tell you that Petey and Matt are bloody awesome, but it's up to you to discover this for yourself .... Jeff has done a splendid job on this book and I will forever be a big fan of Matt and his pup. I am very excited for PUPPY LOVE 3 and I just know it's gonna be awesome. One of my favorite gay series."

—Three Dollar Bill Reviews

DUMB JOCK

"If someone were to tell me I had to spend three months on a deserted island and I could have ten books with me, Jeff Erno's DUMB JOCK would be one of those books. Mr. Erno tells this story of two high school boys who fall in love in such a way that the characters almost become real."

—Rainbow Reviews

THE LANDLORD

"There was a nice balance of drama, humor and sex, alongside a subject matter that was sometimes difficult to swallow, but showed bravery on the part of the author. I liked that the characters didn't always take the easy route, that they had their flaws, and yet underneath they were decent men trying to make the best out of unexpected, difficult and yet also wonderful change in their lives. I would recommend THE LANDLORD with a grade of 'Very Good.'"

—Well Read Books

BULLIED

"I have nothing but praise for this book. It's heartfelt, saddening, and hopeful. It made me want to make a difference in the world, or at least my part of it. It made me want to support my friends instead of teasing and mocking, which comes so easily. True, its messages read like an after-school special (but with better characters, plot, dialogue, and acting), but it's not trying to hide that. I'd recommend this to most everyone."

—Between the Covers Book Reviews

"These stories may be fiction, but they felt quite real to me. They made me think, broke my heart, and reminded me that while the teenaged years may be a carefree time for some young people, this time can spell darkness and torment for others. Hopefully, collections such as BULLIED can help raise public awareness of this issue, because we must first acknowledge that the problem exists before we can addresses the terrible harm that it does. Excellent job, Mr. Erno."

—Book Wenches

SECOND CHANCES

SECOND CHANCES

Jeff Erno

CAMEL
PRESS
Seattle, WA

CAMEL
PRESS

Camel Press
PO Box 70515
Seattle, WA 98127

For more information go to: www.Camelpress.com
www.jefferno.com

Cover design by Tuesday Dube and Sabrina Sun

Second Chances
Copyright © 2012 by Jeff Erno

ISBN: 978-1-60381-876-6 (Trade Paper)
ISBN: 978-1-60381-877-3 (eBook)

Library of Congress Control Number:
2011943764

10 9 8 7 6 5 4 3 2 1

Printed in the United States of America

Prologue

"It's breathtaking," the doctor said.

"Rubbish," The artist shook his head in disgust as he stared at the canvas before him. "It's utterly serene. Boring!"

"Jacob, I have to disagree with you. This is perhaps the most magnificent scenic piece you've ever created. I think it is by far your best work."

Jacob sighed, turning quickly away. "There's more to life than outward appearance or physical beauty. If there is no activity—no *action*—it's pointless. When I look at this scene all I see is serenity, but nothing is happening! There is no purpose."

The doctor placed his hand on his lover's shoulder, gently directing him so that Jacob turned once again to face the painting. "It's nature," he whispered. "It's growth. It's the dawning of a new day—the celebration of new life on a beautiful spring morning. How can you say there is no activity?"

"I don't know." Jacob frowned. "Forgive me, but when I look at this painting, all I see is regret. It reminds me—"

"It reminds you of *him*."

"I'm sorry, Timothy," Jacob confessed. "He was all about that sort of thing. He was all about appearances. He was all about how things looked on the outside. He was all about living his life in a way that appealed to others, a way that met with their approval ..."

"And he was utterly boring, just like the painting?"

Jacob again stared at the canvas sadly, nodding.

"But you loved him so much," Timothy sighed.

"I have no regrets," Jacob said honestly. "I have lived a wonderful, fulfilling life." He took his lover's hand in his own and gently squeezed. "And yes, I did love him. I loved him with all my heart, but Harold is my past. He made his choice and he must live with the consequences."

"Baby, your life isn't over," the doctor said. "You speak as if you have a death sentence."

"Timothy, I'm dying."

"No," Timothy said in his most reassuring voice. "I promise you, I'm not going to let that happen! I'm going to find a cure. I'm going to give you a second chance."

"Shh," Jacob said, turning to face his lover. "Promise me to just enjoy the time we have left together, Timothy. I don't want any false hope."

"Jacob!"

"Promise me … please!"

Reluctantly, the doctor nodded. "I promise you, Jacob Klein, I will cherish every moment we have together, and we both will make the most of every single moment."

"I love you," Jacob whispered. "When I thought my life was over, it was you who gave me a second chance. I don't know how I'll ever repay you."

Tears filled the doctor's eyes as he embraced his dying lover. "I love you, too, Jacob, and I'll never stop trying to save you. I really will give you a second chance … if you'll let me."

One

The old man stared out the window and allowed a silent tear to trickle down his cheek. He was overwhelmed by a wave of emotion as he contemplated the years that had escaped him. He knew the end was near. He knew every time he reached for the oxygen mask. He knew every time he attempted to hoist his frail body up out of the leather recliner. He knew when he was overcome by one of the coughing spells that nearly ripped his feeble frame in two. His body was used up, and his time had nearly expired.

Harold Wainwright had not at first accepted the diagnosis. At seventy-eight he was a fairly healthy man. He'd always taken for granted the best healthcare that money could buy. After all, he had for years been the CEO of the world's largest health insurance provider. He had also lived his life prudently. He'd made wise decisions in terms of his health, never smoking or drinking excessively. For the past thirty-plus years, he'd followed a fairly strict low-carb diet and exercised daily.

But he'd ultimately learned a harsh and unforgiving reality about cancer. It was no respecter of persons. His wealth had not protected him from the disease, and his connections had not delivered the salvation that he so desperately sought. He was rapidly drowning, and sadly there was no life raft.

It was a lonely way to die, there in that mansion by himself. Sure he had his staff. He had an around-the-clock nursing team. He had a chauffeur and a chef and a slew of housekeepers. He even had a gardener and a maintenance crew. But there was no one special in Harold's life. He had no spouse or partner … no one to love and to be loved by in return. When he looked into the eyes of most of his employees, all he saw was pity. Most of them probably felt sorry for him, and perhaps they also felt sorry for themselves, wondering what they would do for employment after he was gone. But he knew that none truly loved him.

Why should they love him? He'd never given them any reason to feel any affection for him whatsoever. In Harold's youth, he'd prided himself on being a strict and authoritative boss. He'd always been demanding, and he'd never hesitated to fire and replace the employees who had not performed according to his expectations. Harold was never one to believe in second chances. If someone was going to screw up one time, they'd do it again. He had very little sympathy for those who made poor decisions.

This was why it had never particularly bothered Harold when he observed the disparity between the rich and the poor. He knew that accumulating wealth was all about making the right decisions. People lived in poverty because they were unmotivated. They chose not to educate themselves. They chose not to jump through the necessary hoops or to take the steps needed to climb the ladder of success. They were lulled by their own sense of apathy into accepting mediocrity.

Harold Wainwright had decided at a very young age that he would never be one of these people. It was true that his parents had paid for his education, but he was the one who'd done all the hard work. He graduated at the top of his class. He'd gone right on to complete his post graduate work and earn his MBA. With his business degree he'd landed a six figure job, and this was back in 1950's. Within a decade, he was a vice president of the company.

He knew all about the politics of succeeding at a corporate level. It was all about impressing the right people. It was far more about who you knew than what you knew. Sentimentality and sensitivity were merely barriers. He'd never allowed these obstacles to become his own personal hurdles. There'd been times when he had to climb over those who stood in his way, and he honestly had not felt any regret in doing so. In fact, as he sipped his scotch and puffed his fat Cuban cigars, he used to brag, "I never worry about going around the people who get in my way. I simply charge straight ahead and go right *through* them."

Harold Wainwright had made his company millions of dollars by revising the policies concerning pre-existing medical conditions. By delving deeply enough into the histories of each client's medical files, you could almost always find a condition that would justify exclusion. His favorite phrase had become "failure to disclose," and it was this excuse that his company had used to cut off the insurance benefits of thousands who were ill, thus saving the company billions of dollars in claims over the years. These savings had led to enormous bonuses and promotions for Harold, and by the time he was fifty, he had become the CEO of the company.

There was a time, albeit just a brief interlude, when Harold had shared his life with someone special. Well, it was not exactly that he'd "shared" his life, but he had momentarily allowed this other person into his personal world. His name had been Jacob, and Harold had met him one night at a pool party. It had been one of those discreet gatherings hosted by a friend of a friend. Such events were all rather hush-hush back in those days, and there never were any females in attendance. For the most part, they were dinner parties sponsored by affluent middle-aged homosexual men. Young attractive guys such as Jacob were invited mainly as eye candy.

Harold had been in his thirties at the time, already very successful, and the initial connection he'd felt with Jacob had been powerful. Certainly the twenty-three-year-old college student was physically attractive, but it was more than that. He had other qualities that appealed to Harold. Jacob was bright and ambitious. Harold took him home that night, and six months later, the boy still had not left. If he'd been honest, Harold would have admitted that he loved Jacob. He loved the way the young man made him laugh. He loved his sincerity and his zest for life. He loved the way Jacob did things spontaneously and impulsively. He loved the thick dark eyelashes and dark brown eyes of his young lover.

But eventually Harold ended it. He finally had to ask Jacob to leave. The relationship was just too risky for his career. It was too complicated. Nobody in Harold's circle of corporate friends would ever understand what he had with Jacob. Nobody would accept it, and he knew that if he did not free himself of this extra baggage, he'd never get that promotion he'd been gunning for.

Jacob hadn't seemed angry that day. In fact, he didn't even seem surprised. He'd looked upon Harold sympathetically. "I love you, Harold," he'd said calmly, "and I know you love me, too. But you love your career more." Then he left, and that was that.

Harold never heard another word from Jacob. He never ran into him at any social functions. He never received any phone calls or letters. He came upon Jacob's obituary one day in mid 90's as he was reading the morning paper. The photo was of the same Jacob whom Harold had known and loved, only he was older in the picture, in his fifties. Reading between the lines, Harold realized that Jacob had died from AIDS complications. He'd become a successful painter, with his own studio. Harold didn't attend the funeral, nor did he send flowers, but he did pay a visit to the studio. He bought the most expensive of Jacob's originals and had it hung in his sitting room. It was an outdoor scene, very picturesque.

Harold looked up at the painting as he sat there alone in his leather recliner. He thought about how things could have been better had he made different choices in his own life. The strict standard by which he'd judged others for so long was now a bitter pill to swallow as he judged himself. If he'd remained with Jacob, perhaps they'd have grown old together. Jacob and he might have remained monogamous. Harold might have been bypassed for his promotion, but at least he wouldn't have grown old alone.

What good was all the money? Sure, he'd been able to buy all the luxuries he'd ever wanted. He had Porches and Jaguars and even a Lamborghini. He'd traveled the world. He'd rubbed elbows with famous celebrities and politicians. He owned summer homes in three states and property throughout Europe. But as he looked back on his life, all he felt was regret. What had been the point? He had money and fame and status, yet he was lonely. And now here he was in his darkest hour, at the end of his long life ... utterly alone.

All of Harold's family had passed on before him. He'd had an older brother and a sister two years younger. They both were gone already. His parents had died nearly two decades prior. There were cousins and nephews and nieces, all of whom he expected would soon be fighting over the inheritance he would leave behind. He had a will, of course, but he knew damned well it was sure to be contested. They were all vultures, every last one of them.

As he sat there staring up at the painting, a tear trickled down his cheek. He sighed, and prayed it all would just be over soon. Perhaps the disease was really a blessing. Maybe it was finally time to cash in his chips. He turned to look at the door when he heard a faint knock. Quickly he brushed the tear from his face and called out in a gruff voice, "Yeah! Come on in!"

"Mr. Wainwright, sir ... I'm sorry to disturb you." It was his housekeeper Ellen. "But there is a gentlemen asking to speak with you—a Doctor Timothy Drayton."

"He from the service?" Harold asked, referring to the homecare service that usually sent nurses and aides.

"No sir," she answered. "He says he's here from

Switzerland, and that he has important news for you about a cure ... for your cancer."

Wainwright laughed. "Ellen, I've been to every top specialist in the fuckin' world, and there is no cure. Tell him to get lost."

"But sir ... forgive me. He said you would say that. He wanted me to tell you that he knew Jacob. I don't know what—"

Harold straightened himself in his chair. "He knew Jacob?"

"That's what he said, sir."

"Very well, send him in."

A few minutes later a thin, middle-aged man carrying a briefcase entered the room. "Mr. Wainwright?" he asked.

"How did you know Jacob?" the old man responded.

The doctor cleared his throat and looked at the elderly gentleman, apparently waiting for an invitation to be seated. Realizing that his host was not planning to be so gracious, he gingerly placed his briefcase on the floor at his feet and smiled. He rubbed his hands together nervously. "Jacob Klein was one of the original participants in the research project I'm here to discuss with you, sir."

"Which is—?"

"Which is what we have come to refer to as 'The Rebirthing Project,' " he said. "May I sit down?"

Wainwright ignored his question. "Jacob was involved in some sort of scientific research project?" he asked.

The doctor scooped up his briefcase and took two steps over to seat himself in a chair opposite Harold's. "Yes sir. Jacob had volunteered to be a research test subject."

"Jacob is dead," Harold replied, "so I guess your project didn't work. And why is it called a 'rebirthing project'? I thought you told my housekeeper it was a cure for cancer ..."

"Mr. Wainwright, I have information in this briefcase that will answer all of your questions. Mr. Klein signed onto the project in the early eighties shortly after he'd been diagnosed with Acquired Immune Deficiency Syndrome. Unfortunately we were unable to perfect the procedure in time to save him. You were listed by Mr. Klein as a potential future candidate for the procedure … Apparently Klein thought you would be interested—"

"I hadn't talked to Jacob in over twenty years … before he died. I find it hard to believe he'd list me … or even remember me."

"Perhaps when you learn about the specifics of the project, you will understand his potential motive, sir," the doctor offered.

"So why don't you tell me, and quit beating around the bush?"

Drayton nodded, and again nervously wrung his hands. He sighed, and then took a deep breath. "During the AIDS pandemic of the '80's, a group of scientists from around the world converged to brainstorm on possible cures for the disease. At the time, the task seemed daunting, to say the least. There was little hope of a vaccine, and we were frustrated by the magnitude of the challenge. So many brilliant minds were being lost … so much talent. We felt so helpless—

"Mr. Klein was initially contacted by our organization because of his artistic talent. We were motivated to recruit him and others like him. People who were tremendously gifted yet were falling victim to this horrible disease.

"The idea behind the Rebirthing Project was to find a method of preserving the consciousness of gifted or brilliant individuals such as Jacob Klein. Even if we could not save their bodies, we hoped to preserve their minds."

Harold laughed. "This is crazy!"

"I assure you, sir, this is very serious. In 1982 we developed a computer chip. Please, allow me to show you …" He hoisted his briefcase onto his lap and snapped it open.

"This chip, when implanted in the cerebral cortex, will store the entirety of an individual's conscious memories ... conscious *and* subconscious, actually. At the time of Mr. Klein's death, however, we had not yet developed the technology to transfer the data from the computer chip into the brain of a donor."

"And I suppose you have that technology now," Harold scoffed.

"Sir, I realize how difficult this must be to believe. Truly, I do ... but I assure you that I'm being one hundred percent serious. We do now have the technology, and we have used it successfully ... with primates."

"But not humans?"

"Chimpanzees," Drayton said.

Harold laughed. "And you expect me to believe that you transferred the mind of one chimp—"

"The consciousness ..."

"The *consciousness* of one chimp into the brain of another? How would you even substantiate this? How could you prove it?"

"Mr. Wainwright, I have a DVD documentary in my briefcase that chronicles our research. We started by training a chimpanzee from birth. Her name was Charlee. She was one of the most advanced primates in terms of language skills, sign language, and manual dexterity. We then successfully transferred her consciousness into that of a donor chimp. This other chimp was taken from the wild and had no communication skills whatsoever. You will see on the video that the evidence is indisputable. Charlee is alive today—in a different body."

The smirk on Harold's face slowly began to fade as he considered the words of the doctor sitting before him. What he offered was pure lunacy, and Harold knew this. It was something out of a science fiction movie, but the thought of it somehow being possible was astounding, almost beyond comprehension.

"Well, let me humor you for a moment," Wainwright said. "Suppose you did have a subject such as myself. And suppose I agreed to this procedure ... then what? How would you find a donor? Who would just give up their body for someone else?"

"Donor subjects are young victims of horrific tragedies," Drayton said. "They are people who have suffered brain injuries that have rendered them ... well, brain-dead. They are vegetables."

Wainwright frowned. "And how is it that by simply transferring another person's memories into their already damaged brain, they suddenly can function again?"

Drayton smiled. "Sir, you ask very perceptive questions, for this very issue was our biggest challenge. In the early test cases, it appeared that what you're describing is precisely what occurred. We transferred consciousness from one brain to the other, but the subject was unable to regain consciousness in their donor body."

"And I suppose you've now solved this problem as well?"

"Not exactly, sir," Drayton admitted. "We have to be very selective of our donors. The injury or condition that has rendered them unconscious must be something that can either be physiologically corrected or it must be a condition where the restoration of consciousness will automatically result in restored motor skills, speech, etc."

"I don't follow," Harold said flatly.

"If the victim has suffered a debilitating stroke, for example, they would not be a receptive donor. Restoring consciousness would merely be placing a functioning brain into a non-functioning body. If the donor had suffered a closed-head injury, however, they might well be a candidate for the procedure.

"The way it works is, we implant a similar chip into the donor brain. When the transfer takes place, the entirety of the subject's identity is transferred. What I mean is that if you were to become our subject, your memories, motor skills, speech, thinking patterns, tastes, preferences—literally everything about you—would be transferred. When you awakened in your new body, it would be precisely that. A new body. Mentally you would be the same individual that you have always been, but you would simply have a new body."

"And what about *this* body?" Harold asked.

"It would be vacant. It would be vegetative in the same manner that the donor body had been prior to the transfer. After a period of time, we would euthanize your former body—if it had not already expired of natural causes."

"You still haven't explained why Jacob suggested you contact me," Harold observed.

The doctor smiled sheepishly and looked the old man in the eye. "Sir, don't you see? Mr. Klein wanted to begin a new life with you. He apparently had tremendous affection for you, and he wanted to give you a second chance. He wanted to give your relationship with him a second chance."

As if a light bulb had been switched on in his mind, Harold suddenly understood. Jacob had been in love with him for all those years. He suspected that Jacob also realized that the feeling was mutual. He must have known that Harold had gone all that time carrying the burden of regret for his decisions, and he wanted a second chance.

"But it's too late for that," Harold said, suddenly becoming misty-eyed. "It didn't work … Jacob died anyway, so why are you here?"

"With all due respect, Mr. Wainwright, I have my own motivation for recruiting you to the project. We are in desperate need of funding."

"You want my money. Ah, of course."

"We *need* funding in order to continue, and you're one of the wealthiest men alive. Forgive me for pointing this out, but soon you will be gone. Your money will be of no use to you at that point."

Harold began to laugh. "So this is your last-ditch attempt to scam a billionaire out of a big chunk of cash? You were very convincing. I almost bought it."

"Sir, all I'm asking is that you think about it. Please watch the videos, and if you decide that you may be interested, simply call the number on my card." He placed a business card on the stand beside him. "In all honesty, Mr. Wainwright, you have nothing to lose. If I am conning you and the result is that I bilk you out of a bunch of money, you will be no worse off. You're going to lose all of your money when you die anyway."

Harold raised his eyebrows at the doctor's frank statement. "But you'd still be a hell of a lot richer, and I'd be dead, so I'd never be able to expose you."

"As I've said, sir, I am legitimate, and so is the Rebirthing Project. We are not running a scam, and we are not trying to bilk you out of your money. We would ask you to pay an initial signing fee of one million dollars immediately. After the transfer of your consciousness has been completed—after you're in your new body—you would complete the payment."

"How?" Harold asked.

"Prior to the death of your current body, you would deposit the money in a Swiss bank account and memorize the access code. You will then be asked for that code after your consciousness has been transferred into your new body. If you elect to provide it, we will euthanize your former body and you will begin your new life. If you elect not to complete the transfer of funds, we would reverse everything and transfer your consciousness back into your dying body."

"How much money are you talking about?"

"Three hundred million U.S. dollars."

Two

"**M**om, I've gotta go! I'm gonna be late for practice." The young man was standing by the kitchen door, duffel bag in hand. He wore a green and white track suit with running shoes and sported a crisply shaven military-style haircut. He was blond, blue eyed, seventeen-year-old Jesse Warren.

"Honey, give me just a couple minutes, okay?" his mom called from the dining room. "I've got to get this email sent …"

Jesse sighed and placed the duffel bag down on the floor. He stepped over to the archway that separated the kitchen and dining room. "It's okay, Mom," he said. "I'll just go. It's only two miles. I can get there faster by running than with the car anyway."

"Jesse, I said I'd take you. I'm almost done here."

He stepped over to his mom and leaned in to give her a quick kiss goodbye, laughing as he did so. "Don't worry about it. I'm gonna head out. I'll see ya in about three hours."

"I'm sorry, honey," she said. "Be careful, and have a good practice."

Jesse dashed out the front door and immediately broke into a steady paced run. His long, muscular legs made it seem effortless to him, and truthfully it was. He could sprint the entire two miles without being so much as winded. As he bounded toward the sidewalk he glanced up and saw his neighbor, Phillip Covington. He nodded and quickly waved at his dark-haired classmate and best friend.

Jesse had known Phillip all his life. They'd been close since the second grade, and it pained Jesse to realize that this friendship would in all likelihood be cut short. Two years ago,

Phillip had been diagnosed with leukemia, and his prognosis wasn't promising. After beginning radiation treatments, he'd lost all his hair and grown rail thin. Jesse wondered if he would even make it through that horrible time, but amazingly Phillip bounced back. The cancer had gone into remission, and Phillip started looking a lot better—like his old self again. He re-grew his hair and beefed up a bit. Jesse decided he'd call Phillip after practice. Maybe they could spend time together over the weekend like they used to do.

In another week Jesse would turn eighteen, and he couldn't wait. Being eighteen wouldn't change his life all that much, but being an adult would. He'd be old enough to buy lottery tickets and cigarettes—not that he'd ever dream of smoking. And of course, he'd be old enough to vote. Then, within the next two months, he'd be graduating. He could hardly believe it. His high school years were really almost over.

He was thinking of these things as he rounded the corner, only a block from the school's track field. He quickly glanced both ways at the intersection, not even bothering to slow down. Seeing that it was clear, he quickened his pace. Just as he strode out into the intersection, seemingly out of nowhere, a pickup truck appeared in his field of vision. All he saw was the front grill as it crashed into him.

The sound of squealing tires was the last thing Jesse heard as his body was hurled thirty feet into the air. The duffel bag flew from his grasp as he sailed helplessly across the intersection. The back of his head slammed violently against a cement curb as he landed, instantly engulfing him in darkness. Jesse Warren's future was suddenly non-existent. He was brain dead.

****

Phillip's heart skipped a beat when he glanced up to see his friend Jesse across the street. He couldn't believe how incredibly hot he looked in his track gear. Phillip had harbored a secret crush on his "best friend" for many years, and the more time he spent with him, the deeper his feelings grew. Sometimes just seeing him like this took Phillip's breath away.

There was no one in the world that Phillip idolized more than Jesse. In a way, it was like Jesse was his hero. He was so confident and intelligent. He was a track star at school and also a straight-A student. He had the looks, the popularity, and the personality to make him any girl's (or gay guy's) dream date. Plus, Jesse was just so incredibly nice.

When Phillip was sick and undergoing cancer treatments, he'd felt so awkward about losing all his hair. He'd never left the house without a cap or hat of some kind. That was, until his best friend showed up sporting a clean-shaven, cue-ball head. Phillip started laughing hysterically as he embraced his best bud. "I can't believe you did it!" he exclaimed as he threw his b-cap into the corner.

"Only the coolest guys are bald," Jesse bragged. And now, nearly a year later, Jesse still kept his hair cut short. It no longer was completely shaved off, but the style was a crew cut. Phillip had always thought Jesse's wavy blond hair was incredibly sexy, but now that he'd seen the butch look on him, he didn't miss the longer hair. Jesse was just scorching hot, as far as Phillip was concerned, especially with the macho hair style.

Phillip wanted so badly to confide in Jesse and tell him about his true feelings. There were times when he wondered if Jesse might feel the same way about him. Phillip remembered when they were fifteen and had fooled around a bit. Really it had been kind of innocent. Jesse had gotten a hold of a porn magazine from somewhere and they jacked off together. Phillip wanted more than anything to touch his friend, but he hadn't had the nerve to do so. The way Jesse had looked over at him and smiled when it was over seemed to indicate that it was more than just boys being boys.

But that had been an isolated incident. Afterwards, the two had never discussed their sexual indiscretion. It was as if it had never happened at all, and not too long after that, Phillip had gotten sick.

The one encouraging sign Phillip couldn't help but notice was that Jesse never had a steady girlfriend. You'd think a hot, popular guy like him would have lots of girlfriends in high school. Phillip knew that Jesse had taken girls out on dates. Of course he had a date for the prom. He'd asked girls to dance at high school dances. He'd even suggested one time that they double-date, but Phillip had never worked up the nerve to actually ask a girl out.

Phillip hadn't been able to bring himself to tell Jesse about his true feelings because he was afraid of ruining their friendship. He couldn't bear the thought of losing Jesse. It would be so awkward and embarrassing if Phillip confided in Jesse, and then his friend said he didn't feel the same. Phillip knew it would likely destroy their friendship.

But their high school years were nearly over, and time was running out. Phillip didn't know how long the cancer would remain in remission. He didn't know what would happen after Jesse went away to college in the fall. He wondered if perhaps Jesse had similar feelings and struggled with the same fears. What if Jesse wanted to broach the topic but was just afraid of what might happen?

Phillip knew he had to do it, though. He had to bite the bullet and tell Jesse what was in his heart. If Jesse rejected him, it would be devastating, but at least he would know, once and for all. And in all honesty, Jesse had a right to know. They were best friends, and shouldn't best buds be honest with each other about things like this?

Phillip decided he was going to just do it. He would

watch for Jesse tonight, and when Jesse got home from practice, Phillip would call him. He was going to tell Jesse how he truly felt. He was going to tell him how much he loved him before it was too late.

****

Harold lay in his bed with the laptop on a tray in front of him. He'd just finished replaying the video from Doctor Drayton. This was the fourth time he'd watched it. Initially it had seemed absurd. Certainly it was just a harebrained scam, a very creative way to cheat a rich old man out of a lot of money. It was brilliant, though, he had to admit.

How could something like this possibly be true? It was beyond comprehension, really. But how were they able to fake the things they showed in the video? Had they trained those chimpanzees? Was it all staged?

As he pondered the possibilities, Harold thought about what the doctor had said. Harold Wainwright was a multi-billionaire, and he knew he was about to die. Being cheated out of a million bucks was of little consequence. Even if it was all a scam, what would it matter after he was dead? And really, the effort put into this scheme was undeniably commendable. The doctor deserved an academy award for his performance.

He picked up the phone beside his bed and quickly dialed a number he knew by heart. "Thomas, Wainwright here ... I need you to run a background check." He paused as the private investigator questioned him about his health. "I'm fine. Look, this is important. I need it yesterday. Got it? Okay ..." Harold then gave his friend the name of Drayton and his company, Ingenico Corporation. "And get me any information you can find on something called 'The Rebirthing Project.' I want names, dates, details—no matter how insignificant you think they might be. I want you to drop everything you're doing and focus solely on this, and I want the information to me by tomorrow morning!"

He listened as the detective assured him he was on it. "And one more thing. No matter what you find, do not discuss it with anyone. I want you to hand-deliver the information. Got it? Bye." He hung up the phone abruptly.

At nine o'clock the following morning, the private investigator Chris Thomas joined Harold in his sitting room. The elderly gentleman removed his oxygen mask when the detective walked in. "What did you find?" he asked.

Thomas handed a file folder to his employer. "Some very interesting stuff, sir," he said. "Ingenico has been around for about thirty years, and they're a global enterprise. Their home base is in Switzerland, and they specialize in the development of youth-enhancement products. Anti-aging remedies, etcetera."

"And Timothy Drayton?"

"He's a neurosurgeon who was at one time regarded as the leading specialist in his field. He worked at the Mayo Clinic until he was hired by a government agency as a consultant. It was a branch of the intelligence department, and the projects he worked on remain classified to this day. He left the agency in the early '80's when he and several renowned doctors from around the world started Ingenico. It baffled a lot of people that he would go into this new age shit. It was not the sort of prestigious field you'd expect to see someone of this talent waste his time with.

"Well, for whatever reason, Ingenico has been quite successful. They have expanded their operation over the years and now are in more than a dozen countries. They sell a lot of these fountain-of-youth products under various labels. Anti-aging creams, hair re-growth liquids, shit like that."

"And what about the Rebirthing Project?" Harold asked.

"I couldn't find anything about it. What I did learn is that the parent organization operates under numerous grants from governments around the world. They have several research projects, and many of them are rather ambiguous."

"Does this Drayton have any kind of a rap sheet?" Harold asked.

Detective Thomas shook his head. "Clean as a whistle. Dude ain't got so much as a parking ticket."

"Did you find criminal records on any of the other key members of this Ingenico group?"

"Nada," he said. "They're all clean. They're all pretty much successful doctors and scientists. My gut tells me the anti-aging business is just a cover. They probably sell that shit to keep their research afloat."

"So they're generating revenue from these commodities they're selling, and they're also receiving funding from grants. Must have a separate, non-profit branch of the company that operates independently."

"Exactly, sir. The research side of their operation is referred to as Ingenico Frontiers, and their sales branch is Ingenico Enterprises."

"Were you able to get a financial statement?"

Thomas nodded. "It's in there."

"Ah," Harold said as he scanned the P & L statement. "Now I see why they need money. They lost forty million dollars last year."

"The economy, sir," Thomas surmised. "It sucks."

"Indeed it does. Indeed it does." Harold nodded somberly and then reattached his oxygen mask.

Three

Timothy Drayton looked out the window of his Chicago office as he pondered the case files in front of him. Slowly he rubbed his temples, trying to will away the headache that had been building as a result of stress. If he didn't find a way to generate some revenue to keep his research project solvent, all he'd worked for over the past thirty years might well be lost.

He had feared for years that this may eventually happen. All of the cosmetics and snake oil potions they'd been manufacturing eventually would fail. People would realize it all was crap, and they'd stop buying it. With the global recession that was currently threatening the world economy, people were just not wasting money like they used to.

The grant money for the Rebirthing Project had also about dried up. Drayton had applied for several grants over the years, and the money had always been readily available. It really was a matter of knowing the right thing to say, following the proper protocol. The government seemed to be dying to dole out money; you just had to have your hand out at the right time. Unfortunately that time had passed. Nowadays even the government was not so generous.

He'd hated the idea of approaching Wainwright in the first place. In fact, the thought of giving that slimy bastard a second chance at life made Drayton want to puke. Wainwright represented the polar opposite of the ideals upon which the Rebirthing Project had been established. He was a leech, a bottom feeder of the lowest form. He'd spent his whole life amassing a fortune off the backs of innocent people, denying them the healthcare they so desperately needed.

How ironic that Drayton would now extend a lifeline to this selfish prick who had denied others the same compassion for so many years. It didn't seem fair, but what else could he do? The company needed the money to eventually help others.

He looked down again at the desk and opened one of the donor case files. It was from a thirty–year-old executive who lived in southern California. He'd been injured from a fall while rock climbing and was sure to never regain consciousness. Drayton knew that this body would be the perfect match for Harold. He'd be able to slip easily into this other man's life, and in a matter of months he'd probably be back to enjoying the luxurious lifestyle he'd been accustomed to for so many years. Drayton frowned and slid the file folder to the corner of his desk.

He picked up the next folder and looked at the photo of the young man. Jesse Warren of Dayton, Ohio. It was so sad … so utterly tragic, really. The kid had just turned eighteen and was in a coma. He had been hit by a truck while jogging to school. It now appeared he would never regain consciousness. He existed merely on life support.

The Warren family was not at all affluent. In fact, they were barely what you'd consider middle class. The father, Paul Warren, was an assistant foreman at an auto parts factory, and the mother Margo ran an eBay store on line. Their combined income wasn't even fifty grand per year. How utterly devastating it must have been for them to lose their only child this way.

Of course, the Warren's still held out hope for their son's recovery. Undoubtedly they were at the hospital every day, camped out at his bedside. Drayton suspected they'd offered thousands of prayers, clinging to the hope of a miracle.

It was within his power to grant them that miracle … well, sort of. He could give them back a boy who resembled their son. The horrible thing about it, though, was that it wouldn't really be their Jesse. It would be an imposter. It would be a crusty, old, selfish bastard who should be dead.

Drayton smirked when he saw the name of Warren's insurance provider in the file. It was Wainwright's company, and they were trying to deny coverage. They were claiming the right to drop his coverage since the boy had just turned eighteen. Oh wasn't this just the most deliciously ironic twist? If they had their way, Wainwright's own company would pull the plug on the boy who might be Wainwright's only hope for a future existence.

Nah, he knew he should do the right thing. He should simply tell Wainwright that the only available and suitable donor was Dennis Kauffman, the man in California. He should leave the Warrens be and destroy the boy's case file. They deserved to remember their son as the beautiful human being he had been.

And the geographical location of the Warren boy was just too coincidental. Drayton was already monitoring another subject from that locale. It would be too risky.

But wouldn't it be poetic justice to place a man like Wainwright into a family such as this one? Wouldn't it serve him right to be forced to face the struggles and heartaches of an average person? He would begin his new life with a mountain of medical debt and a battle with the insurance company he had personally established.

The ringing of his phone startled him, and he shook his head slightly before answering. "Hello, Timothy Drayton." After a pause, he said, "I see. Very well, thank you." He sighed as he hung up the receiver. Shaking his head again he sadly picked up the folder of Dennis Kauffman and tossed it in the trash receptacle beside his desk. Kauffman was dead.

****

Paul and Margo Warren sat huddled together at their son's bedside. "I'm so sorry, baby," she whispered. For the past three months she had been torturing herself, begging God and her son to forgive her for not getting up out of that fucking desk chair to drive Jesse to practice that fateful day.

"Honey, don't," Paul said. "We've been over this … it's not your fault."

She wiped the tear from her cheek and looked up at Jesse's bed stand, where a framed diploma was proudly displayed. The school had awarded him his diploma in spite of the fact that he hadn't been available to complete his finals. His grades were high enough that he didn't need the final test results in order to earn the qualifying credits. Trophies and ribbons were also on display around the hospital room, representing Jesse's athletic accomplishments. A picture of Jesse and Phillip, their arms wrapped around each other's shoulders, sat in front of one of the huge sprays of flowers that had been delivered.

During the first two weeks after the accident, young Phillip Covington had refused to leave the hospital. He sat by Jesse's bed talking to him, holding his hand and trying to evoke some kind of response from his best friend. Margo had been touched by the boy's devotion, but eventually she'd asked Phillip to leave. She feared that the experience was not good for Phillip, and she knew he'd already suffered a challenging life of his own. She promised the boy she would notify him immediately if there was any change, and she encouraged him to stop in or call whenever he wanted. She just did not feel it was prudent for him to be camped out at the hospital this way. She said Jesse would have insisted he move on with his life.

"Mr. and Mrs. Warren," a voice from behind startled them. They turned and saw a familiar face. It was that of Jesse's doctor, Eric Shelton.

"Doctor Shelton," Paul said as he stood to greet him.

The doctor extended his hand and the two exchanged the cursory gesture of a handshake. Margo stood as well, hoping for news, any shred of hope. She glanced at the gentleman standing behind the doctor, wondering if he might be a consultant of some sort. Perhaps he was there to help.

"I'd like to introduce you to one of my colleagues," Doctor Shelton said. "This is Doctor Timothy Drayton, and he specializes in cases such as your son's."

Margo quickly stepped forward to shake the doctor's hand. "Oh sir, it's a pleasure to meet you."

"I'd like to have a conference in my office to discuss some possible treatments for Jesse ..."

"Can't we discuss it here? Now?" Paul said.

"I specialize in a procedure that may help your son," Doctor Drayton spoke for the first time. "It'd be best if we sat down together, in the office, so I can explain it in detail."

"Yes, yes of course," Margo said. "Of course we're available."

"Let's meet back at my office in a half hour, okay?" Shelton said. "I think you'll be pleased by what Dr. Drayton has to tell you."

"We'll be there," she said. "Thank you. Thank you so much."

Twenty minutes later the Warrens sat nervously in the waiting room of Dr. Shelton's office. When the receptionist called them in and led them down the hallway to the doctor's office, Margo's heart skipped a beat. She said a silent prayer, asking God once more for the miracle they so desperately needed.

"Please have a seat," Shelton said as he greeted them. "I just felt it would be better to discuss this matter in the office. Doctor Drayton is a neurosurgeon who specializes in these sorts of cases. He is regarded as the most skilled neurosurgeon in the world."

Margo glanced over at her husband and nodded hopefully.

"Mr. and Mrs. Warren, I've extensively reviewed your

son's case, and I have to be honest with you … it is pretty bleak." He eyed them sympathetically. "But if there were no hope for his recovery, I wouldn't be here. In years past we would have probably encouraged you to simply remove him from life support, because truthfully, in his current state he has already expired … mentally, that is.

"Your son is what we refer to in laymen's terms as 'brain dead.' We do not detect any activity in the CATT scans that would indicate any possibility of recovery."

"I don't understand," Margo said. "I thought you said there was hope …"

The doctor reached into his lab coat and removed a small article, handing it over to Margo. "This is a computer chip my research company developed. We have had some success by implanting this chip into the brain of patients such as your son. We are often able to stimulate brain activity—"

"You're saying he needs surgery?" she asked. "He's already had two brain surgeries."

"This will be quite different, ma'am. This surgery will involve the implantation of a chip like the one you're holding."

"And you think this chip will restore Jesse's consciousness?" Paul asked. "How is that possible?"

"All of Jesse's memories are present within his brain. It's just that his brain has stopped functioning. The chip will allow us to jump-start his consciousness, so-to-speak."

"Have you done this before?" Margo asked. "Successfully?"

"We have had very promising results …"

"But it hasn't worked … not completely?"

"Mrs. Warren, it is my belief that with the implantation of this device into your son's brain, we will completely restore his consciousness. He will, however, awaken in a confused state. He may have difficulty recalling many of his memories and seem bewildered about certain things. Eventually, though, his memories will return."

"Oh Paul," Margo gasped as she placed her hand over her mouth. This really could be the miracle she'd been praying for. "Yes, of course we want to try ... I don't care how much he may have forgotten. We'll work with him. We'll help him learn everything again."

"He is likely to have memory of all his motor skills. He will know how to walk and talk and do all of the things he normally has done. He may, however, not remember events or people in his past."

"How is this possible?" Paul asked. "If he can remember all that other stuff, why not everything?"

"Memories are stored in different parts of the brain," the doctor explained. "The chip will stimulate the part of the brain that controls motor function. It is our hope that all his memories will eventually return. You will ultimately have your son back completely, but it may take time."

"How much does this procedure cost?" Paul asked. Margo glared at her husband in disbelief.

"We don't care!" she exclaimed. "Paul how could you—"

The doctor interrupted her. "It is a valid question. The procedure will not cost you a cent."

Paul's brow furrowed as he looked at the doctor suspiciously. "It's free? You're going to do this pro bono?"

"My research and experimental work is paid for by grants that fund our non-profit organization. We specifically look for cases such as your son's where we can help people who may otherwise have no hope."

"So it *is* experimental?" Paul asked.

"Yes, very much so. But I need to be honest with you. Please forgive me, but your son is, for all intents and purposes, already dead. Technically the surgery is experimental, but your son has no other options. In his current state, he is nothing more than a human vegetable."

Margo grimaced at the doctor's remarks. "Paul, please ..."

27

Doctor Shelton spoke. "Paul and Margo, please understand that I would never have suggested Doctor Drayton if I did not trust his judgment. What he's telling you is true, and we're frankly very fortunate to have this opportunity. Yes, there is a risk involved in this surgery. Jesse could possibly die as a result of it, but the way he is now, he is pretty much already dead."

"But he could wake up, right? I mean you hear about people waking up from comas, sometimes after many years—"

Drayton shook his head. "Not with this sort of injury, sir. I'm sorry."

"Paul!" Margo said, "They're telling us they can help Jesse wake up! They can restore his consciousness—"

"But without his memories, how is he Jesse?"

"Paul, for God's sake! We'll make new memories. We'll have our son alive! We'll have Jesse back."

Paul smiled at his wife lovingly. "I know. I'm sorry, of course you're right."

"We want to try it," Margo said. "When?"

"I'd like to perform the procedure early tomorrow morning … at six a.m."

Margo reached over to take her husband's hand. "Thank you, Doctor," she said tearfully. "Thank you so much."

As they walked out of the office, Margo reached in her purse to fish out her cell phone. "I have to call Phillip," she told her husband. "He's going to be so happy!"

****

Phillip Covington had not cried so many tears in his entire lifetime as he had since learning of Jesse's accident. It pained him terribly to realize that on the very day he planned to bare his soul to his best friend, such tragedy had occurred. It was just so wrong. Nobody deserved to suffer an injury like that, least of all such a wonderful person as Jesse Warren.

None of this should be happening. It was Phillip who was supposed to die, not Jesse. Phillip had long ago accepted the reality that he would have a short life. The most he could hope for was one or two more years, but he might have as little as a few months. This had been the reason he'd decided to face his fears and tell Jesse his true feelings. He wanted to make the best of the little time he had left.

Why had he waited? Why hadn't he just told Jesse the week before? He could have stopped Jesse and spoken to him that afternoon as he ran by the house. Had he done so, the collision might never have happened. Jesse would be fine.

Everyone told him that when a person is in a coma, they can hear and sense things around them. This was why Phillip so adamantly insisted that he remain at the hospital beside his friend's bed. During the times they were alone, Phillip confided his feelings to Jesse. He told him over and over how very much he loved him. He'd even kissed him, ever-so-softly, on the lips.

But Jesse never did respond. He didn't so much as twitch a finger. No matter what Phillip said or did, he could not evoke a response from the comatose boy he so deeply loved. Jesse just lay there like a statue, connected to a machine that forced air into his lungs. Another machine pumped intravenous nutrients into his bloodstream. He had catheters and electrodes and wires of all sorts attached to various body parts, and Phillip knew that if they were removed, Jesse would cease to exist.

This was why he cried. He felt as if Jesse were already gone.

When Mrs. Warren called Phillip that June morning to tell him she had good news about Jesse, he wanted to know immediately if Jesse had awakened.

"No honey, not yet … but this is what I need to talk to you about. We're on our way home now, and I want to stop over to talk to you. Don't worry, it's good news."

"Do you want me to just come to the hospital? I can leave right now."

"No honey, we'll be there in a few minutes. We're leaving now."

So Jesse was not awake, but they had good news. What could it possibly be? Had he responded in some way? Maybe he'd moved his hand or fluttered his eyelids. But if this were the case, certainly they would not leave the hospital. They'd stay right there with him to see if he responded in any other way.

Phillip was literally pacing when the car pulled in across the street. He raced out the door and headed over to the neighbor's yard. "Mrs. Warren," he said, "I have to know … what happened? Did Jesse respond somehow?"

She smiled at him sweetly. "Come on inside, Phillip. We'll explain everything."

The three of them made their way into the house and situated themselves in the living room. "Do you want something to drink, dear?" she asked.

Phillip shook his head. "No thank you. I just … I need to know about Jesse."

"Well," she said, "he's having surgery tomorrow morning."

Phillip sighed dejectedly. "Again? What's wrong now?"

"Nothing," Mr. Warren responded. "A doctor from Switzerland is doing an operation to implant a chip in his brain. It's supposed to help him regain consciousness."

Phillip looked puzzled. "Really? I've never heard of such a thing."

"Honey, it's pretty much our only hope. It's an experimental procedure, but according to this doctor, it will stimulate Jesse's brain and cause him to wake up. This doctor is the best brain surgeon in the world."

"Oh my god! I can't believe it."

"But there are some risks," Paul said. "He might die …"

"There are always risks with surgery, sir," Phillip said. "Did he tell you the odds?"

"He told us that without the procedure Jesse would never be more than a vegetable. The odds of that are a hundred percent. We feel it's worth it, no matter what the risk."

Phillip nodded, tears welling in his eyes. "I want to see him ... today. I want to see him before the surgery."

"Of course," she said. "We're going to go back to the hospital after we eat, and you can go with us. The operation is at six tomorrow morning. If you'd like, you can go with us ..."

"How could you even ask? Of course I'll go with you. I'll spend the night there."

"No," she said and smiled at him sweetly. "We're going to come home and try to get some sleep; then we'll head up to the hospital at five tomorrow morning."

"Okay ... Oh my god! I just can't believe this. Jesse is gonna be okay ... maybe."

"Well there's another thing we have to talk to you about, Phillip," Margo said. "When Jesse wakes up, he may have amnesia. He may not remember any of us ... right away. The doctor said it may take time for him to regain his memories."

"It's okay," Phillip said quickly. "I can't wait to remind him!"

Margo smiled at her husband. "That's what we said."

Phillip was both elated and terrified. Jesse might have a chance. He might just be okay after all, or he might die. "I'm gonna go home and change real quick," he said.

"Why don't you meet us back here at about four o'clock? We need to shower and get a bite to eat."

"Okay," he said. "I'm gonna go tell my folks about everything. Thanks ... thanks for letting me—ya know—be there with you."

"Phillip, Jesse's lucky to have a friend like you. Thank *you* for all you've done. You're an angel." She walked over to him and kissed him on the forehead.

"Okay ... I'll be back in a couple hours."

As soon as Phillip was inside the house he closed the door and leaned back against it, sighing to himself.

"Oh God, please! Please let Jesse be okay. Please let him live. I'll do anything ... I'll die in his place—"

"Phillip Covington, don't say such things!" his mother said as she stepped into the hallway. "Come here!" She held her arms out and embraced her son. "God's not going to let anyone die. Not you and not Jesse Warren. You hear me?"

Four

When Harold Wainwright left his home that morning, his employees were told that he was being taken to a research facility in Switzerland for an experimental cancer treatment. Instead he was flown to Dayton, Ohio and taken to a specially-designed operating room. The building appeared to be a warehouse, and it was located within a mile of the hospital where a young boy lay in his comatose state awaiting surgery.

In spite of Harold's frail condition, he had painstakingly made all of the arrangements. In his will he had left a large sum of money to a boy named Jesse Warren, but the contingency was that the boy must provide proof of identity as well as a fourteen digit alpha-numeric code. Without this information, the payment would be denied and the money given to charity.

A deposit of three hundred million dollars had also been made to a Swiss bank account under the name Timothy Drayton. This account was also protected by a numeric code. The account was only temporary, however. In sixty days the money that remained therein would automatically be transferred back to Wainwright's estate.

Wainwright had memorized the code he would give Drayton when he awoke in his new body, but he did not know the alpha-numeric code that had been assigned to the will. He had instead arranged for Chris Thomas to mail a certified letter to Jesse Warren. Harold feared that he would not be able to recall the digits after the transfer, and thus he wanted to safeguard against the possibility that he forget and lose the money.

In truth, the money was not of great concern to him. If

there was one thing Harold had learned during the course of his long life, it was that money did not buy happiness. He'd resolved to use his second chance to focus upon the things in life that were truly important. He merely wanted to provide himself a safety net in case he needed money for any reason. The amount he transferred to himself was minimal compared to everything he was leaving behind.

He had spent his waking hours the past several days poring over every bit of information he could learn about Jesse Warren and his family. He knew of all Jesse's athletic achievements and had read his complete elementary and secondary-level educational transcripts. He knew the names of Jesse's family members and had seen photos of his parents. He'd learned about Jesse's best friend Phillip, who lived next door. They had been classmates and pals for many years.

When Wainwright had first been given Jesse's file, he'd urged Doctor Drayton to fake the boy's death and give him an entirely new identity. Drayton had flatly refused, however. He insisted that such a scheme would be extremely dangerous and might put the entire project in jeopardy. If the body were allowed to die, it would be worthless, and there was no way to fake such a death. The family would want to see the corpse. They'd need a burial or cremation.

The other possibility would have been to convince the Warren family to donate the body and simply tell them the truth. Drayton had insisted that this was also not feasible. The Warrens would never freely make such a donation. Who would willingly allow the body of a loved one to be inhabited by the mind of a stranger?

Wainwright knew that Drayton was correct on all counts. The only way to make this work was for him to assume the identity of his donor. Harold also realized that once the transfer had taken place, there absolutely would be no way that anyone would ever believe he was anyone other than Jesse Warren. Neither were they likely to believe he had been reincarnated.

Harold Wainwright realized that this was his very last day on earth as Harold Wainwright. As he lay on the gurney awaiting the arrival of Doctor Drayton, Harold wondered what his new life would be like. He thought about how wonderful it would be to breathe normally again. He thought about how thrilling it would be to look down at his body and no longer see wrinkles and sagging skin, but instead a smooth, tight abdomen and long, powerful runner's legs. He thought about making love again, about playing sports, about dancing and jogging and riding fast motorcycles. The possibilities were endless.

He smiled weakly at the doctor when he saw him walk in.

"Are you ready, Mr. Wainwright?" the doctor asked. Harold nodded. "I have your documents, and I was pleased to hear that the check for your initial payment has already cleared. Have you memorized the number to the bank access code?"

Harold again nodded, unable to speak through the oxygen mask.

"Very well. There are a few things I need to go over with you prior to the transfer. I suspect that as the transfer takes place, you will not be aware of any physical sensation. When you awaken, however, you will no longer feel any of the physical pain associated with your current body but will feel everything your new body is experiencing.

"Remember, this boy has been in a coma for several weeks. You may awaken to cramping muscles. You may feel stiff or sore. Your throat will be raw from the respirator tube, and you are likely to experience terrific thirst.

"Adjusting to your new body might be difficult. As you attempt to apply the motor skills you know now to your new body, you are going to see that you have to re-learn a lot of your behaviors. Your body will be stronger, and it will require less effort to do things that you currently find very taxing.

"You will have just gone through brain surgery so your head will be bandaged. There will be pain and soreness associated with the incision. You're likely to have an excruciating headache, but we will administer pain medication as needed.

"Jesse Warren has 20/20 vision, and this will be a remarkable change for you. His body is physically fit. All of his senses are sharper than what you are currently used to. From a physical standpoint, he's in the prime of his life. According to his family, he runs and completes an exercise routine every day … or did, up until the accident.

"You also will be assuming his body at a time when it is in its sexual prime. You are likely to experience sexual arousal numerous times a day. You will again have a libido."

Harold smiled to himself in anticipation.

The doctor continued without acknowledgement. "The boy's family has been told that their son is likely to have amnesia upon his awakening. You would be wise to use this as an excuse when you find yourself in situations where you find it difficult to maintain the ruse of your new identity.

"Eventually, though, you must completely assume this new identity. After today, Harold Wainwright will be dead. You will henceforth be Jesse Warren, for better or worse. It's going to be up to you to make it work."

Harold nodded as he looked the doctor in the eye.

"One more thing …" The doctor sighed as he looked down at his patient. "I need to be honest with you. Including you in this project has been very difficult for me. I feel as if I've compromised my ethical standards."

Harold stared up at the doctor with a perplexed expression on his face.

"I don't feel you deserve a chance like this. You've been a selfish motherfucker your whole life." He picked up a scalpel from the counter beside him, holding it within the old man's field of vision. "I hope you will appreciate the fact that you've been given a unique opportunity. I hope you will use your new life to do a little good … to make the world a better place. I hope you will appreciate the family you've been given …

"If you don't, I swear to you I will do everything within my power to send you to Hell where you belong. Do you understand me, Mr. Wainwright?" As he wielded the scalpel, the overhead light reflected off the shiny metal.

Harold stared at the weapon somberly and then looked the doctor in the eyes and slowly nodded.

"Good," he said. "I'm glad we have an understanding." He placed the scalpel back on the tray. "My assistant will be arriving shortly and will begin administering the anesthesia. I've already implanted the chip in the brain of Jesse Warren, but his family believes he is still in surgery. When the transfer takes place, I will already be back at the hospital. My face will be the first you see when you awaken. Do you have any questions?"

Harold shook his head as he felt a wave of excitement wash over him. It all seemed surreal, like a weird dream.

"Very well," the doctor said. "Just lie there and rest until we're ready to begin."

The next twenty minutes seemed to be the longest of Harold's life, and as he lay on the gurney he contemplated the threatening words the doctor had said. He knew it all was true. He knew what a selfish and foolish bastard he'd been. This was his second chance, and he resolved to become a better man in his next life. He was flooded with memories, recalling scenes from his past that he'd be glad to put behind him forever. He remembered Jacob. He remembered the pain he'd caused so many people. Tears flowed down his wrinkled cheeks as he allowed the regret to overwhelm him.

"Mr. Wainwright, are you okay?" It was a new voice, that of a middle-aged woman. She had a thick foreign accent Harold could not quite identify. "I'm Doctor Russell, your anesthesiologist. We are about to begin the procedure. Do you have any final words before I administer the anesthesia?"

Feebly he reached up and pulled the oxygen mask from his mouth. "Thank you," he said as he looked into her eyes and smiled. These were the last two words ever spoken by Harold Wainwright.

****

It was nine a.m. and Phillip Covington had not slept a wink the entire night before. He was now with Mr. and Mrs. Warren in the small hospital waiting room, sitting hunched over with his elbows resting on his knees and his hands folded together in front of him. It seemed an appropriate posture, for his mental state was one of supplication. He'd been praying for hours, silently repeating his pleas to God. "Please let him wake up. Please let him be okay."

The night before, Phillip had been afforded some time alone with Jesse, and he had once again declared his love for his dearest friend on earth. He'd whispered into the comatose boy's ear how deeply he cared for him. "Jess, I don't know if you can hear me. I just want you to know I love you with all my heart. I love you so much …"

The issue of Phillip's sexual orientation had never been much of a concern in the Covington family. Instead they were focused upon the boy's health. When he was sixteen, he'd confided in his mom about his feelings, telling her that he thought he liked boys more than girls. She never so much as batted an eye. "I love you just the way you are, no matter who you find attractive," she said. Then she kissed him sweetly on the forehead and pulled him into her loving embrace.

His mom was actually the only person he had told, and from that point forward it never seemed to be a big deal. When the two of them were alone together, she'd sometimes make comments to him about other boys she thought were cute. It seemed weird to Phillip to hear such remarks from his own mother, but he had to admit that she had pretty good taste.

Phillip realized how blessed he was to have the wonderful parents God had given him. Even though he didn't feel quite comfortable enough yet to come out to his dad, he knew it would not be a problem when the time was right. His father, Kyle Covington, was a manager at a supermarket, and one of his best friends from work was gay. His name was Donald, and he was the produce manager. He remembered how one day his father had come home and shared a story about a disturbing incident that had happened at work. Apparently someone had gone into the produce preparation room and vandalized the drywall. They'd spray-painted it with graffiti that stated, "Donald Price is the biggest FRUIT in produce." Phillip's father had been so furious that he swore he would find out which employee had done such a malicious thing and fire their ass on the spot. Phillip was so proud of his dad that day.

Phillip didn't know exactly why he had felt more at ease talking to his mom about these things than he did with his dad. It wasn't that he feared his father's rejection. He didn't even think his dad would be disappointed by the fact that his son was gay. It just felt awkward. He secretly wished his dad would broach the topic. He wanted to tell him, but he just never felt brave enough to do so.

Nobody had ever considered Phillip Covington a sissy. When he was really young, he'd seemed like any other boy. He liked to play with the boys' toys, and as he got older he became a big sports fan. He was even on the track team with Jesse in junior high. He'd had to drop out when he started the chemotherapy, but it certainly wasn't because he wasn't man enough to mix it up with the guys.

There were some aspects of Phillip's personality, though, that made him stand out from his peers. He was fairly quiet and introspective. Most people regarded him as shy and reserved. He also seemed overly preoccupied with his physical appearance. He made it a point to keep up with the latest fashions. He was a bit of a neat freak who always wanted to look his best. This was why it had been so difficult for him when he began to lose his hair. He was the type of guy who absolutely hated having a bad hair day.

It made Phillip smile when he thought about the way Jesse often teased him about being so preppy. Jesse was a lot more carefree than Phillip—one of the characteristics Phillip admired most about him. Phillip didn't think Jesse had ever even had a bad hair day, and if he did, he didn't give a shit one way or the other. Jesse was spontaneous while Phillip was far more cautious. Jesse liked to be the life of the party.

Phillip wondered if the Jesse he had known and loved all this time would be the same when he woke from his coma. The doctor had said that he would likely have amnesia, and Phillip worried that Jesse might not even know who he was. He might not remember the countless nights they'd stayed up talking into the wee hours of the morning. He might not recall the spontaneous road trips that they'd taken after Jesse first got his license. He might not have any recollection of the hockey games they'd gone to together or of the music they both loved.

But as long as Jesse was alive again they could make new memories. They could rediscover each other, and this possibility alone was exciting. Although Phillip was saddened by the thought that Jesse might not remember their good times together, he also relished the possibility of a fresh start. Maybe this would make it a little bit easier for Phillip to finally come out to his friend. On the other hand, the opposite could happen. Jesse could end up freaking when he learned his friend was gay. It could all backfire. However, the only thing Phillip could do at this point was remain positive and hope for the best.

****

Harold Wainwright felt himself drift into restful sleep and slip into darkness. During his surgery he dreamed of

Jacob. He was young again, and they were together. He was cradling his lover in his arms, assuring him how much he enjoyed his company. "I love you, Harold," the young man said to him. Harold pulled him close against his chest and kissed the side of his face. Why couldn't he respond? Why couldn't he say what he really felt?

Suddenly he was standing at the end of a dark tunnel, and he could see a dim light at the other side. He stepped in, slowly making his way toward the light. A figure appeared before him, standing in the center of the light. At first it was merely a silhouette, but then, as he got closer, the details became clearer. It was Jacob. He quickened his pace, rushing toward his lover. "Jacob!" he cried. "Oh Jacob, I love you too!"

As he stretched his arms outward, preparing to embrace the man for whom he'd pined all these years, he suddenly felt himself drifting backwards. As hard as he tried, he could not get any closer to the light. It was as if the tunnel was becoming longer. "Jacob!" he cried. "I do love you, Jacob!" The light in front of him grew smaller and smaller, and he felt himself flying backwards, away from it.

As he tried to scream, he suddenly felt a jolt of electricity pass through him, and he was once more surrounded by darkness. He groped at the space in front of him, realizing for the first time that his eyes were closed. He quickly opened them and was instantly blinded by the bright light above his head.

"Jesse," the voice of Doctor Drayton greeted him. "Can you hear me?"

He strained to focus, allowing his eyes to dilate and adjust to the bright light. He tried to open his mouth to speak, but it was as if he'd swallowed cotton. "Wa-" was all he could say. He needed water!

The doctor placed a straw between his lips. "There you go, Jesse. Sip slowly ..."

"Drayton!" he said, not even recognizing his own voice. "It didn't work!"

"Jesse," the doctor laughed, "calm yourself. Everything's going to be just fine. You were in an accident and were unconscious for some time. You're awake now, though, and you're okay."

He lifted his hands in front of his face but did not recognize them. Instead of the wrinkled, arthritic hands he was used to seeing, he saw a pair of big, strong, youthful ones. He flexed his fingers, moving them back and forth.

"Yes, you can move your limbs just fine. You suffered no lasting physical injuries. You will notice, however, that your head is bandaged. You had to have a surgery on your brain."

He reached up to feel his skull, realizing for the first time that he had an excruciating headache. "It hurts," he complained.

"Yes, we're going to give you something for that. We needed you to regain consciousness first." The doctor turned to the anesthesiologist and nurses who surrounded him. "I need a few moments alone with the patient, please." They looked at him, puzzled. "Please inform the boy's family that he is awake, and that they will be able to see him shortly."

The other medical personnel were perplexed by the doctor's request. Generally the doctor left after completing an operation, and the staff remained behind to provide the post-op. Once they were alone, Drayton stepped over to a counter at the side of the room and retrieved a large circular mirror. He carried it back with him to the bedside of his patient.

The boy was craning his neck to stare down at his young body. He moved his legs, wiggled his toes, and bent his knees. "Go ahead," Drayton said to him, "explore your new body. The transfer *did* work." He held the mirror up to the young man's face.

It was beautiful! So smooth and free of wrinkles or blemishes. Slowly he reached up to touch his cheeks. He stared directly into his own brilliant blue eyes, and then he smiled. "You did it! Oh my God … you …"

"I completed the transfer as we agreed. Now you must keep your end of the bargain. Give me the access code." He pulled the mirror away and placed it face down on the tray beside him. He took a notepad and pen from the pocket of his lab coat. "Give me the number!" he demanded.

The young man smiled as the reality of his situation began to sink in. He had survived! He was alive and well, and he had a brand new body … and oh what a body it was! He was no longer the old, decrepit, cancer-stricken miser. That man was now dead … and he was an entirely new person. He was Jesse Warren!

"I'll give you the number, Drayton," he said, still marveling at the sound of his own deep voice. "I'll give it to you—"

"Now!" the doctor demanded. "Give me the number now, or I swear I'll reverse everything."

Jesse laughed. "You don't get it, do you? Do you think I care about the money? You can have it. You can have it all. I don't want any of it! The number is 377-79-7699."

"That's a social security number," he said.

"It was Harold Wainwright's social security number," he said.

"You used your own social security number as the access code?"

Jesse laughed again. "I wanted to make sure it was a number I wouldn't forget."

"This better be correct," the doctor threatened.

"It's correct," the boy said calmly. "Go ahead and call the bank. The money is there, and it's all yours. All three hundred million."

"If it's not there, you'll hear from me again soon. Otherwise, have a nice life." The doctor turned and quickly crossed the room, sliding the notepad back into his pocket as he exited through the double doors.

Jesse reached over to the tray beside his bed and picked

up the mirror, holding it once again before his youthful face. He smiled contentedly and then placed the mirror back down. God his head hurt! He took another sip of water and then closed his eyes involuntarily. He was still so groggy. Within seconds he was sound asleep.

Five

"How can he be awake already?" Phillip asked. "They just brought him out of surgery."

"The doctor awakened him before he left the operating room," the nurse explained. "With this type of surgery, they needed to see if the implant was successful. After he had awakened, though, he immediately fell back to sleep. He's still receiving a heavy dosage of pain killers."

"But he *was* awake? He was talking and everything?" he asked excitedly.

"He was fully conscious," the nurse said, smiling at the family.

Margo held her hand over her mouth and gasped. Tears streamed down her face.

Phillip was overcome with excitement. "Oh thank God! Thank you, God!" he exclaimed. He rushed over to embrace Mrs. Warren.

"Can we see him now?" Paul Warren asked.

"Of course. They're taking him to the recovery room now. I will come get you as soon as he's ready."

Phillip couldn't believe that the procedure had worked and that Jesse had actually regained consciousness. It seemed as if all his prayers had been answered after all. When he'd received the news the previous day that Jesse was to undergo an experimental surgery, it had all sounded too good to be true. Who would have imagined that medical technology had advanced to the point that a patient classified as "brain dead" could be revived? And it was all done by implanting a computer chip in his brain!

Honestly, though, Phillip did not care *how* it had happened; he only cared that it had been successful. Now his biggest concern was how Jesse would react when he saw them for the first time. Would he remember them? Would he recognize their faces and recall what his loved ones meant to him? The doctor had told the Warrens that he most likely would remember who they were, but would have forgotten much of his past. It would take a team effort to help Jesse overcome his amnesia.

Phillip immediately called his mom to inform her of the good news. He was still talking to her when the nurse came back into the waiting room. "I've gotta go, Mom. The nurse is here."

"You can see him now," the nurse said as she smiled at the threesome. "Follow me." They stepped in line behind her and briskly followed her down to the recovery room.

****

When Jesse awoke, he was disoriented. At first he did not remember where he was. He didn't even remember *who* he was. As he looked up into the eyes of the recovery-room nurse who stared down at him, it suddenly came back to him. He was a new person now, and he had a new life.

"Hello Jesse," the cheerful face greeted him. "Welcome to the land of the living. My name is Rose, and I'm the nurse who will be taking care of you for the next few hours. Do you remember why you're here?"

He nodded as he stared up at her. Slowly a grin crept across his face. "An accident," he said softly.

"That's right! You had a terrible accident, and you've been in a coma for quite a long time. Several weeks—"

"Can I get out of this bed?"

She laughed. "No honey, not yet. You need to get some rest and heal from your surgery."

"But I've been resting," he argued.

"Hey, I've got some good news for you," Rose changed the subject. "Your family is here, and they're coming in to see you. Would you like that?"

Jesse squinted at her, unsure of how to respond. Once again he slowly nodded. "Yes … or yeah. Yeah, I would."

As if on cue, Paul and Margo approached the side of Jesse's bed. He looked up into the eyes of the woman he would soon regard as his mother. "Oh baby!" she cried. "Oh Jesse, you're awake."

"Mom," he said. Quickly she reached down and grabbed his hand. This was the very first physical contact that Jesse had felt in his new body. The softness and warmth of her touch soothed him.

"Oh honey, we're so glad to see you awake. We're so glad you're back with us!" She reached up to wipe a tear from her cheek.

Paul spoke next. "Are you okay?" he asked. "Does it hurt too bad? Your head, I mean."

The boy shook his head. "No Dad, it doesn't hurt. Not at all." It was true. Jesse was not feeling any pain in his head, in spite of the incision. Of course his current condition was hardly comparable to that of his former body. Previously he had been in constant pain, with every joint aching. He'd been constantly exhausted, and every breath had been difficult. The current discomfort in his head from the incision was nothing in comparison.

"We have good news, son," Paul said. "You're done with school, and you graduated with honors."

"I did?"

"We have your diploma back in your hospital room," his mom said. "And Phillip is here too." She turned and motioned for Phillip to step up to the bed where Jesse could see him.

As Jesse looked up at the dark-haired boy who was approaching his bed, his mouth fell open. He almost could not believe his eyes. Purely as an automatic reflex he said the only word that came to his mind. "Jacob!"

Margo looked down at her son, puzzled by his

exclamation. "This is Phillip, Jesse. Phillip Covington. He's our neighbor, and he's been your best friend since you were a little boy."

"It's okay, Jesse," Phillip said. "Don't worry if you can't remember. We have lots of time to work on helping you regain your memories."

"I'm sorry," Jesse said. "Um … It's just that you … well, you look exactly like Jacob!"

"Honey, who is Jacob?" Margo asked. "Is he someone you know from school?"

"I knew him a long time ago."

"Ya know what?" Phillip said. "My middle name actually *is* Jacob. My name is Phillip Jacob Covington."

"Baby, do you remember Phillip?" his mother asked.

"I do," Jesse lied. "I do remember him … I think."

"Well he's your dearest friend. I'm sure all your memories will come back in time."

Finally the nurse spoke up. "It's not unusual for patients to have memory loss and confusion after surgery on their brain. It'll come back though. I can tell already. He's very clear-headed and sharp. He'll be just fine."

"Thank you," Margo said.

"Would you like to meet us back at Jesse's room? I think we're about ready to get him transferred out of recovery."

"Oh yes. Yes of course."

"We'll see you in a bit, son," Paul said.

"See ya, Jesse! I'm so glad you're awake," Phillip said.

Margo leaned in to kiss her son on the forehead. "I love you, honey. We all do."

Jesse stared up at her wide-eyed, unsure how to respond. Thankfully the three of them quickly turned and exited.

How was it possible that this boy looked so much like Jacob? It was much more than a resemblance. This young man was the spitting image of Jacob Klein. It felt as if he were in a time warp. Of course it had been many years since he'd seen Jacob, and perhaps his mind was merely playing tricks on him. Maybe he'd been so obsessed with the memory of Jacob after the dream he'd experienced during the transition that he was imagining that the resemblance was more striking than it actually was.

But the image of Jacob's face was burned into his mind. For all those years he had clung to that very memory. He'd lived the last two decades of his life regretting the day he had sent Jacob away. Now all of a sudden there was this boy—this young man who looked exactly like the Jacob he'd always loved. The facial features were identical. The smile. The stature. *The eyes!* How could this even be?

Jesse asked the nurse if he could get out of bed. He wanted more than anything to walk around. He needed to test his legs, look at himself in a full length mirror, and examine the parts of his body that were still unfamiliar. The nurse discouraged him, though. She said that he needed more bed rest after the surgery but promised that sometime in the late afternoon they would get him up for a walk. He was still connected to a catheter as well as IVs and heart monitors.

Once he was transferred to a bed in his hospital room, the family was again allowed to visit. "So we've known each other since we were kids?" Jesse asked Phillip.

"Yeah, we're best friends," Phillip said. There was a hint of disappointment in the boy's voice that was troubling to Jesse. For some reason it hurt him a little to even think of disappointing this beautiful young man, this *clone* of his former lover.

"I'm sorry. I'll try harder to remember ..."

"No!" Phillip said. "I'm sorry. I don't want you to worry about stuff like that. Don't be silly. You can't help it if you can't remember. In time it will come ... I'm not worried."

"Maybe if you brought some pictures, some photo albums or something. Maybe that'd jog some memories."

"Oh, good idea!" Margo said. "We have lots of pictures

of you, of both of you, from the time you were really small. It'll be fun going through all those old albums."

Jesse looked around the room, staring at the athletic trophies and sprays of flowers. It surprised him to see so many bouquets. It had been several weeks since the accident. What the new Jesse did not yet comprehend was that he was a very popular young man. He was well-liked and admired, and a lot of well-wishers had continued to send their heartfelt expressions of hope for his recovery.

How odd it was to see such affection. In his former identity, he'd been ill for a great long time, and he hadn't received so much as a single get-well-soon. Nobody—none of the connections he had made in the business world—had cared whether he lived or died. His life had basically been meaningless. After he'd retired from his position as CEO of the insurance company, he had been quickly forgotten.

"I don't understand why … well, why do I have all these flowers still? The accident was a while ago."

"Honey, you get flowers almost every day." Margo laughed. "So many people have been praying for you. In fact I bet you're gonna get a ton of visitors as soon as word gets out that you're awake."

A look of shock and concern crossed his face. "How will I remember them?"

"Don't you worry, sweetie. If you're not up to visitors, you don't have to receive any. If you are, though, we'll be here to help you."

"Can we just, ya know … keep it to the four of us for now?"

"Of course …"

"Jesse, if you want, I can go and come back when you're feeling more up to company …" Phillip began to suggest.

"No!" Jesse quickly responded. "No, I want *you* to stay … please!"

As he looked up into his friend's eyes, Jesse could have

sworn he saw an expression of genuine love and gratitude. It was the same look that Jacob used to give him.

"Thanks, Jesse," Phillip said. "I'm glad you want me here, 'cause I really wanna be with you, too."

Jesse smiled at him sweetly.

"Man, I can't wait to get out of this bed! I want to try testing these legs."

The three of them laughed. "It's obvious you're a runner," Mr. Warren said. "Don't worry, son, your legs are fine."

"You didn't really sustain that many physical injuries during the accident," Margo explained. "You were bruised up pretty badly and had some broken ribs, but other than that the only real damage was to your head. You had a closed-head injury and were unconscious."

"Well maybe this afternoon they'll let you get up and move around a bit," Phillip suggested hopefully. "If so, I'll walk with you. I know this whole hospital like the back of my hand."

"You do?" Jesse asked. "Do you work here?"

Phillip laughed. "No, I'm a patient … or I have been. I've spent a lot of time here, and it seems like I know just about all the nursing staff. "

"Really?" Jesse said. "You've been ill?"

Phillip again smiled at his friend. "I've had some problems … some health issues … but I'm all better now."

As Phillip was speaking, an orderly entered the room carrying a tray of food. It was Jesse's lunch. "Anybody hungry?" she asked.

"Famished!" Jesse confessed. The hospital worker placed the tray on the L-cart beside Jesse's bed and slid it over to him.

Phillip stepped forward and leaned in to whisper something to his friend. "The food here sucks, dude. But I can call the kitchen for ya and place a special order. I know all the cooks down there. Or better yet, I can make a Burger King run ..."

Jesse looked up at his friend. "Burger King? Do I like *that*?"

"Oh man! It's your favorite—double Whopper with the works."

Jesse looked over to his mother for confirmation. She nodded and said, "Why don't you stick to the hospital cuisine for today? We'll have plenty of time for Burger King—or whatever you want, when you get home."

Jesse knew nothing about double Whoppers other than the television commercials he'd occasionally seen. He'd never stepped foot in a Burger King and never intended to—at least in his former life. He was a vegetarian and planned to remain one. When he removed the silver dome lid covering his plate, he discovered the hospital had no idea that he didn't eat meat.

"What is it?" he asked, shaking his head.

Phillip again laughed. "It's called Salisbury steak but is more commonly referred to as 'mystery meat.' "

"Oh ... I can't ... I can't eat that!" He pushed the tray away and reached for the salad. As he began to unwrap it he noticed cubes of ham mixed in with the lettuce. "And this salad, it's got meat in it."

"It's a chef's salad, honey," his mother said. "It's got meat and eggs, and all kinds of good stuff. You used to love it with lots of ranch dressing."

"Ranch dressing?" Jesse said as he stared at his mother disbelievingly. "I think I'd prefer vinaigrette ... or perhaps Thousand Island."

Phillip busted up laughing. "Dude, you haven't lost your sense of humor! That's like the stuff old people eat. Nobody under the age of sixty likes Thousand Island dressing."

Jesse stared at his friend, realizing immediately that the boy was right. He had a lot to learn, and he was going to have to be willing to make compromises on some of his personal tastes and preferences if he was going to pass as Jesse Warren. He grinned and laughed obligingly at his friend. "Just kidding," he said. He then picked up the small cup of ranch dressing and removed the lid. He dipped his index finger in the buttermilk dressing and licked it clean. "Not bad," he confessed.

It wasn't easy to force himself to eat the salad, but he did so, trying as much as possible to avoid the meat and eggs. Surprisingly, it wasn't as bad as he imagined it might be. On the other hand, he was utterly famished. He knew, however, that there was no way in hell he could even think of touching the Salisbury steak.

"You sure you don't want me to call down to the kitchen and order you something special? I can have them make you tacos or even a meat-lover's pizza!" Phillip eagerly offered.

"Oh, no … thank you anyway. This is fine … but thanks for the offer."

Jesse finished most of the salad along with a jell-O cup and a dinner roll. He left the rest of the food untouched. Afterwards, he confessed to being extremely sleepy. His mom encouraged him to rest, stating that they'd have lots of time to visit when he was fully recovered. Before he knew it, he had drifted back to sleep.

****

"Jacob, I'm so sorry," he cried. "You were right. I do love you, but I was just scared. I was afraid of what everyone would think, and I feared I would lose everything—everything I'd worked so hard to attain."

The dark-haired young man lay beside him, cooing into his ear. "Shh," he whispered in an attempt to calm his lover. "It's okay, now. I understand, and I'm just so happy we're finally together …"

"But how?" Harold asked. "How is it possible? That was so long ago, and look at you. You haven't changed, not one bit."

"Look at yourself, lover," the raven-haired beauty responded. "Look at how young and attractive *you* are!"

Harold propped himself up on his elbows in the bed and stared across the room. In the full length mirror he saw an image of two young men, immediately recognizing one of the figures. Of course it was Jacob. He was seeing his boyfriend's reflection. There he was lying on the bed, stretched out comfortably. Beside him, though, was a person he did not recognize. It was another boy, young and blond, also strikingly handsome.

Harold stared at the reflection intently. He took in the broad shoulders, the penetrating blue eyes. The smoothness of the boy's unblemished complexion was striking, and it was all he could do to refrain from reaching out to touch it. He repositioned himself, sitting more upright. As he moved, so did the reflection. Slowly he raised his hand. The boy in the mirror did the same, mimicking his action. When he finally reached up to run his shaking fingers across his own cheek, it suddenly dawned on him.

He was no longer Harold Wainwright. He was now Jesse Warren!

"Jacob!" he cried. "Oh Jacob, look at me!"

He continued to take in his reflection, utterly mesmerized by its undeniable beauty. He barely noticed that his lover had not responded. "Jacob," he repeated, this time in a whisper. "Jacob, look at me ..."

When Jesse turned to once again gaze upon the one he loved, a wave of fear and panic instantly washed over him. On the bed beside him lay not the dark haired angel he'd gazed upon just seconds before. In his place lay a shriveled up old man. A corpse! The body belonged to Jacob, but it was no longer youthful and angelic. It was the body of a man who'd battled against the ravages of a horrific disease. It was a skeleton.

The eyes, wide open and glazed over, appeared sunken.

The face itself had lost all its fleshiness and was now merely skin draped over bones. Wrinkles and abrasions disfigured this once-perfect complexion. His body was covered with deep, purple lesions, and the magnificently thick, jet-black hair was now nearly gone.

Jesse gasped and cried out. "No, Jacob, no! I was too late, and now you've left me forever!" He covered his face as he screamed.

"Jesse!" the voice cried, pleading with him. "Jesse, I'm right here. I'll never leave you. Wake up! Please, Jesse, wake up!"

As he pulled his hands away and opened his eyes, he saw the boy again. There he stood, leaning over him. It was Jacob, his angel. "Oh, Jacob! Thank God!"

"Jesse, it's me. It's Phillip. You were having a nightmare."

Six

Jesse's heart continued to beat rapidly as he stared up into the eyes of his friend—this one who bore such a striking resemblance to the only man he'd ever loved. The only man Harold Wainwright had ever loved, that was. It was all so bizarre. It seemed too much of a coincidence that he could possibly encounter this remarkable soul in not just one, but two lifetimes.

"Are you okay?" Phillip asked him. The soothing and compassionate tone of his voice aided Jesse greatly in his efforts to calm himself. He nodded.

"Yeah. I don't know why I'm having these horrible dreams ..."

"Oh Jesse," the boy reassured him, "you've been through so much. It's probably normal. Were you dreaming about the accident?"

"Jacob," he responded.

"The one you talked about earlier?"

"He looks like ... or you look like him. Like he used to look."

"Jesse, where did you know him? It's so weird, because you never talked about him before."

"Where are my parents?" he asked, changing the subject. "What time is it?"

"It's like around seven o'clock. They went home to eat, but they're going to come back to pick me up and check on you ... unless you want me to stay. I know I can stay all night with ya. I'll just go talk to the nurses. I'm sure they'll let me."

"Really?" Jesse asked. "No ... I don't want you to have to do that."

"I want to!" he exclaimed. "Jesse, you've been away for so

long. You were in a coma. I wanna spend as much time as I can …"

"But I'm back now, and both of us need our rest."

"What if you have another nightmare? I wanna be here for you."

Jesse smiled up at him. "Thank you," he said, "but it's okay. It was just a dream. Everything's going to be fine now. It's gonna be perfect."

His friend returned the smile and gently placed his hand on Jesse's arm. A shiver traveled through his body in response to the tender touch. "Have we always … um … been close like this?"

Phillip's face suddenly looked flushed. "I've … um … well, I've always cared about you. Like I said, we've been best friends for years. I'm sure you'll remember soon."

"Maybe you can remind me," Jesse said. He sensed there was more. He could see it in the boy's eyes. He knew that Phillip wasn't telling him everything.

"Are you hungry? They brought you your dinner."

"Didn't I just eat?"

Phillip laughed. "Dude, that was like seven hours ago. It was your lunch, and you've been sleeping ever since."

"I have to use the bathroom," Jesse confessed.

"I don't know how to tell ya this, man, but … um … you have a catheter in ya. It's like a tube that goes into your bladder. If you feel like ya gotta go, just let 'er rip."

Jesse cracked up. "You're not serious!"

"I *am*! Man, I'm sorry. I know it's gross. I've had that before myself, when I was in the hospital. You get used to it though. It sorta feels like you gotta go all the time."

"That nurse earlier, she told me I'd be able to get out of bed today and walk around."

"I think they decided to let you sleep. I bet they'll take out your catheter tomorrow and let you get up. You just had brain surgery, ya know. You should just chill."

"No more chilling! I've been chilled for the past … well, since God knows how long."

"Twelve weeks. You've been in a coma all that time. It's a miracle you survived the accident." Phillip's voice cracked slightly, and his eyes were moist with tears.

"Thank you," Jesse whispered. "Thank you for caring so much. I can't tell you what it means to me …"

This time Phillip boldly grabbed his friend's hand and squeezed it. "Like I said, I care about you. I … um …"

"W-what's for dinner?" Jesse asked, knowing his new friend was struggling to say something and wanting to spare him the discomfort.

Phillip pulled away and turned to the tray beside him. "Let me see. I think it's probably cold by now. It's been sitting there awhile. Looks like tuna casserole."

"Oh dear God," Jesse said.

"Oh dear God?" Phillip repeated. "I can't believe some of the expressions you use … you're so funny."

"I didn't used to talk like this?"

"It's cool, man. It's like you've become so grown-up all of a sudden. I guess maybe it was from being unconscious. You matured in your sleep or something."

"What else is on that tray? Any vegetables?"

"Green beans, it looks like."

"Okay, I'll have them."

"Seriously?" Phillip asked. He laughed as he pushed the cart closer to his friend. "I guess your taste has changed, too. You used to hate vegetables."

"You can have the casserole if you want," Jesse offered.

"I had pizza from the cafeteria. I was gonna bring you some …"

"This is fine," Jesse assured him. "So tell me about us. How did we meet? How'd we become such close friends?" *And why do you look so damned much like Jacob Klein??*

"I don't exactly remember when we first met," Phillip

said. "Seems like we always knew each other. I've lived in the same house all my life, and I think you have, too. You've been my neighbor for as long as I can remember." Phillip stepped over to the other side of the bed and sat down on the edge of the mattress, allowing Jesse to continue to eat.

"You used to have really big birthday parties. I think you were like eight or nine the year you had a huge outdoor party. Your birthday is in the spring, and it was really nice weather. It was a slumber party, and we slept outdoors in tents. You and me slept in the same one, and I got scared in the middle of the night. This is kinda embarrassing ..."

"Please go on! Don't be embarrassed ... please."

"Well, I was crying, and I wanted to just go home. I was gonna get up and go back across the street to my house, but you wouldn't let me. You told me to crawl inside your sleeping bag with you."

"I did?" Jesse smiled. "And did you?"

Phillip smiled back at his friend and nodded. "Yeah. It was so warm, and you made me feel so safe. I think that was when I first knew ..."

"What do ya mean?" Jesse asked.

"I mean ... um ... well, that's when I first knew we were gonna be best friends. It always felt like you kinda looked out for me. You were always the one who was so fearless. You never seemed to be afraid of anything, and just knowing you made me feel braver."

"So you were kind of insecure, then? I mean, when you were on your own."

Phillip paused a moment before answering. "Yeah, I guess I was, actually. I just think you were the outgoing one. I was always a little more cautious, but you were the daredevil. You had so much confidence. I'm the type who wants to do a lot of different things, but all I really do is think about them. I'm a dreamer, I guess. For you, though, to imagine something is to do it. Once you decide you want it, you will eventually get it. I always admired that about you."

The boy's honesty was tugging at Jesse's heartstrings. As he looked into his friend's big brown eyes, he felt the sincerity of his words. He wanted to touch him. He *had* to, and he reached out and gently took his hand into his own as the boy continued to talk.

"Jesse, the day of your accident, I saw you right before it happened. I saw you as you ran by my house on your way to practice. You waved at me, and I decided something. I knew I had to tell you how I felt, and I planned to do it that night.

"I was too late though. When I found out about what had happened, I was afraid I'd missed my chance." Big tears streamed down Phillip's face as he squeezed Jesse's hand. "Jesse, I love ..."

Phillip immediately pulled his hand away as he heard someone enter the room. He turned to see Margo in the doorway. Paul was behind her. "Someone's awake?" she asked.

"Hi Mom," Jesse said, a little too cheerfully. "I'm just having my dinner, and Phillip's telling me about us ... about our friendship."

She and her husband stepped into the room and approached the foot of his bed. "And are you remembering?"

"Some of it," he said, trying to sound convincing. "I think he's trying to build up my ego or something. He's only told me the good things about myself—nothing bad yet."

"That's 'cause there *is* nothing bad," Phillip insisted.

"See what I mean?" Jesse said, laughing.

Margo smiled as she reached over to hand Jesse a bag she was carrying. "Here, we brought you something. You didn't seem too excited about the hospital food this morning, so we stopped at Taco Bell."

Jesse stared at the bag for a moment before reaching out to take it. "Oh thanks," he said, trying to fake his approval. "I'm gonna save this and eat it a little later. I just finished my supper."

"Jesse, you took like two bites of green beans," Phillip observed. "Go on and pig out! Enjoy yourself, and let your mom spoil you."

"This could be your only chance," Margo teased. "You might not remember yet, but I'm not always so nice."

"Ain't that the truth?" Paul chimed in, and they all laughed.

"Mom," Jesse said seriously. "Do you think you could do me a favor?"

"Of course, honey. Anything."

"Can you check at the nurses' station and see if they can unhook some of these tubes and wires … and this catheter? I need to get out of this bed!"

Just as he made his plea, a nurse walked through the door. It wasn't Rose this time, but a male nurse. He smiled at the family. "I see our patient is awake finally," he said. "My name's Roger, and I'm your nurse tonight. If you'll excuse me, I need to check this young man's vitals. How's the pain, Jesse?"

"I don't have any," he said. "But I want you to take this thing outta me. I hate having the catheter."

Roger smiled down at him. "I know what ya mean, and you know what? I think I can do that for you. We were going to remove it earlier but you were sleeping. Visiting hours are over at nine. Do you want to wait 'til then?"

"Phillip is staying," Jesse said. "He's spending the night."

"Jesse!" his mom chided, "Phillip needs to go home. If you want someone to stay with you, I will."

"Well," Roger said, "hospital visiting hours end at 9 p.m. Except in emergency situations, we don't allow overnight visits."

"Please!" Phillip begged. "Look, I was a patient here before, lots of times, actually. They used to let my family stay with me when I was afraid. And Jesse—he's having terrible nightmares. Earlier he woke up screaming—"

"Oh honey!" his mother exclaimed.

"Well, let me check with my supervisor," Roger said. "I'll see if we can allow it. I might also be able to get the doctor to give you a sleeping pill, something to calm you. It's not abnormal for accident victims to suffer from anxiety and stress, and to have bad dreams."

"I don't need drugs," Jesse said. "I need Phillip. I want him to stay. Only him." He looked over at his friend, who was smiling down at him proudly. "No offense, mom," he added.

"Dear, it's okay. Whatever you need … whatever you want. Of course I'm not offended."

"Okay then, I'll check and see what I can do. Open up," Roger stepped over and slid a thermometer under Jesse's tongue.

****

An hour later, Jesse felt his face redden as the nurse peeled back the covers to expose him. He was preparing to remove the catheter from Jesse's bladder. "Is it gonna hurt?" Jesse asked.

"Nah, it'll be over before you know it."

Jesse looked away, staring at the curtain that had been pulled around the bed. His parents had already left the hospital, and Phillip had excused himself from the room until the nurse was finished. "It's kind of embarrassing," Jesse said.

"Try not to be embarrassed. You have nothing to be modest about," Roger said.

"What's *that* supposed to mean?" Jesse demanded, turning to look the man in the eye.

"Oh, I just mean we do this stuff all day long—all the time. I've seen so many naked people that I don't even think about it anymore. It goes with the job. Plus I would think a guy like you wouldn't be shy. You're an athlete, right?"

"Yeah, what's that got to do with it?"

"Well, you're probably used to being in the locker room, having other guys see you naked."

"But they're not touching me!"

"True. Just relax, it will only take a couple seconds. You're a track star, right?"

"I was on the track team, yeah. Not anymore though. I graduated."

"Well, you're one lucky guy," Roger said. "After what happened to you, we never expected to see you sitting up and talking again. Everyone here is amazed by your recovery."

"Oww!! I thought you said it wouldn't hurt! Damn!" Jesse grasped the bed sheets as the tube was withdrawn from his penis.

"All done!" Roger said.

"Shit! Oh god, that was awful."

"But it's out of you now, and you're back in business," Roger laughed. "I'll send your friend back in." The nurse gathered up his medical supplies as Jesse quickly pulled his hospital gown down to cover himself and draped the thin hospital blanket about the rest of him.

As Roger left the room, Jesse lay there, still concealed by the curtain. He was back in business. Yes indeed, he was. He reached down and touched himself, realizing he had yet to examine his own equipment. He didn't even know how well-endowed he was. Slowly he rubbed the bulge that was starting to grow beneath the covers.

"Can I come in?" He heard Phillip's voice from the other side of the curtain. "Are you decent yet?"

"Sure," Jesse said, withdrawing his hand from his crotch and resting it against his chest. Phillip stepped around the curtain to peek in.

"Feel better?"

"I will in a minute, I think. Kinda hurt when he pulled it out."

Phillip made a face. "Sorry, man."

"Come sit with me. We got interrupted earlier, and you were telling me something—something important."

Phillip smiled sweetly at him. He slowly stepped over to the bed and again sat on the edge of the mattress. "I was just telling you how I'd planned to talk to you that day, the same day as your accident."

"You were going to tell me how you really felt—"

"Jesse, I'm afraid—"

"Don't be."

"I love you ... and not just as a friend."

Jesse stared at his friend and once again noticed the tears in his big brown eyes. "Phillip, I wish I could remember ... I wish I could say I felt the same, but I just don't know you yet."

"But you *will* remember. The doctor said it would all come back. But you're not repulsed by the fact that I'm ... well, that I'm in love with you?"

"I'm flattered," Jesse said, smiling sincerely at his friend. He reached out to take the boy's hand. "You're absolutely beautiful."

"Oh Jesse!" he cried. "I was so scared to tell you. I was afraid you'd hate me, and that we'd never be friends again. I've never told anyone that I'm this way ..."

"Homosexual?"

Phillip laughed through his tears. "Well, can't we call it 'gay'?" he asked.

"Oh right. Guess I'm talking like an old man again."

"Yep!" Phillip cracked up. "It's okay, though. Talk however you want."

"Phillip, I'm gay, too ..."

Phillip reached up and covered his open mouth with his hand, staring at Jesse in shocked disbelief. "Jesse," he gasped, "for so long I've been praying I'd hear you say those words."

"Let's just be friends, okay? We'll see what happens ..."

Phillip smiled at him and slowly nodded, then without another word he leaned in and gently kissed him on the lips. Jesse felt the bulge start to grow again.

Seven

This wasn't their first kiss. While his friend had been unconscious, lying there in a coma, Phillip had kissed him several times. He'd whisper in Jesse's ear every single day how much he loved him. He never could be certain that Jesse was even able to hear him, but he told him just the same. Perhaps it had paid off, for when Phillip finally did have the opportunity to say the words to the fully-awakened Jesse, he hadn't been rejected.

It was so beautiful the way Jesse responded to his kiss. His lips were so soft against his own. Jesse leaned into him, parting his lips slightly, and reached up to gently place his hands on the sides of Phillip's face. As Phillip slowly pulled away, Jesse smiled, and they looked into each other's eyes.

"Well, I'd say that's a pretty good start," Jesse said.

"Oh Jesse," Phillip whispered, just as he heard the sound of a throat being cleared behind him. Quickly he turned to see Roger, who immediately pulled away the curtain.

"Boys," he said. "Normally the hospital only allows overnight visitors in cases of emergency; however, after I explained to my supervisor how frightened Jesse was, she agreed to make an exception. This is not a slumber party, though. Jesse needs his rest. Phillip, I will set up a cot alongside the wall. But if you plan to stay up all night talking, you'll be asked to leave."

"Thank you, Roger," Phillip said. "I promise, I'll let Jesse rest. I'll just be here if he needs me."

"I do need him," Jesse said, and Phillip's heart swelled. "I need him to sit here with me until I fall asleep. But it's still early. I'm not ready to go to sleep yet. I wanna get out of this bed and take a walk!"

Phillip looked up at Roger imploringly. "I could walk with him down to the solarium. I used to go there all the time when I was a patient. We won't bother anyone … I promise."

Roger looked at the couple suspiciously. He held up his left hand to reveal a single gold band on his ring finger. "See this?" he asked. "It's my wedding ring. I received it last year in Vermont when I married my *husband*. You two aren't fooling me. I can tell how much in love you are."

Phillip beamed from ear to ear. He felt himself blushing. "Well, it's not exactly like that … but we are … um …"

"Gay?" Roger asked.

"My parents don't know," Jesse said. "Please don't tell them."

"Your secret's safe with me, but you need to remember this is a hospital. Save the romance for when you're completely better and back home."

"Aww, come on, Roger! I've been in a coma for like three months."

"Exactly! That's why you need to just chill out and get the rest your body needs. Once you're better, you two can go at it all night if you want … at home."

Phillip started laughing. "It's not like that. We aren't boyfriends or anything. Right now we're gonna just be friends and see what happens. Jesse doesn't even remember a lot of stuff yet."

"Looked like he remembered how to kiss well enough."

Phillip felt a little embarrassed, knowing that Roger had seen them. "Yeah," Phillip agreed. "He definitely remembered that just fine."

Jesse winked at him.

****

It all seemed surreal to Phillip. For so many months—years, actually—he had harbored this crush on his best friend, secretly imagining the day when he'd be brave enough to bare his soul. Now it had happened, and the response he'd received was better than in his wildest dreams. Instead of being shocked and freaked out, Jesse had taken Phillip's admission in stride. He'd told Phillip that he was flattered and had even called him beautiful.

Most significantly, though, they had kissed, and it had been magnificent.

"Thank you, God!" Phillip whispered as he leaned against the wall. He was standing outside the bathroom waiting for Jesse. This was the very first time Jesse had been out of bed since waking from the coma.

Although Phillip was aware that Roger assumed the only reason he was staying with Jesse overnight was because he had the hots for him, Phillip was indeed worried about Jesse. It was so strange seeing him stand up for the first time. He was so unsteady on his feet, and his first few steps had been rather tentative. It was like he was afraid, and who could blame him, really?

What had really given Phillip pause, though, was the remark Jesse had made as he began to walk. "This is my first time in this body."

"Jesse," Phillip had said, "you may not remember, but you've walked a lot in this body. In fact, you were a runner, and a damned good one. I know it must feel weird. It probably really does feel like you have a whole new body."

In spite of his wobbly stance, and regardless of the skimpy, unflattering hospital gown he was wearing, and notwithstanding the bandage on his head that covered most of his now-bald skull, Jesse looked strikingly handsome to Phillip. As Jesse straightened his body, pushing his shoulders back and thrusting his chest slightly forward, it was all Phillip could do to keep from sighing out loud at the sight of his magnificence.

"Let me help you with this," Phillip offered, as he pulled the back of the hospital gown together and tied the cords.

"Don't want you to be em-bare-assed."

Jesse laughed. "I can't believe it Phillip!" he said excitedly. "It feels so incredible."

"You mean being out of bed finally?"

"Yeah! I feel so strong ... so healthy!"

"Well I've got to be honest," Phillip said. "You look pretty darned good for a guy who just had brain surgery. You actually do look healthy."

Jesse held out his hand to his friend. "Will you help me? I'm going to try making it over to the bathroom."

"Sure," Phillip answered. "Of course I'll help you, but you seem to be doing great on your own."

And that was when Jesse began to walk. At first he took small steps, almost like a child learning to walk for the first time. Phillip slid his arm around Jesse's waist. It was more of a reassuring gesture, for Jesse didn't really appear to be in danger of falling. Once they arrived at the bathroom door, Jesse turned to his friend and gently kissed him on the forehead. "Thanks," he whispered. Then he opened the bathroom door and slipped inside. "I'll be right out. Wait for me."

"Sure," Phillip said.

Now some ten minutes later, Phillip still stood outside the door, waiting for his friend to come out. He was a little worried, wondering what was taking so long. Just as he was about to call out to Jesse, the door opened.

"Ready for our walk?" Jesse asked.

"Definitely!"

"I wish I could find a way to describe how this feels," Jesse said. "It's like ... well, like being born again. When I was in the bathroom, looking at myself in the mirror, I just couldn't believe it!"

Phillip looked up into his friend's animated face. "Jesse, do you not remember how you were before? Is everything brand new to you?"

Jesse sighed and held out an arm for his friend to take. "I remember some facts. Just the basic things like who my parents are, and my address. I just don't know details. I don't remember how anything feels, or how it's supposed to feel. When I took my first steps a few minutes ago, it seemed like I was walking on pillows ... ya know like I was on the surface of the moon or something."

"Really?" Phillip asked. "That's kinda cool ... isn't it?"

"It was rather strange," Jesse admitted.

Phillip laughed. "Rather strange? See, it's like you grew up while you were sleeping. You seriously say things a lot different now. Before you'd have said it was freaky, but now you say 'rather strange'." He saw Jesse's face redden slightly, and he quickly added, "But it's totally cool. Maybe it just means you're maturing. You're growing up."

Jesse placed his hand against the wall with his right arm, and with his left he held onto Phillip as they began to walk towards the door of the hospital room. "I can't really say why I'm talking differently. I can assure you, though, that it's not deliberate."

"Jesse, don't worry about it, okay? I shouldn't have said anything. To be honest, it's kind of sexy. I like a guy who is mature."

"Thanks, Phillip. I like you too. I really do ..."

"I like how you kiss, too," Phillip whispered.

"Am I the first ... the first guy you've kissed?"

Now it was Phillip's turn to blush. He looked down at the ground.

"Hey, it's okay. You're probably the first guy I've kissed, too. I mean, if there were any others before you, I don't remember."

"But you remembered you were gay." Phillip looked up into Jesse's eyes. "How'd you remember that when you have forgotten so many other details?"

"Phillip, you make it very easy for me to remember." He

leaned in and again kissed Phillip tenderly on the lips. This time the kiss felt even more passionate to Phillip. He sensed Jesse's urgency as he pressed against him.

"Oh god!" Phillip sighed as he pulled away. "Are you sure you wanna go for that walk?"

Jesse laughed. "Yeah, I'm sure. Sorry, I just couldn't resist …"

Phillip giggled. "No problem, dude! I … um …" Suddenly Phillip felt the emotion wash over him. "Jesse, you have no idea how long I've been dreaming of this—how much I've prayed you'd … um …"

"Be attracted to you?"

Phillip nodded. He looked over toward the door and once again grabbed Jesse's arm. "Let's go on our walk—"

"It's true," Jesse said, ignoring Phillip's attempt to change the subject. "I do find you attractive, and I don't just mean your looks."

"But you don't really remember me, Jesse. As far as you know, I could be an axe murderer."

"I knew the second I laid eyes on you, you were no axe murderer." Jesse laughed. "You have a kind heart, and I hope you can teach me—"

"The things you forgot?" Phillip asked.

"No, I hope you can teach me how to be kind …"

"Oh Jesse, I really wish you did remember because you are the kindest person I know! When I was sick …" Phillip was starting to get choked up. "Jesse, when I was sick, you shaved your head for me!"

Jesse laughed in spite of himself. "And that was kind?"

"Yes! It was the kindest thing anyone ever did for me. I had lost all my hair, and you shaved yours off so I wouldn't feel so bad."

Jesse suddenly became somber. "Phillip, do you have cancer?"

"It's in remission. I'm fine now, and I don't even have chemotherapy anymore."

"I'm so sorry," Jesse said. "I know about cancer ... or I mean, I remember. I remember how horrible it is."

"Do you remember me having cancer, Jesse?"

Jesse became silent and smiled sweetly at his friend. "I'm sorry Phillip, not yet. It's just confusing to me. I remember things but I don't know why. I mean, I can't specifically relate them to anything."

"Well I'm kind of glad you don't remember all that. I don't want you thinking of me as being ... um ... like a victim or something. Plus, I don't want you to feel sorry for me."

"What about me?" Jesse asked. "When I was in that coma and you didn't know if I would ever wake up, didn't you feel sorry for me?"

"But Jesse, you're awake now, and you're proving just how strong you are. You overcame something that was almost impossible. And now you have a lot of challenges ahead of you—relearning so many things—but because I know exactly how strong you are, I know you can do it. I don't feel sorry for you—not at all! When we thought you might die, I felt sorry for *me*. I didn't wanna lose you—"

"And that's how I feel about you, Phillip. If you are strong enough to fight cancer, you're no victim. You're a survivor."

"We both are. We're both survivors."

"And in a way, both of us are starting over. It's a whole new beginning, and we're facing it together."

"Let's go," Phillip said. "The solarium is straight ahead, down the hallway. After we get there, I'll race you back."

****

Less than twenty four hours ago Harold Wainwright had lain dying, an old and lonely man in a body besieged by illness. Now he was an entirely new person, and his former self no longer existed. As Jesse stood in front of the full-length bathroom mirror and took in his reflection for the first time, it was startling, to say the least.

71

Jesse Warren's body was magnificent! It was toned and defined, and his broad shoulders framed his perfect physique magnificently. His face was so beautifully smooth, the skin taut and unwrinkled, not a single line or blemish. His eyes were bright and sharply blue, and his teeth gleamed flawlessly white. He looked down at himself, taking in the tightness of his core. His abdomen was smooth and ripped, so different from the flaccid body he'd grown used to. In fact, he didn't seem to have an ounce of excess anywhere.

Tentatively Jesse pulled the hospital gown away from his body, exposing his private parts. "Yes!" he whispered, "there is a God!" Not only had he been blessed with a stunningly handsome face and athletic body, but he also had nothing to be ashamed of in the personal equipment area. Just seeing himself for the first time elicited a response. Oh, the joy of again experiencing an eighteen-year-old body! He instantly remembered what it was like, getting erections for apparently no reason at all, being able to achieve orgasm and then only moments later finding himself ready to have another go at it. He remembered the stamina that he used to have, and he recalled how he'd taken it for granted.

This time would be different. He was going to savor every second of his life. He was not going to take any of life's blessings for granted—especially not Phillip. It was so unnerving to Jesse how much this young boy looked like his former lover Jacob. Could it be that he was the offspring of the man he'd once loved? But Jacob's obituary made no mention of surviving children. There was no reference to an ex-wife, and honestly Jesse could not believe that Jacob would have married a woman under any circumstances. Jacob had been so much like Phillip, it was mind-boggling. Phillip seemed to Jesse to be the reincarnation of Jacob Klein.

He knew that Phillip was waiting for him, standing on the other side of the door, but he could not stop staring at his own reflection. Slowly he lifted his arm and flexed it while examining his bicep. He turned to the side to see his profile, then turned even farther in an attempt to examine his behind. As he devoured the image of his youthful body, he became fully aroused, and he could not resist reaching down and touching himself.

"Oh God!" he sighed. It had been so long since he'd experienced that sensation. He almost couldn't believe it was happening. *Phillip is waiting for me*, he told himself, yet he just couldn't stop. He grinned at his reflection as he began to stroke. Slowly at first, he pumped his fist up and down, never taking his eyes off the mirror. His pulse quickened. He began to sweat. Oh, it felt so wonderful! He was so close ... and then his body trembled as the orgasm washed over him. "Unghh," he cried, trying to stifle the sound of his moaning.

He nearly laughed out loud as he shivered violently. "I love this body," he whispered to himself. Then he cleaned himself up, washed his face and turned to exit the bathroom. Of course Phillip was waiting for him, and when Jesse leaned in to kiss him for the second time, he realized what it meant to die and go to heaven.

As the boys walked together down the hallway, arm-in-arm, Jesse knew it was just the beginning of a beautiful friendship.

Eight

On his way to his new home, Jesse stared out the window of his parents' Ford Fusion. He sat silently in the passenger seat, taking in the sights of the suburban neighborhood. The houses all looked so much alike, and they were all so small. It was a warm summer day, and children were outside playing in their yards. An ice cream vendor had stopped his truck at the corner of the block, and kids from the neighborhood gathered 'round, waiting to purchase their chilly treats. Jesse smiled as he observed the scene. He was sitting in the passenger seat, and his mother was driving.

He had only remained in the hospital for four days after awakening from his coma. His doctor said there was no medical reason why he needed further hospitalization. He no longer wore the bandage on his head, only a small, white knit cap. The doctor said his incision could heal just as well at home as it would in a hospital bed.

Jesse was beginning to get used to his new body. He was starting to understand exactly how much physical strength he had. Walking was now no longer something that felt weird to him. In fact the previous day he did little else. He walked up and down the hallways of the hospital with Phillip.

Phillip seemed to know so many people. They had stopped at several of the nurses' stations, and Phillip had proudly introduced Jesse to the staff members that he knew. "This is my friend Jesse. He's the track star who was in a coma for three months." Everyone was aware of the details of the accident. Jesse was a bit of a celebrity, and it warmed his heart to see how so many people had been concerned about his recovery.

His mom seemed exuberant. She chattered endlessly

during their drive home. She apologized to Jesse that his father would not be there for his homecoming. He had finally returned to work the previous morning. While Jesse had been unconscious, his dad had used up all his sick pay benefits in order to maintain a vigil at his bedside. Money was going to be tight for a period, she explained, but everything was going to work out. They would be fine once Paul's regular paychecks started to roll in again. She also was going to refocus her efforts on her Internet store.

Margo assured Jesse that they would have a special homecoming dinner for him. Phillip and his parents were coming over, and they were barbecuing in the back yard. Jesse was going to get a chance to see some of his extended family as well. His grandparents and cousins were supposed to stop by as well as his track coach.

"Do I have a computer?" Jesse asked his mom.

"Of course you do, baby," she smiled as she glanced over to him. "You don't remember?"

"Sorry. I thought I had one, but I wasn't sure. I don't remember any of my passwords ... I mean for my email addresses and stuff."

"Well, hopefully you have some of them stored ... or written down somewhere. Don't worry, I'm sure you can reset the passwords that you don't remember."

"Is it a laptop?"

His mom laughed. "No honey, I'm sorry, it's not a laptop. It's a PC, and it's a couple years old. You've been bugging me for a laptop for the past year or so. We haven't been able to afford it, but we'll get you one soon."

"So I don't have a job? I mean, I didn't work anywhere to make spending money?"

"You did have one for a while. You worked at the grocery store where Phillip's father is manager. With your sports, though, it seemed like a job was too much. We felt it was best that you focus on school. You had talked about going back this summer and working to save money for college in the fall, but I think you should just relax and concentrate on fully recovering first." She reached over and placed her hand on his knee. "All that matters is, you're back home, and you're healthy again."

Jesse was beginning to realize how much of an adjustment his new life was going to require. He'd been used to having any material possession he desired. He had a computer in practically every room of his mansion-style home. He had pool tables, swimming pools, and even an in-house movie theater. The rec-room area alone was bigger than most of the houses in his new neighborhood. He had told Drayton rather pointedly that he didn't give a rat's ass about losing the money, but now that he was facing the reality of a middle-income lifestyle, he wasn't so sure the sacrifice was as insignificant as he'd thought it would be.

"Is this the only car we own?" he asked.

"Oh no, sweetie. Your dad has a car he uses mainly to drive back and forth to work. It's a Ford Escort. We just got this nice car last year ..."

"This is the *nice* car?" Jesse asked.

Margo laughed. "It's the nicest car I've ever owned. I love this car. It has everything I need."

"Have we always owned Fords?"

"Well, your grandpa worked for Ford, so we have always gotten a discount. There was a period a few years ago when we had a Chevy. It was our beater car. Your dad has always kept an older car for running around in. He lets me drive the nice vehicle."

"One of these days I'll buy you a decent car," Jesse said confidently.

"Well, like I said, I love my car. Don't be worried about buying me anything. You just concentrate on getting better."

As Jesse looked over at his "mom," he was momentarily taken aback by the dawning realization that he was reverting to his old self. It had been a matter of hours since he'd willingly left behind the world of materialism that had once consumed him in exchange for a second chance at life. Now, faced with his first exposure to a normal, middle-class existence, he was already yearning for a return to the good life.

That sincerity in her eyes, that genuine emotion—it was priceless. "You know, Mother," he said, his voice cracking, "I think you're right. This really is a nice car … and I don't need a laptop computer." A single teardrop slowly trickled down his cheek.

"Baby, you've never called me that before," she responded as she reached up to wipe the tear from his face. "In all these years you've always called me Mom, or Mama … or when you were young it was Mommy, but never Mother."

"I'm sorry," he whispered.

"Sweetheart, don't be sorry! Why are you suddenly so emotional? Maybe we should postpone the barbecue …"

"It's just that …" Jesse paused a moment before continuing. "It's just that I know the sacrifices you've made for me. I know how tough it's been, and here I am worrying about cars and computers—things that don't matter."

"Jesse, you're a teenager, and you're being a typical teen. Of course you want the best computer. Of course you want a cool ride. I understand. Don't be so hard on yourself, okay?"

"I have everything I need. I have you and Dad, and I have Phillip. Everything's going to be just fine."

"Everything's gonna be perfect. You're back with us—back among the living. How could life be any better?" She grabbed his hand and squeezed it affectionately as she pulled the car into their driveway.

****

"I'm thinking of shaving off all my hair," Phillip told his mother.

"But honey, your hair just grew back. Why would you want to shave it all off?"

"Don't you remember how Jesse shaved his head after I started chemo? He did it for me, and now he's a cue ball himself because of his surgery. I wanna do it for him."

"Well, I think you should wait. Does it seem like he feels bad about being bald? Does he act self conscious about it?" She was standing at the sink peeling potatoes as she spoke to her son.

"Nah, but he has that big bandage over his head. When they take it off, I bet he will feel weird." Phillip cocked his head and glanced out the window, thinking about Jesse and his turban-style headgear. "Ya know what?" he asked, suddenly realizing something. "You're right; I don't think Jesse will be embarrassed at all. He's just that way; he doesn't really care what anyone else thinks about his appearance."

Phillip's mother smiled at her son affectionately as she turned on the tap water. "I'm sure he'd appreciate the gesture, Phillip, but I doubt that it'll bother Jesse Warren to have no hair for a few weeks 'til his grows back. He's a good looking kid with or without hair."

"You got that right!" Phillip replied, a little too readily. "He's here!" Phillip exclaimed as he noticed the white Ford pulling into the driveway across the street. He continued to stare out the window, watching for Jesse to get out of the car and wondering if he should go greet his friend at his homecoming. Nah, he'd better wait. It had only been a few hours since he'd left Jesse's hospital bed.

"So how are things going with you and Jesse?" his mom asked. "Is he starting to remember?"

"Bits and pieces," Phillip explained. A broad smile crossed his lips. When he thought about Jesse he could barely contain himself. "Things are going good though ... *really* good."

"Oh?" she said.

"Mom, we kissed," Phillip whispered. "Jesse told me … um … he confessed to me about himself."

She turned off the water and grabbed a kitchen towel to dry her hands. "What do you mean?" she asked.

"He's gay, too," Phillip said. "He's gay and he said he thinks I'm beautiful, even though he doesn't remember all of our past."

"So he remembers that he's gay, but he doesn't remember you? That's interesting."

"Don't say anything, though, please. He hasn't told his mom and dad."

"You know I'd never say anything, sweetie. But I want you to be careful. "

"Mom! Be careful? I don't want to be careful. Not now. I almost missed my chance with Jesse, and now …"

"And now Jesse has to start his whole life over again. He has a lot of things to figure out, and I don't want you getting yourself hurt in the process."

"Jesse would never hurt me, Mom." Phillip scowled, somewhat offended by his mother's skepticism.

"Just do me a favor, okay? Take things slow. Make sure you're not rushing into things before you both know what you want, and give Jesse the time he needs to get adjusted to life again."

"We're just gonna be friends for now. We both want to wait and see if Jesse remembers more. Can't you for once just stop worrying about me and let me enjoy my life? I almost died, and so did Jesse! Can't you let us enjoy each other?" Phillip felt his face reddening. It was unlike him to snap at her this way, but she'd struck a nerve.

"I know, Baby. I'm sorry. I just don't want you getting hurt. I don't want either of you getting hurt. I'm just asking you to be careful."

His anger shifted inward as he felt the tears well in his eyes. He didn't want her to think that she had made him cry, but when he became defensive about something, it seemed the tears were always there. "Mom, I love Jesse Warren! I've always loved him, and if you really cared one bit about me, you'd realize it."

"Phillip, I love you with all my heart." She tossed the towel in the sink and placed a hand on her son's shoulder. "But there's another reason I want you to be careful. You know I've never had a problem with your sexual preference …"

"It's not a preference, Mom. It's who I *am*. It's my identity."

"Okay … with your *orientation*. You know I have no problem with it, and I'm sure your father will have no problem with it. We'll always love and support you exactly as you are—for *who* you are. But I don't know Jesse's parents well enough to say for certain that they will feel the same way. What if they have a problem with having a gay son?"

"Jesse's eighteen now. They can't stop him from seeing me," Phillip stated defiantly.

"But he still lives at home, and if they don't support him, it could be very difficult for him."

"I think Margo will support him. In fact, I know she will. It about killed her when Jesse was in that coma. I know how much she loves him."

"You're probably right, honey. I hope you are, anyway. But think about what I said. Take it slow and enjoy each other. Let him get to know you again. I'm positive he is going to fall head over heels. But no matter what, let it happen naturally."

Phillip reached up to wipe the tears from his cheeks. "I know, Mom," he whispered. "Thanks.

"Hey, ya know what is funny? When Jesse first woke up he thought my name was Jacob. He kept calling me that. I told him that was my middle name."

She smiled lovingly at her son. "Jacob was my uncle. I named you after him, and he was like you."

"What do you mean?" Phillip asked.

"He was gay. His name was Jacob Klein, and he was a famous artist. That painting in the living room above the sofa, it's one of his prints."

"Really? I had a gay uncle?"

"Your great uncle. He was your grandmother's brother."

"Isn't that weird? Jesse kept saying I looked like some guy named Jacob, and it turns out my uncle was named Jacob. Do you think I look at all like him?"

"You're the spitting image of him when he was your age."

"Wow! What a coincidence."

****

Jesse stood in the doorway of his ten-by-twelve foot bedroom feeling rather claustrophobic. "Wow," he said, "so this is my room, huh?"

"Exactly as you left it," his mother quipped. "Well, I did tidy it up a bit, but you'll find everything pretty much the same—I mean if you can remember."

"I don't really … sorry. But it's fine. And this is my closet?" He stepped over to the sliding doors, opened them, and peered inside. "I guess maybe I was a bit of a slob, huh?" Stacks of sporting equipment, shoes, and clothing were piled on the closet floor.

"Oh, I've seen it much worse," Margo laughed. "Are you saying you're about to turn over a new leaf and suddenly be Mr. Neat and Tidy?"

"Um … I hope a little better than I've obviously been so far," he vowed. Jesse looked over at his mother and smiled sweetly. "How did you put up with my slovenly behavior?"

"Oh baby, I've missed your slovenly behavior. I'm just so glad to have you back with us. I don't care how much of a slob you were—or are." She stepped over to him and rubbed his back affectionately as he pulled the closet door closed and stared at their reflection in the full-length door mirror.

The white beanie Jesse wore on his head effectively covered the still-gruesome looking stitches of his incision. He gently pulled the cap up to reveal his scalp. Hair was already starting to sprout on the crown of his head. "Look, I'm getting some peach fuzz already," he laughed.

"Your hair has always grown quickly. You'll have it back in no time. "

"What time's Phillip coming over?" he asked as he stepped over to the twin-sized bed and pressed his palm firmly on the mattress. He depressed it, checking its firmness.

"Oh, I'm not sure," she replied. "Any time you want."

"I really like Phillip. I like him a lot," he said sincerely.

"You two have always been close. Even if you don't remember him, I'm glad to see that you are bonding with one another." She sighed and took a step closer to her son. "You know, he almost died himself a few months ago. He had cancer."

"He still has it," Jesse gently corrected her, "but it's in remission."

"I really thought I understood the hardship that family was going through. I was wrong, though. I didn't understand anything until we almost lost you." Her voice was beginning to choke up.

"But you didn't lose me," he said as he turned to take her into his arms. "I'm here now, and I'm fine. I'm not going anywhere."

"Yes!" she said, struggling to remain composed. "Yes, young man, you're not going anywhere, and you're going to be just fine."

Jesse felt the softness of her hair brush against his cheek as she embraced him. She smelled of lilac, one of his favorite fragrances. It was so tragic really, because this woman he was holding believed it was her son she was embracing. She believed that a medical miracle had rescued him from the clutches of death, while in reality she had truly lost him. The Jesse Warren she had given birth to and then raised and loved for eighteen years was dead. A new Jesse had taken his place, and he was an imposter.

But what was Jesse to do? Even if he elected to be honest and tell the Warren family the truth, they would never believe him. They would think that their son was delusional, possibly insane. Additionally, even if he were to convince them of who he really was, it would accomplish nothing; it would just hurt them. Not only would it hurt Paul and Margo, but it would also crush Phillip.

It was too late to question the ethical ramifications of his decision to go through with the transfer. He was beginning to realize what an incredible young man the real Jesse Warren had been, how loved and cherished. Glancing up at the walls of the small bedroom to see the numerous academic and athletic awards on display, he was acutely aware of the big shoes he had to fill.

Thus far his one aim had been to live a better life than he had previously. He had considered this adventure a second chance, a means of righting some of the wrongs he'd committed in his previous existence. Now, though, he realized that he bore an even greater burden. He owed it to Jesse Warren to live a life that would honor him. He owed it to Jesse's family, and of course to Phillip.

"I swear I'll be better," he whispered to himself. "I swear I won't hurt this family. I'll cherish the ones who love me."

"Oh Jesse," Margo cried. "I don't know what you're talking about! You have never hurt us. It was an accident, and if I'd have just driven you to practice that day—"

Apparently she thought he was blaming himself for the accident, and was in turn claiming responsibility for the tragedy herself. "It's not your fault, Mother," he whispered. "It was just an accident. It wasn't your fault, and it wasn't mine ..."

"Then why, Jesse? Why are you so distraught over hurting us?"

He pulled away from her in order to look her into her eyes. "I love that perfume," he confessed. "It smells like lilacs."

"You bought it for me last year … for Mother's Day. Of course you love it."

"Oh," he laughed through his tears. "I guess I had good taste."

"You always have."

He sighed as he looked at her endearingly. "I just want to be a good son, that's all. I want to make you proud."

"You already have, Jesse. You always have."

"Thank you," he whispered. "I think I'm going to try to fire up this computer before the … um … the social event."

She laughed in spite of herself. "The *party*!" she clarified. "It's your homecoming party, silly!"

"Yes, that. What does one wear for a homecoming party?"

She shook her head as she stared at the boy in front of her. "You look perfect just as you are, but you can wear whatever you want. It's a barbecue, very informal."

He leaned in and kissed her on the cheek. "I love you, Mother."

"I love you, too."

Nine

Phillip was greeted by Margo when he arrived at the Warren doorstep that afternoon. "Come on in!" she said cheerfully. "Jesse's upstairs in his room. Why don't you go right on up?"

"Oh thank you, Mrs. Warren," he said. "My mom and dad will be over later. She made potato salad."

"How nice." She smiled at him sweetly. "You really didn't have to bring anything. Phillip, I want to thank you for all you've done, the way you've been so supportive. It's meant a lot to our entire family, especially Jesse. He was telling me this afternoon how much he likes you."

"Thanks." Phillip looked down at the floor in front of him, suddenly embarrassed. Then he willed himself to look back up into her eyes as he said, "I can't tell you how much he means to me. He's my best friend, and I just can't believe I almost lost him."

"And he almost lost you. You've been there for each other."

Feeling as if he might be on the verge of tears, Phillip quickly shrugged off the emotion. "Better go see how he's doin'," he said and then dashed down the hallway and up the stairwell.

As Phillip stood outside Jesse's bedroom and gently knocked on the door, he suddenly realized he could hear music. But wait, it couldn't be. It sounded like …

"Is that classical music you're listening to?" Phillip asked as Jesse opened the door.

Jesse's smile was warm. "Hey! I'm home!"

Phillip wanted to hug him … or more, but he just stood

there grinning. Jesse leaned in and softly kissed him on the lips. "Did you miss me?"

"Oh my God, yes!" Phillip confessed. "You got your bandage off?" He pointed to Jesse's small white cap.

"Yeah, and you should see the incision. I look like Frankenstein."

"Really? I never realized what a hottie Frankenstein was, then."

Jesse laughed. "Come on in. You can help me pick out music for the party."

"It's so weird to hear you listening to … what is this?"

"It's Horowitz. A piano concerto."

"And you had this? It was with your CDs?"

Jesse laughed. "No. Oh my god, you should see my CDs. I don't recognize any of the artists. I must have forgotten them all. This is public radio I'm listening to."

Phillip was again puzzled. "How strange," he admitted, "that you don't remember any of your favorite singers, but you know about this classical stuff."

"Oh … um, well they announced who it was. They said his name before the piece started playing. I liked the sound of it, so I kept listening."

"It's … well, it's really pretty. I like it, too, I think."

"Why don't you pick something out? Remind me of what I used to like before the accident."

Phillip looked over at Jesse's twin bed and saw an array of CDs strewn across the mattress. "Do you remember him?" Phillip asked as he held up a CD. "It's Kris Evans, the winner of American Idol last year."

"I think I vaguely remember him. He was the cute one, and I didn't think he stood a snowball's chance of winning. I thought that other guy would win … the really radical one."

"Adam Lambert," Phillip clarified.

"Right," Jesse nodded and smiled.

"I wanted Kris to win, and you wanted Adam," Phillip reminded him.

"Ahh … but still I bought his CD?"

"We both liked them both, but Adam was a little too outrageous for me."

Jesse laughed. "So I liked the outrageous one?"

"You've always been like that," Phillip said. They were staring into each other's eyes. "You were always a little edgier than I was. You never really gave a damn what anyone thought of you."

"And you … were you always this—?"

Phillip grinned at him as he hesitated. "What?"

"Sexy?"

He felt his face starting to redden. "Oh Jesse," he whispered, and then he giggled. He felt so conspicuous all of a sudden.

"I'm embarrassing you, and I'm sorry. But you really *are* sexy. Your eyes are so big and dark, and you have this compact-yet-solid body. Short with bod."

"You *do* remember! That's what the girls at school say. They call guys like that SWB's."

"Well that's what you are. You're *my* SWB."

Phillip was unable to tear his eyes away from Jesse's penetrating gaze. It was almost magnetic, the way they were being drawn closer together. Then suddenly they were in each other's arms, and the CD was lying on the floor behind Jesse.

"And you smell good, too." Jesse sighed as he buried his face in Phillip's neck. "What is it? Polo?"

"You … ahh … you're remembering more … um … Jesse!" Jesse nuzzled his chin into the crook of Phillip's neck and it tickled. "You're remembering more all the time."

"I like it," Jesse confessed. "I could eat you up."

They kissed again, this time far more passionately. Phillip felt a wave of euphoria sweep him away as he swooned in Jesse's strong arms. He felt Jesse's tongue probing against his own, tasted the crisp, minty flavor of Jesse's breath. Most noticeably, though, he felt his own arousal.

He was gasping as he pulled away. "Oh Jesse ... we ... uh ... we better behave. The party—"

"Screw the party," Jesse said.

It was the sound of footsteps in the hall that brought them back to reality. They pulled apart as Paul stepped into the doorway. "You're home," he stated the obvious.

"Hey, Dad," Jesse said. "How was work?"

His father shrugged. "'Bout the same as always, but at least today I had something to look forward to. I knew my son would be here when I got home."

"Thanks, Dad," Jesse smiled at him. Paul then stepped in and wrapped his arm around Jesse's shoulder.

"We've really missed you," he said, and then, uncharacteristically, he leaned into his boy and kissed the side of his head. "*I* really missed you."

"Dad!" Jesse said, "Um ... thanks, man."

An awkward silence ensued for a few moments, and then finally Paul squeezed his son one more time in an affectionate-yet-masculine manner before releasing him. "I'm gonna hit the shower before the party gets started, but I just wanted to welcome you home. Sorry I couldn't be here when you first got out of the hospital."

"It's cool, Dad. Thanks." They exchanged a smile before Paul exited.

"Jesse, can I ask you something?" Phillip said after Jesse's dad had left. Jesse nodded. "What do you think they'd say? Your parents, I mean. What would they say if they knew about us ... being gay?"

Jesse grinned and shrugged. It was a gesture of uncertainty. "I honestly have no idea," he admitted. "I ... well ... I know this sounds strange, but I just don't know them well enough yet. I feel how much they love me, and I think they will be supportive no matter what. Then on the other hand, sometimes prejudice is a powerful thing. Prejudice and fear."

"Fear?" Phillip asked.

"People are sometimes afraid of the truth. Afraid of what others will think. Afraid of being embarrassed. Afraid of being looked down upon, being judged. Afraid of the shame that they think they will feel."

"But not your mom and dad. They're just not like that, Jesse."

"Probably not. Only a fool would be that way, really."

"Exactly!" Phillip agreed.

****

It had been during that time alone in his bedroom before Phillip's arrival that Jesse first began to make some interesting yet startling discoveries about who the real Jesse Warren had been. When he logged onto his computer, he initially found the expected. Jesse's homepage was bookmarked with numerous sports' pages. Hundreds of emails filled his inbox, which Jesse did not even attempt to go through. Instead he searched through the "sent" folder, where he found numerous jokes, humorous photos, and other lighthearted forms of communication typical of an average teenager. He then opened Jesse's Facebook and Myspace pages, where he found a lot of information about the music the boy had liked. This is what had prompted him to begin rifling through the CD collection, which was now strewn across the bed.

It was by opening the Web browser history that Jesse came upon the surprises. Jesse Warren had frequently visited a site called gay.com. He also seemed to have a keen interest in gay athletes, and he'd visited several sites dedicated to this theme. Most interestingly, though, was that Jesse Warren had been hooked up with some wickedly hot gay pornographic websites.

There was no doubt in his mind after the first ten minutes online that Jesse Warren was indeed homosexual. He always had been—even before this imposter took over his body.

As he sat there staring at the screen, Jesse felt a wave of relief wash over him. He knew he was being silly, for in truth it didn't matter one way or the other what the real Jesse Warren's sexual orientation had been. Still, he felt better knowing that as he moved forward in his new life, his innate physical attractions would in no way be contradicting or tarnishing the identity of the original Jesse. Perhaps it was his own internal homophobia that led him down this path of reasoning, an assumption that heterosexuality was in some way superior. Perhaps it was merely that he was beginning to greatly admire the person that Jesse had been, and he just felt at peace with the fact that he shared this characteristic with the real boy. Or maybe it was that he was starting to earnestly think of himself as actually being Jesse Warren rather than Harold Wainwright. Whatever the reason was, he felt an overwhelming sense of satisfaction in knowing that Jesse had been gay.

He then dug a little deeper into the item file and discovered that Jesse had an online journal. He nearly cried with joy upon this discovery, for he knew it was going to be his key to convincingly assimilating his new identity. And as he began to read through the entries that the real Jesse had posted, he did indeed weep. Tears of joy and sadness streamed down his face as he learned of the struggle that Jesse had endured during his period of self-discovery. It also became clear to him just how close he had been to Phillip Covington, and how deeply he had loved the boy he believed to be dying.

This was how Jesse had learned the term "short-with-bod" or "SWB." It was Jesse's code name for Phillip in his journal. Oddly the real Jesse had vowed never to tell Phillip of his true feelings. He was afraid it would destroy their friendship. He didn't want to risk alienating his best friend in what he feared were the remaining months of his life. Jesse Warren, who had harbored intense and unrequited feelings for Phillip, had sworn himself to secrecy, and he'd done it out of love.

This was why Jesse was so quick to pull Phillip into his embrace when he saw him that day. This was why he'd so affectionately nuzzled his face into the boy's neck and inhaled the sweet scent of his cologne. This was why he'd kissed him first so tenderly and then ravenously. Only two days prior he had told Phillip that they should just be friends and see what happened, yet now already he wanted so much more.

"I've made a decision," he said earnestly as he looked the shorter boy in the eye. "I don't want to live like that. I don't want to be controlled by fear. Look at what we both have been through! We both almost died, and I want to be my genuine self. I want to live in truth—"

"Oh Jesse … me, too," Phillip whispered.

"I've been reading. Did you know … um … were you aware that I used to keep a journal?"

Phillip shook his head, staring intently into Jesse's eyes. "No. I had no idea."

"I found it. I found the journal on the computer, and … Phillip—"

"What? Please Jesse, tell me," he pleaded.

"I've always loved you. Even before the accident, I was crazy about you."

Phillip's eyes filled with tears as he covered his mouth in shock. "Really?" he gasped.

Jesse nodded and smiled, becoming teary-eyed himself.

"And I … I'd decided never to tell you. I thought you would reject me. I thought you would hate me."

"Oh Jesse, that's what I thought! How long? How long did you know … I mean about how you felt?"

"Let's sit down," he said, taking Phillip's hand into his own. They moved in unison toward the bed and sat side-by-side. "I'm not sure how long I've been in love with you; I haven't yet read all the journal entries. Some of them, though, are pretty intense."

"But is it helping you to read them? Do you remember writing them at all?"

Jesse shook his head sadly. He couldn't lie about this any longer. "I may never remember, Phillip, and I hope you can accept this. I sincerely hope that the fact I can't remember our past will not change how you feel about our future."

"No," he said immediately. "No, it doesn't matter. It doesn't matter at all. Even if you never regain any of those memories, we can just make new ones."

Jesse squeezed the boy's hand. "I was hoping you'd say that."

"Can I see them? Can I read the journal?"

Jesse smiled broadly. "Yeah … of course. They're about you, after all. But I want to wait. I don't want to share them tonight because … well, like I said, they're so intense. I want us to read them together when we can be alone."

"Okay. Do you want to come over to my house tonight … after the barbecue?"

"I don't want to be away from you ever again," he confessed. "But I'm not sure. I don't know what my parents will say about me doing a sleepover on my first night home. Why don't you stay here instead?"

Phillip grinned at him. "Okay." His dark brown eyes widened. They were so temptingly alluring when he smiled like that. Jesse placed his hand gently against Phillip's cheek.

"I want more than your friendship, Phillip Covington. I want so much more …"

And then they kissed again.

****

Phillip was so overjoyed by the news Jesse had shared with him that he felt if he didn't tell someone he just might burst. He had to be discreet, though. He couldn't risk exposing Jesse to his parents and family. His coming out had to be something that Jesse controlled. He was the one who had to make the decision about who to tell and when to tell them.

The smile on Phillip's face that evening was telling, though. He was so ecstatic and so head-over-heels for Jesse that he didn't even think it possible to wipe that cheesy grin off his face. When he saw his mom looking at him and smiling herself, he suspected that she must have figured it out. Then again, she might just assume her son was merely happy to have his best friend home again.

Phillip liked the fact that Jesse had to rely upon him so heavily that evening. It was Phillip who ran interference. He whispered details about the guests into Jesse's ear, providing him at least a semblance of foreknowledge prior to conversing with them. "Hey Jesse, ten o'clock," he whispered, indicating that he was talking about someone who was approaching, slightly to Jesse's left. "See the guy with the really bad toupee? He's your uncle Seth, and he always has really bad breath. He's a big Chicago Cubs fan, and you always talk baseball with him."

Jesse nodded. "Uncle Seth! What about those Cubs this year?" Jesse then launched into an in depth conversation with his uncle about the team, surprising Phillip with the degree of knowledge he obviously recalled about the players.

"That's wild," Phillip said after the old man had left. "You can remember all that information about a sports team but you don't have your memories of family and friends."

Jesse shrugged. "I wish I could explain it," he said.

There were about thirty people who showed up that evening, and all of them were thrilled by Jesse's remarkable recovery. Phillip knew almost everyone present, and he had fun sharing his impressions of each of them with his best friend. "That woman over there with the really big A-double-ess, her name is Shirley, and she is one of your mom's friends. She buys a lot of stuff from your mom's Internet store, and one time she sat down in a lawn chair and broke it right in two."

Jesse's mouth dropped open in surprise. "No way!"

Phillip laughed. "You should have seen it … well, actually you did, but I wish you could remember. She was wailing like a banshee, and you had to help her up. But you were about pissing yourself because you couldn't stop laughing. Then your laughing made me laugh. We got into so much trouble from your mom."

"Oh no, what did she do?"

"She just yelled at us, but I could tell she was almost laughing herself. Oh my god, it was so funny when it happened. That Shirley is really loud and overbearing, and she doesn't really like either one of us. She hates boys or something. She has two girls, and both of them are obnoxious brats … and ugly."

"Wow, I wonder why she came tonight, then," Jesse said. He glanced over to her and then back at Phillip.

"Free food," they said simultaneously. They watched her as she shoveled a huge forkful of potato salad into her mouth and nodded in agreement. They then both started laughing.

It seemed to Phillip that even though the specific memories that he and Jesse shared were now lost, the camaraderie they'd always shared was in full force—stronger than ever, in fact. Jesse had initially seemed timid and confused after waking from his coma, but now the real Jesse was starting to emerge again, and Phillip felt almost as if he liked this new Jesse even more than the person he'd known before the accident.

Perhaps it was that this new Jesse in his life did not have to sort through his feelings and attempt to redefine his "best friend" status. They were like two strangers meeting for the first time, sharing that euphoria that couples experience at the onset of a relationship. Some called it the "honeymoon." Jesse had been Phillip's protector. He'd always been there to stick up for him and offer him constant reassurance. It meant so much to Phillip that he actually had an opportunity to return the favor.

Phillip sensed, however, that Jesse would quickly rebound and come into his own again. Seeing the confident way he mingled with the guests at the party reminded Phillip that Jesse was a true leader, the sort of person who could face any challenge. When the world handed him a lemon, he made lemonade. That was just who he was, and with or without his memories, Jesse would always be that strong-willed, confident individual. Wasn't this why Phillip had always idolized him?

While Jesse was across the yard, conversing with his track coach, Phillip leaned against the fence and simply watched. Jesse was wearing a pair of basketball shorts and a loose-fitting tee. He looked hot as hell, and Phillip sighed audibly as he took in the sight of the tight fabric stretched across Jesse's posterior. He liked Jesse's long, powerful legs, perfectly toned from years of running and physical fitness training. His broad shoulders, v-shaped torso, and narrow waist made Phillip's mouth water. He was just too-good-to-be-true.

The idea that Jesse had loved him for a long time was beyond Phillip's comprehension. It was also a bit disconcerting. They had wasted so much time. They had both been yearning for each other, yet each was too frightened to voice his feelings. Jesse had been so right when he'd said that life was too short to live in fear. He had almost missed his opportunity to be with the one he loved. Both of them had nearly missed their chance. Had Phillip's cancer not gone into remission, Jesse would never have been able to tell him how he really felt. Had Jesse not awakened from the coma, the same would be true of Phillip.

It was almost too much of a coincidence that they had both undergone these near-death experiences. Destiny clearly meant them to be together. They'd both been given second chances, and nothing was going to prevent them from achieving genuine happiness.

Phillip wished more than anything that all these people would leave so that he and Jesse could be alone again. He smiled as he thought of Jesse's kiss and how lovingly he'd held Phillip's hand. The frisky way he'd burrowed his face into Phillip's neck was so incredibly sexy that he felt himself starting to feel aroused merely from the memory. He looked over the side of the fence, staring across the street at his own house. He moaned quietly as he automatically closed his eyes, allowing himself to imagine a future with Jesse.

For a moment he wasn't sure if it was part of his fantasy or if Jesse was physically there with him. Strong arms wrapped around him. Jesse's hard body was pressing against his back, his cheek against his own cheek. "What are you thinking of?" Jesse whispered.

"You … us," Phillip whispered. "I think I—"

"I think I need to get you alone … and soon," Jesse interrupted him, "before I have my way with you right here in front of all these people."

"On the picnic table?" Phillip laughed.

"Okay," Jesse teased. "The one where Shirley's sitting."

Phillip cracked up. "Jesse, I wanna kiss you."

"I know."

"But … but I can't."

"I know."

Phillip turned and stared into Jesse's eyes as he wrapped his arms around Jesse's waist. "Thank you ..." Phillip whispered.

Jesse smiled at him lovingly. "No, I should be thanking you. I ... um ... I really appreciate all you've done. Thanks for never giving up. I think you're the reason I'm here. I think it's destiny."

"Yes," Phillip sighed as he gazed into the taller boy's eyes. "I think so, too."

And then Jesse pulled him again into himself, enfolding him in a bear hug, completely unconcerned about how that hug might be interpreted by the thirty-some people behind them.

Ten

There was no denying that Jesse's initial attraction to Phillip stemmed from the fact that he looked and acted so much like his Jacob. Yet it was also becoming clear to Jesse that his feelings for Phillip transcended mere emotional transference. He was beginning to become enamored of the unique, sensitive, funny, and charming personality of this boy who physically resembled his former lover but possessed qualities that even Jacob had lacked.

If Jesse had ever met a more selfless and compassionate human soul than Phillip, he could not recall. His sincerity melted Jesse's heart. The boy's entire demeanor projected openness and honesty, and it inspired Jesse to be a better person.

What struck Jesse most, though, was Philip's ability to make him laugh. During the many lonely years of his earlier, humorless existence, he had yearned for the companionship of someone who could make him smile. And now Phillip had the power to draw the joy from Jesse's soul. It bubbled up uncontrollably, this blissful helplessness that amazed and delighted him.

It was getting late, and some of the party guests were leaving. When Phillip suggested they go for a walk, Jesse was eager to do so merely as means of gaining privacy.

"Let's go over to my house," Phillip offered. "I'll show you my room, and maybe it will spark some memories. We used to spend a lot of time together there."

"Sure," Jesse said, "good idea," and winked at the smaller boy.

After excusing themselves from the party and promising to "be right back," the boys headed across the street to the modest, two-story home with a perfectly manicured lawn and bountiful sprays of colorful flowers set in beds along the front walkway. "My mom loves flowers," Phillip explained. "She says they add life to a home."

"She's right," Jesse said. It was remarkable to him how this simple and unpretentious house had the feel of a "home," far more so than any of the mansions in which he'd previously dwelled.

"Come on," Phillip said as he opened the front door. "I'll show you around."

As soon as the two stepped into the foyer and closed the door behind them, all thoughts of the house vanished from Jesse's mind. He spun Phillip around and wrapped him in a passionate embrace, this time cupping the boy's face in the palms of his hands as he kissed him. The eager, hungry way Phillip responded to him sent a surge of yearning through Jesse's body, and he opened his mouth in order to probe him with his tongue.

The feel of Phillip's soft hands on his chest was electrifying, as the boy slid his arms up and under his loose-fitting tee shirt. Jesse pressed against him, backing him against the wall. "Phillip," he gasped. "I want you!"

Phillip sighed and looked into Jesse's eyes. "Oh god … yes, I want you too, but we don't have time. Not right now."

Jesse kissed him once more before pulling away. He smiled broadly, once again staring into the big brown eyes. "Okay," he conceded. "Show me your house."

Phillip laughed and then reached down to grab hold of Jesse's hand. Turning, he led him down the hallway and into the living room. "This is our front room," Phillip declared.

The sofa, loveseat, and arm chairs did not immediately catch Jesse's eye, nor did the coffee table with the large floral centerpiece. He barely noticed the widescreen television or the floor lamps. Instead all he saw was that incredible painting.

"Oh my God!" he gasped, as he took a step backwards.

"Jesse! Are you remembering something?"

"It's … uh … how? How is it possible?"

"What is it, Jesse?" Phillip's voice was filled with concern. "Please …"

"The painting," Jesse said.

"Do you remember something about the painting? It's the same one we've always had hanging there."

"But where did you get it?" Jesse whispered. He recognized the print, which was identical to the original he'd purchased after Jacob had died.

"Do you need to sit down?" Phillip asked, attempting to guide Jesse toward one of the chairs.

Ignoring the attempt, Jesse went on. "Phillip, I know this painting. I know the artist who created it."

Phillip stared up at him lovingly, gently shaking his head. "Jesse, I'm sorry, but that's impossible. My uncle painted this picture—my mom's uncle actually—and he passed away a few years ago."

"Jacob Klein," Jesse's voice was barely audible.

"Yes … Jesse, how did you know?"

And now Jesse did feel as if he needed to sit. Slowly he slid himself into the chair, all the while continuing to stare up at the picture that canvassed the wall before him. "I'm … uh … I'm not sure."

"Is this the same Jacob you were talking about earlier, when you first woke up from your surgery?"

Jesse nodded, unable to think of what he could possibly offer as an explanation.

"I don't understand …" Phillip stared at him, confused. "I've known you all my life. We're the same age, so you couldn't have known him. Yet … you know his name."

Although Phillip was obviously confused, the situation was suddenly becoming crystal clear to Jesse. This boy bore such a striking resemblance to his former lover because the two were genetically connected. Phillip was Jacob's nephew.

"Maybe …" Jesse struggled to find the words. "Uh … maybe it's a deep-seated memory. Maybe you showed me this picture before and told me about your uncle … and I'm just now starting to remember."

Phillip, kneeling beside the chair, slowly shook his head as he looked up at Jesse. "I just learned who painted this picture today. I knew I had been named after an Uncle Jacob—my middle name, I mean—but I had no idea he was an artist."

"I don't know," Jesse was trying to sound rational. "Maybe your mother told me. Someone must have mentioned his name. How else would I know?"

The look of concern on Phillip's face started to fade and was replaced with a genuine smile. "Hey," he reasoned, "this is a good sign, don't you think? You're truly starting to remember things! And they must be true memories, not just stories I've told you. You're remembering things that I don't even recall."

Jesse nodded and then reached down to take both of Phillip's hands into his own. "Come here," he urged him, and Phillip slid onto Jesse's lap. "It doesn't matter," Jesse said. "I don't really know how I came to learn about your uncle, but even if I did remember, I don't care about him. I care about *you*."

And then they kissed, this time beneath the panoramic outdoor scene painted by Jacob Klein.

****

It was after ten o'clock when the last party guests bid their farewells to Jesse. He'd never been hugged and kissed by so many different people in all his life, in all of either of his lives. So this was what it felt like to be loved. This was what it meant to be cherished and valued and needed by real human beings. It was so vastly different than the satisfaction that

Harold Wainwright had felt when he was valued by his employer. Jesse knew that companies like those he'd worked for in his previous life only judged people by the number of dollar signs above their heads. He realized now how pitifully dispensable he had always been.

Before going into the house and retiring for the evening, he walked out to his mother's car. Phillip was by his side, probably wondering what was going on. "Phillip," he said, "I love this car!"

Phillip looked at him quizzically. "Okay." He smiled sincerely at his best friend. "And where did that come from? It's an okay car, but it's hardly what I'd call 'rad.' "

"Phillip, think about what this car represents," Jesse said. "Think about my parents, and about how they've both worked so hard all their lives. Everything they've done has been for me. Isn't that what parents do? Normal ones, I mean. Don't they focus all their energy and devotion on raising their families? They want their children to have better lives than theirs. Their kids become their hope … their future."

"And this has *what* to do with the car?" Phillip laughed.

"It has everything to do with the car!" Jesse stepped closer to Phillip, placing his hands on the boy's shoulders. "Okay, think of it this way. You and I, we're just starting out in life, and both of us have dreams for our future. These dreams include our careers, our families, our material possessions. We have a mental image of how we want our lives to be in, say, twenty or thirty years, when we are our parents' age.

"Well I bet my mom and dad—Margo and Paul—I bet they had dreams too. I bet they fantasized about owning luxury cars and fancy houses. My dad may have imagined himself rising to the top of his company. My mom may have dreamt of being a singer, or a dancer, or a famous actress.

"But what they actually achieved in life is by far more meaningful than any of these material possessions or claims to fame. They achieved success as excellent parents! And when I first saw this car, I felt such disappointment. I felt like they had settled for mediocrity. It seemed like a joke to me that my mom would be so proud of owning a Ford.

"But I know now that they made all these sacrifices for me. They supported all my athletic endeavors. They worked their butts off to make sure I had the best birthdays and Christmases. They provided for all my needs, first and foremost, and they compromised on their own dreams. But you know, in the end, I think they have proven to the world what success really is. It's not a luxury automobile … it's a family filled with love!"

Jesse was talking so animatedly and with such passion that he did not notice at first that Phillip's eyes were brimming with tears.

Phillip nodded at Jesse, smiling sweetly. "You're right," he said. "It really is a beautiful car."

"Just like you," Jesse said. "You have such a soft heart. I love that about you."

"I can't even begin to list everything I love about you," Phillip countered.

"Let's go up to my room, and we can work on the list together."

Phillip held out his hand, and Jesse reached down to grasp it firmly. "Come on," Jesse whispered, and led his best friend back to his house.

****

Jesse asked Phillip to put on a CD, and the two of them sat together on the small bed. Jesse had found one of the family photo albums, and Phillip was telling him all about the pictures therein. Jesse only heard half of what he said though, because although he stared at Phillip with seemingly rapt attention, all he could concentrate on was how desperately he wanted to make love to him.

Phillip continued to prattle on and on, pointing at photos of Jesse with his cousins, Jesse at the theme park, Jesse on the track field. He repeatedly mentioned how cute or handsome Jesse was. He bragged about Jesse's sports' awards and laughed at Jesse's silly antics as he hammed it up for the camera. Phillip was a virtual magpie, and Jesse just sat there, allowing him to blather on endlessly.

Finally Jesse reached over and gently placed the palms of his hands flat on top of the open page of the photo book. "Shh," he whispered, slowly pulling the book off Phillip's lap and letting it drop to the floor. "You need to shut up now, baby."

Phillip smiled at him nervously. He nodded. "Okay." His voice was suddenly so quiet.

Jesse reached over and slowly grasped the bottom of Phillip's tee shirt. "Let me undress you please."

"Jesse," Phillip sighed. "Oh Jesse... I ..."

"Are you afraid?" Jesse asked sincerely. "You know I would never hurt you."

"I'm not afraid of that," Phillip said. "I know. I know you'd never hurt me, but I'm afraid you won't like what you see ..." The pained look in Phillip's eyes was nearly earth-shattering to Jesse.

"What, baby? I already know I will love every inch of you."

"Jesse ... I have a scar."

Jesse grinned at him, slowly reaching up to lift up his beanie. "So do I."

"It's from the cancer," Phillip said as the tears welled in his eyes. "In my neck, they had to put a tube, and it came out my chest. That was how they drew blood and gave me medicine."

"Let me see it ... please," Jesse implored him. He reached back down to grasp the tail of Phillip's shirt and slowly pulled it up over the boy's head. Jesse stared at the smooth, bare chest before him, taking in every single inch of its absolute perfection. Then he leaned in, sweetly pressing his lips against the scar on Phillip's neck. He kissed it, not once, but multiple times. He gradually descended down his chest and kissed the second scar created by the exit wound. He kissed that as well, delicately and reverently.

"I love your scars," he whispered.

"I love yours!" Phillip cried, as he leaned forward and sweetly kissed the side of Jesse's head.

"Did you think the imperfections of your body would make me love you less?" Jesse asked sincerely.

"No! Oh Jesse, no, of course not. I just … I just didn't want to disappoint you."

"Consider me un-disappointed," he said sternly. Then he pressed his mouth firmly against Phillip's nipple and sucked it into his mouth, grazing it ever so softly with his teeth. Slowly he pushed him backwards on the bed until he was lying flat on his back; all the while Jesse continued to tweak his sensitive nipples.

"Oh God, Jesse!" he cried. Jesse delighted in the way his boy squirmed beneath him.

"Phillip," he whispered, as he pulled his face away from Phillip's smooth skin. "Have you ever …?"

"No," he whispered.

Jesse continued to kiss his way down the boy's body, savoring the clean taste of his skin. He wrapped his hands around Phillip's lithe midsection and ran his fingers down the sides of his tight abdomen. Phillip sighed and squirmed as Jesse slid his tongue teasingly into the boy's navel. Soon Jesse's deft fingers found the waistband of Phillip's shorts, and he began to tug against them, attempting to pull them downward. Phillip thrust his pelvis upwards just enough for Jesse to slip off the pants, and as he did so, along came the boxer briefs.

"Oh Jesse!" Phillip cried excitedly. "Did you lock the door?"

"Mmm hmm" Jesse responded while continuing to lick and kiss just below Phillip's belly button. He could smell the slight muskiness wafting up into his nostrils, a scent he had never expected to experience again, and his own erection throbbed in his shorts.

Now on his knees beside the bed, Jesse slid in between Phillips outstretched legs and began to tauntingly lick his testicles. He grabbed hold of the thick shaft and slowly started stroking it as he continued to tease his lover with his expert tongue.

Phillip was so excited that Jesse could feel his cock throb in his grip. It was fiery hot and hard as steel, yet so sensuously smooth to the touch. Unable to restrain himself any longer, Jesse thrust himself upwards and quickly wrapped his lips around the head. As he did so, he looked up at his boyish-faced lover and saw him staring wide-eyed at what was being done to him. He suspected what was going through the boy's mind. Jesse remembered his first experience, all those years ago. It seemed quite surreal, almost as if it could not possibly be happening. Oh god, he had to make this an event that would forever be special to Phillip. He had to make it perfect!

Jesse pressed his tongue against the underside of Phillip's shaft as he ever-so-slowly inched his way downward. He knew the moist and warm feel of the inside of his mouth would be like silk around the sensitive skin of Phillip's cock. Phillip's pleasurable moans told him he wasn't wrong. He allowed himself to at first take in only half of the rigid pole, and then he began to suck. The suction was sure to feel incredible to the boy, whose only prior experience was the stroking of his own hand.

"Oh Jesse," he whimpered. "Oh God, it feels so good!"

Jesse began to slide up and down, taking the cock deeper into his mouth with each downward thrust. Phillip was now writhing beneath him, moaning with pleasure. Gradually he quickened the pace, realizing that going slowly and deliberately would allow Phillip's sexual excitement to build until he finally reached that point of no return.

Of course it did not take long, and this was no surprise to Jesse. He knew the first time would be short and sweet, yet it was in truth beyond his wildest expectations. Tasting and feeling Phillip for the first time was so incredibly exhilarating that Jesse nearly released his own cum load right into his shorts. When Phillip finally reached that delirious state of oblivion where his passion erupted from him, Jesse held him firmly in his mouth. The volcanic explosion flooded his mouth, and he eagerly and hungrily gulped it down, not pausing long enough to even savor the unique bitter-salty taste.

"Unnngh!" Phillip cried as he groped frantically at the bedspread beneath him. "Oh God! Oh my God!" His whole body convulsed as he tossed his head back and moaned. Jesse continued to suck until the boy beneath him was whimpering and trembling.

"Jesse!" he cried. His voice was trembling with emotion. He simply lay there shivering, and Jesse couldn't tell if he was laughing or crying. It sounded like both.

Instantly Jesse slid up on the bed beside him and wrapped the boy in his strong embrace.

"Jesse, Jesse ..." Phillip kept repeating his name. He wrapped his arms tightly around Jesse's torso and clung to him.

"Baby, how was it?" Jesse whispered in his ear.

He knew now without a doubt that Phillip was crying. "It was so beautiful," he sobbed. "It was amazing."

They lay there cuddling for the next hour until Jesse finally sat up and brushed a lock of hair over to the side of Phillip's face. "You're an angel," he whispered. "Let's get some sleep."

"I want to—"

"No ... I don't want reciprocation. Not this time. Please

let this be about you. Let this be the beautiful experience you deserve. We'll have plenty of time for more later."

"Thank you, Jesse," he said. "You made it better than my wildest dream. In fact … you *are* my wildest dream."

"Let's dream together," he said. "We'll have to snuggle real close in this little bed, though."

"Aw darn," Phillip said as he smiled sarcastically.

Jesse playfully swatted Phillip's bare bottom. "God, you're sexy!"

****

Jesse lay there in the dark with Phillip spooned against his body. His arm was around the boy, and his hand was pressed flat against Phillip's chest. He could feel his heartbeat, hear his breathing. The softness of Phillip's hair against his cheek reminded him of another time in his life some forty years prior. No, it hadn't happened in this life … that was then, before the transition.

These moments of solitude were the most disturbing for Jesse. They seemed to provide a melding of two consciousnesses—an overlap. Alone with his thoughts, he still identified mentally as Harold Wainwright, yet physically he felt like Jesse Warren. He wanted more than anything to simply assimilate this identity.

Harold had been a seventy-eight-year precursor to his real life. Harold was the background—the preparation. All those years had been merely one long and horrific lesson. He had used the time to make every imaginable mistake. He had chosen fame and financial comfort over love. He'd chosen prestige over family. He'd chosen image over truth. He'd chosen profit over compassion. Worst of all, he'd chosen material possessions over genuine happiness.

He thought about the money, the nest egg he had arranged to have sent to himself. It would be arriving within a few days, and he would need to decide what to do with it. He could make life so easy for Paul and Margo, provide them with every possession they'd ever imagined or desired. He could take Phillip on the trip of a lifetime, travel the world with his lover.

He knew it wouldn't be possible, though. How would he ever explain the money? How would he be able to convince his parents that this elderly man he'd never met had bequeathed him millions?

The money was tainted. In truth it was blood money, acquired at the expense of beautiful and unsuspecting souls. For all those years as Harold, he had denied the insurance claims of patients such as Phillip. The scar on Phillip's neck that he'd kissed a few hours earlier was caused by the insertion of a central venous catheter. It was part of the standard medical practice used in the treatment of leukemia patients, providing multiple IV insertion points for the numerous intravenous drugs that had to be administered. Without the catheter, Phillip would have been rendered a pin cushion. His veins would have ultimately collapsed from the hundreds of needle pokes and blood draws. Yet Jesse remembered the countless number of claim forms he'd rejected, stating that catheters were an unnecessary expense.

The lump in his throat wouldn't go away. His tears were scalding hot on his cheeks as he lay there embracing his precious Phillip. How could he have made such decisions? How many other Phillips had there been? How many innocent and pure souls had suffered in order to make him one of the wealthiest men alive?

As much as he wanted to use the money to help his new family and provide for Phillip, he knew he could never spend a dime of that fortune. Not now. Not after discovering the true meaning of life. Perhaps there were other ways in which he could help his loved ones. He could make a difference in their lives in legitimate ways. He could go to college, earn a degree and use those credentials to pursue a much different type of success.

His goal would not be the acquisition of wealth. Instead it would be helping people like Phillip and his family. Maybe he'd go to law school, become an attorney, and take on the insurance industry. He'd fight for universal health care With all the secret knowledge he possessed, he'd practically be unstoppable.

He smiled to himself as he lay there in the dark thinking on these things, and then slowly the smile faded. Again, he realized, he was making this all about himself. Yes, he did want to make a difference in the world. Certainly he wanted nothing more than to see the massive insurance companies brought to ruin, yet none of these fantasies even began to compare to a lifetime of happiness with Phillip.

It was perhaps silly of him to even allow himself to think this way. It was too early. He had only known the young man for a few days, and already he was dreaming of taking up a homestead. Phillip would have dreams of his own. He'd have his own goals and aspirations, and Jesse had no right to assume these would include him. Jesse had already lived a full life and had already learned his lessons, but to Phillip it was all brand new. He realized that he, Jesse Warren, was Phillip's first love. Was it even sane to imagine that they'd be together indefinitely?

"I love you, Phillip," he whispered, knowing the boy in his arms was sound asleep and unable to hear him. Gently he pressed his lips against Phillip's smooth cheek. "I love you so much, and I wish you all the happiness in the world … with or without me."

****

Over the course of the twelve weeks Jesse had been in a coma, Phillip had repeatedly whispered his proclamations of love and devotion into the sleeping boy's ear. Numerous times he had kissed Jesse's angelic face, on the forehead, cheek, and even on the lips. And now, as he lay there feigning sleep, his heart swelled upon hearing Jesse do precisely the same thing.

Jesse's postscript, "with or without me," was of great concern. What could he possibly mean? Was Jesse having second thoughts about embarking upon a serious relationship? If so, then why would he confess his love? *He said he loves me!* Phillip wanted to turn to Jesse then and ravage him with kisses. He wanted to swear his undying and eternal devotion and assure this man-of-his-dreams that he wanted him and only him forever.

Instead Phillip simply continued to lie there in Jesse's arms. He felt so secure within Jesse's strong and protective embrace. The warmth of his friend's body surrounded him, and he felt as if it would be nothing less than criminal to ever leave the security of such a serene abode. The hardness of Jesse's toned pectorals pressed firmly against Phillip's back, and the tightness of his abdominals brushed against Phillip's posterior as Jesse snuggled against him. It was as if they could not get close enough.

What Jesse had done earlier for Phillip was enough to blow his mind. Ever since Phillip was old enough to know what an erection was, he'd been fantasizing about being intimate with Jesse, yet in these daydreams it was he who was giving Jesse pleasure. He'd sworn to himself that if ever he were afforded the opportunity to be with Jesse sexually, he would make it so beautiful for Jess. He would literally worship him.

Never had Phillip imagined that Jesse would be the one to bring him this sort of pleasure. Phillip felt guilty for allowing their first encounter to happen that way. With Jesse just getting out of the hospital that morning only a few days after having brain surgery, Phillip should have tended to Jesse's sexual need, and not vice versa.

Oddly, though, Jesse had made it seem that merely by pleasing Phillip he himself had experienced enormous pleasure. It did make sense, now that he reasoned it out. Yes, if their roles had been reversed, Phillip would have felt honored to be allowed to do *that* to Jesse. In fact, he wanted to more than anything! Why should it seem strange to him that Jesse would feel this way as well?

He knew one thing for sure, though, and that was the fact that loved Jesse and always had. He somehow had to make it abundantly clear that there were not now nor ever would be any thoughts of happiness "without" Jesse. He had to find out where these doubts were coming from and convince Jesse that they were in this together, and that they would remain together for the long haul.

How could Jesse have earlier stated to him that he believed it was their destiny to be together, and then now question whether they'd remain together? His confusion had to be related to Jesse's memory loss. Phillip could not fully comprehend how difficult it must be to awaken from a coma, only to realize your previous existence had been all but erased. Of course he would be leery of what the future held. Of course he would be cautious.

Most importantly, though, Jesse had declared his love. As Phillip replayed the declaration repeatedly in his own head, he allowed himself to snuggle firmly against Jesse's torso. He felt Jesse squeeze him a little tighter and then drift peacefully back to sleep.

Eleven

Later that morning Jesse was awakened by the soft touch of Phillip's lips upon his own. "Mmm," he moaned, not yet opening his eyes. Phillip's small, slender body was pressed against his, and Jesse gently wrapped his arms around it, caressing Phillip's naked backside. He could feel his lover's arousal pulsing against his abdominals as Phillip brushed his hands against Jesse's hard chest.

Jesse himself was aroused, though still wearing his boxer shorts. He'd forgotten what it was like to be young, every morning with a raging hard-on. He smiled as he gradually opened his eyes and saw the face of an angel staring back at him. "Morning," he whispered. "What time is it?"

"Dunno," Phillip said as he leaned in to kiss him again, this time with passion. "Morning," he belatedly responded to Jesse's greeting.

"How'd you like sleeping on the floor?" Jesse asked. The boys had told Jesse's parents that Phillip didn't mind using an air mattress. He'd been offered the living room sofa but had declined.

"Oh, I feel kind of stiff this morning." Phillip grinned at him as he slid his hand down Jesse's chest and affectionately groped his hardness. "But then so do you."

Jesse laughed. "You know you make me that way."

"I want to do it to you … I mean like what you did to me last night."

"Mmm," Jesse responded. "You don't have to now. We have time …"

"Yes I do … Yes I do have to do it now!" Phillip insisted, and then he began kissing his way down Jesse's torso, starting first at the neck and slowly descending.

113

"Oh Phillip, you're having your way with me when I'm most vulnerable, not even fully awake … aahh!" He squirmed as Phillip found one of his nipples.

Phillip looked up at him with a devilish grin and then repeated the phrase Jesse had used on him the night before. "It's time for you to shut up, baby."

"Okay," Jesse responded without protest. He closed his eyes as Phillip continued to lavish his body with kisses. He was trying to relax, play it cool while he enjoyed some unexpected morning head, but as he felt Phillip's fingertips tugging at the waistband of his underwear, his pulse began to quicken.

It had been so long since Jesse had felt the silky warmth of a wet mouth that he'd nearly forgotten the sensation. Soon the shorts were history, and the bed sheet was tossed aside. Jesse spread his legs apart and allowed his lover full, unencumbered access to his private parts. He felt Phillip's fingers brushing softly against his inner thigh, tickling him. That touch was so gentle and delicate, just like Phillip himself, and as those same fingers began to fondle Jesse's ball sac, he sighed uncontrollably.

"Phillip!" he cried in a whisper. "You're driving me crazy …"

As Phillip began to reverently kiss his throbbing shaft, Jesse reminded himself to relax and enjoy the sensations. Mentally he downplayed his excitement, reasoning that this was Phillip's first time. He shouldn't expect much from the boy. Of course with no experience he wouldn't yet know exactly what to do with his tongue. He couldn't possibly realize the precise manner in which to do things, how strongly to suck, how much pressure to use, how to take it deep.

When the warm, moist mouth slid around his cock for the first time, Jesse's low expectations suddenly vanished. Phillip devoured the whole of him instantly, swallowing the entirety of his full eight inches in one smooth movement. Phillip's mouth began to glide up and down on his cock with a slickness that was heavenly. It was indeed silky, and the pressure of Phillip's tongue against the sensitive underside of Jesse's cock was absolutely magnificent.

Never once did Jesse feel the graze of Phillip's teeth. Never once did he hear him gag or choke. It was amazing how skillfully and naturally Phillip assumed the passive oral role. He was a born cocksucker, equal to any expert. Jesse's plan to play it cool and relax was soon forgotten as he writhed pleasurably on the bed. The relentless sucking of that incredible mouth on his cock was edging him to orgasm more quickly than he ever would have expected.

"Phillip!" he cried. "Oh my god, you're gonna make me ... Oh, Phillip!"

Jesse's protests seemed only to encourage his lover, who cupped Jesse's balls with one hand while holding the base of his shaft with the other. Phillip then began to bob furiously on Jesse's throbbing prick.

"Oh fuck!" Jesse moaned. "Fuck yeah!" He felt it coming. He was so close. "Baby, I'm so close!!"

Jesse bucked his hips wildly as he reached down to place his hands on Phillip's head. "Ahhh!" he cried. "I'm cumming!" It was like the firing of a canon as Jesse released his load. Phillip eagerly gulped down the first two or three volleys, then quickly pulled away and allowed Jesse to shoot the remainder onto his cherubic face.

Jesse was trembling, still moaning with pleasure. "Oh baby!" he sighed. "Oh god!"

As he looked down at Phillip's cum-covered lips he saw them break into a self-satisfied grin of triumph. "Well?" he asked. "How'd I do?"

"Oh my god, Phillip. This couldn't have been your first time ..."

"Really? So I did okay."

"Come here!" Jesse demanded, and Phillip quickly slid up next to him on the bed. Jesse cupped his face in his palms and kissed him, passionately driving his tongue into the boy's cum-coated mouth.

Gasping for air, he finally released Phillip, and as he did so, he stared directly into the big brown eyes. "Phillip, all I can say is 'Wow!'"

"I guess we should get cleaned up before breakfast. Your mom said she was making you pancakes this morning."

Jesse rolled his eyes. "Let me guess, they're my favorite?"

Phillip nodded. "With those little sausage links. You love those things."

Jesse made a face. "There's only one sausage link I wanna eat," he said teasingly as he reached down to grope his lover.

"We need to strip these bed sheets," Phillip confessed sheepishly. "I got a little excited when I was ... ya know."

Jesse grinned at him in disbelief. "You mean you came? You came while you were blowing me?"

Phillip nodded as his face began to redden.

"Oh baby, that is so fucking hot!"

The sweetness of Phillip's giggle warmed Jesse's heart at almost the exact moment that his leg found the wet spot. "You really did. You really came just from sucking me!" He rolled on top of Phillip and again ravaged him with fervent kisses.

****

Jesse surprised his mother by helping to clear the dishes from the breakfast table. "I'll get that, honey," she said. "Sit down and relax. I just got you home and want to pamper you a little."

"Thank you, Mother, but I don't expect you to wait on me all the time. I'm feeling fine, and in fact Phillip and I are going to go for a run in a bit."

"Baby, are you sure?" She looked at him with an

expression of grave concern. Perhaps she feared he'd be too spooked from the accident to ever run again. "You just got out of the hospital. You just had *brain* surgery."

"I'll be careful, I promise," he assured her. "And I've decided I do want to get a job for the summer. Even if it's not many hours, and even if the pay isn't great. I at least want to be contributing."

Margo crossed her arms and scowled at him. "I'd hoped you would have lost your stubbornness along with some of your memory, but you're still the same. Jesse, it's too soon, and there's no reason for you to work. Besides, we're still hoping the driver's insurance company will compensate us, and if they do, we'll be more than okay."

"Are you suing them?" he asked as he opened the dishwasher.

She shook her head. "No, we don't want to sue anyone …"

"Sue them!" Jesse demanded. "They're an insurance company, and they won't give you a cent unless you sue."

Margo stared at her son in bewilderment. "Jesse! What's gotten into you? Of course they will pay. That's what insurance is for."

"Trust me, Mother, if you don't get an attorney, that insurance company is going to find every excuse they can *not* to pay you. They should have already paid, actually. Who covered the medical bills?"

"Your father's insurance from work was supposed to be paying them, but then we got a letter denying the coverage because it was an automobile accident. They said the driver's insurance had to pay, so we filed a claim with them. So far nobody has paid, but when Dr. Drayton performed your surgery he assured us that all of the medical bills would be taken care of … pro bono."

Jesse sighed and shook his head as he turned to look his mother straight in the eye. "Mom, you're too trusting. Neither

of those insurance companies is going to pay, and it is going
to destroy your credit rating. You're going to be stuck with a
huge bill from the hospital, and as for Drayton, he was merely
waiving his fee for performing the surgery. You're still going
to end up being charged for the hospitalization. Please,
promise me you'll go see a lawyer. I'll even help you find
one."

"Jesse," she said sternly, "now you listen to me. I don't
want you worrying about this stuff. Your father and I are
handling this. Your job is simply to get better. We don't care
about the money."

"But I care! I don't want your lives ruined because of
me!"

Phillip finally chimed in, "Jesse, your mom is right. You
shouldn't be getting upset like this."

"Please, Jesse!" Margo implored him. "Please, let your
dad and me handle this."

****

Running was exhilarating to Jesse. Feeling the strength of
his legs, the wind in his face, and the rapid beating of his own
heart reminded him how virile and totally alive he was.
Halfway through their five-mile trek, both Jesse and Phillip
stripped off their shirts, and Jesse allowed himself to fall
slightly behind his running partner. The sheen of sweat on the
shorter boy's back and shoulders coated his golden skin, and
Jesse felt himself becoming aroused. The fabric of Phillip's
running shorts was drawn tightly across his smooth bubble
butt, and every stride of his toned legs invited Jesse to savor
the natural beauty.

During the last mile of their run, the boys quickened
their pace, almost as if racing. They were feeding off each
other's competitiveness, urging each other on. Jesse wanted to
see just how far he could push himself. He wanted to again
feel the power of a youthful body, to relish the stamina and

118

strength of powerful legs, fully-functioning lungs, and a strong, healthy heart. He surprised himself with his own agility, and the joy that filled him threatened to explode from his chest.

In the last fifty yards Jesse sailed ahead of Phillip, pushing himself with all his might. When he reached the lawn of Phillip's front yard, he finally stopped, leaning over to catch his breath. Gasping for air, he rested his hands on his knees and looked up to see Phillip finally approaching.

"Damn!" Phillip gasped. "You haven't lost a thing!"

Jesse laughed as his chest continued to heave, sucking in big gulps of air.

"Oh my god!" Jesse exclaimed. "That was incredible!"

Phillip dropped to the ground, exhausted, lying flat on his back in the grass. He pulled his tee shirt out of the front of his shorts where he'd tucked it and used it to wipe the sweat from his face and hair.

"You look … amazing," Jesse observed.

"What?" Phillip said, staring straight up into the sky, not yet noticing that Jesse was staring at him.

"I said, you look fucking amazing!"

Phillip grinned but kept his gaze directed upwards. "And I suppose you're going to take advantage of me now, when I'm at my most vulnerable and not fully awake—"

"You're fully awake, and yes, I'd love to take advantage of you right here on the front lawn."

"That's what you said this morning, right before—"

"Right before you gave me the best blowjob in the history of mankind."

Phillip laughed and finally rolled onto his side to look at his best friend. "I wanna do it again."

Jesse shook his head and turned away, smiling broadly. "No!" he insisted. "If you do it again, I'm afraid I'm going to be addicted to you …"

"And your point is …?"

Jesse turned back around and took a step closer to Phillip. "I guess I'm already addicted to you. You realize that, don't you?"

"So ... let's go take a shower. Nobody's home right now."

"Oh really?" He held his hand out as Phillip reached up to grab hold. He pulled his friend to his feet and they walked into the house together, Jesse catching one more glimpse of the most gorgeous ass he'd ever seen.

****

Phillip was kneeling down in front of the bathroom vanity, rummaging around. "Here it is!" he declared with satisfaction. "My mom uses this shower cap when she goes swimming."

Jesse had been concerned about taking a shower so soon after the surgery. It would be a couple more weeks until the stitches were removed. "Thanks," he said, as he reached down to take the cap from his friend. He pulled off his beanie and stared at his reflection in the mirror. "By the time my stitches are out, my hair will be long enough that you won't even be able to see the incision."

"You look perfect just the way you are, with or without hair," Phillip said, still kneeling beside his friend.

Jesse laughed. "But will you still be able to say that when I have a rubber skullcap on my head?" He snapped the shower cap in place, pulling it snugly onto his head.

"You look like an Olympic swimmer," Phillip declared. "A damn sexy one."

Jesse reached down and affectionately ran his fingers through Phillip's thick, black hair. "And you ... you look like ... like an angel. I swear to God, you're just ..." He couldn't even find the words to describe the depth of his attraction to the boy kneeling at his feet.

Phillip reached up and grabbed the waistband of Jesse's shorts. "Let me help you out of these," he offered.

"Phillip!" Jesse laughed.

"You can't take a shower with your clothes on, can you?"

"Seeing you like that—there on your knees—it's making me—"

"Hard," Phillip grinned. "And seeing you hard is making me *hungry!*"

"Don't you want to at least wait 'til I'm clean and not so hot-n-sweaty?"

Phillip shook his head. "No! It turns me on seeing you all hot-n-sweaty. You're a total jock!"

"You're not so bad yourself. You play sports, don't you?"

"Not like you," Phillip said as he tugged on Jesse's shorts, hauling them down past his thighs. "I kind of had to give up on sports when I got sick."

"You have a nice body, though. You're my SWB, remember?"

"Mmm hmm," Phillip said as he wrapped his lips around Jesse's cock.

Jesse grabbed hold of Phillip's shoulders to steady himself as he moaned. "This has to be a dream," he whispered. "Please don't ever wake me up ..."

****

Phillip and Jesse were alone together in Phillip's living room when his mother arrived from work. Jesse was sitting on the sofa, and Phillip was lying beside him with his head in Jesse's lap. When Phillip heard his mother enter, he made no effort to conceal that he and Jesse were sharing an intimate moment. He did lift his head slightly from Jesse's lap, though, to offer his mother a greeting.

"Hey, Mom," he said casually. "How was work?"

"Oh fine, honey. How are you boys today? Enjoying a chance to spend time together again?"

"Yup," Phillip said. "Very much. We went for a run."

"Oh really? Jesse, how're you feeling? I was a little

worried about you having that big party on the first day home from the hospital."

"I'm feeling great, Mrs. Covington. Once in a while I get a headache, but not so much that I've had to take anything."

"Staying for dinner?" she asked.

Jesse looked down at Phillip. "Yes, he is," Phillip replied.

"I guess I should let my mother know," Jesse said. "I'm not sure what she was planning."

"Well just sit there and relax." Sarah Covington smiled at him sweetly. "I've got to call Margo anyway, and I'll make sure nobody's toes get stepped on."

"I appreciate it," Jesse said.

"You know, I don't remember you being quite so mannerly," Sarah laughed.

"Hmm, maybe the accident knocked some sense into me," Jesse quipped.

Sarah grinned at him sweetly as she set down her purse. She took a seat in a chair opposite the boys. Continuing to smile, she sat up a little straighter and took a breath. Then she cleared her throat. "Boys, I have to talk to you about something."

Phillip knew she was serious from her sudden change in tone. He pulled himself upright and sat on the sofa next to Jesse. The two were still sitting closer than necessary for mere friendship. "What's wrong, Mom?" Phillip asked.

"Oh nothing's wrong, but I just noticed something last night, and after our conversation yesterday, I have a concern."

"Concern?" Phillip looked at Jesse, wondering if the direction the conversation was headed in would make him uncomfortable. Phillip hadn't yet mentioned that he'd told his mother about them.

"Well, yesterday you'd told me that the two of you were planning to be just friends. I sense there is more to it than that. Is there something you're not telling me?"

Phillip once again looked over at Jesse and was reassured

by the slight nod of his head. He then turned to his mother and said, "Mom, we're more than friends." Reaching down to take Jesse's hand into his own, he was relieved when the other boy responded by squeezing his hand affectionately.

Sarah again smiled at the boys, and once more she sighed. She reached up to her face and placed her hand gently against her cheek, a gesture of pensiveness. "Well..." she began, adjusting her sitting position and biting her bottom lip.

"What?" Phillip said. "I thought you said you would support me."

"Oh baby, I do. I do support you, and if there is anyone on earth I would want you to have for a ... special friend ... well of course it would be Jesse. I'm just concerned that it's so soon."

"We've known each other all our lives," Phillip reminded her.

"You've known Jesse all of your life, but he doesn't really even remember you yet."

"Mrs. Covington," Jesse said, "I'm positive that there is nothing I could learn about Phillip now that would change my feelings for him."

"Oh, I'm not saying there is. In fact, I'm sure that as you get to know Phillip better, you will only grow fonder of him. I think he's pretty special, and not just because I'm his mother. My point is that from your perspective, Jesse, you've only known Phillip a few days, and that may be a little bit quick to—"

"Mom," Phillip interrupted, "you told me with your own mouth that when you and Dad met, you knew right away that you were destined for each other. It was love at first sight. Right?"

She cocked her head and smiled as she took in the sight of the young couple before her. "Yes, Phillip, you're right."

"Why is it any different for us? Plus Jesse is already

starting to remember things. He's remembering things that I don't even recall."

"Really?" she asked. "Well that's wonderful! Are you remembering your friendship with Phillip?"

"Mrs. Covington, I found something yesterday—a journal I'd been keeping. I had written a lot of stuff about my feelings for Phillip. None of this is new. Even if I don't remember all the details, I know that I have had feelings for him for a long, long time."

Phillip noticed that Jesse hadn't really answered the question, but he let it go. He wanted to tell his mom that he loved Jesse and that Jesse loved him, but since they had not yet made this confession to each other—at least not while they thought the other was conscious—he decided not to use the "L" word just yet. "Can you believe that, mom? All this time I've had this major crush on Jesse, and now I've come to find out he felt the same way—"

"Wow," she said. "You know, that's just ... it's just incredible. So you had been keeping a diary?"

"I'm so glad I had been," Jesse admitted. "I think everyone should keep a journal if for no other reason than if they ever have amnesia, they will have some of their memories recorded."

"I never really thought about it that way, but you're right. I can't imagine what it must have been like for you to wake up and not really remember your past."

"What I care about mostly is my future. In fact, that's all I care about. I had kept my feelings for Phillip a secret for so long, and I don't want to do that anymore."

"Good for you," Sarah said encouragingly. "Which brings me to the next question, have you yet told your parents?"

Jesse shook his head. "The only reason I haven't told them yet is because of everything they've been through. I don't want to add one more thing for them to worry about.

Once I feel confident that they will be okay with the news, I plan to tell them. But I'm not going to keep this a secret for long. I already decided, life is too short to be living a lie."

"Absolutely," Sarah said, and now her eyes were becoming visibly moist. "You know, I always knew that Phillip was special. I sensed it from the time he was really young. I wasn't surprised at all when he told me he thought he was gay. And I could tell how crazy about you he was. I was worried, though, because I had no way of knowing how you felt."

"Please Mom, just be happy for us. Like I told you yesterday, we almost lost each other. We don't want to pretend anymore."

"Well baby, you know that you have my full support. I love you with all my heart, and if Jesse is that special person for you, I know I'll love him like my own son."

"Thank you, Mrs. Covington," Jesse said.

"But …!" she paused for dramatic effect. "You two had better be playing it safe, if you know what I mean."

"Oh no!" Phillip covered his face with his hands. "This isn't gonna be a safe-sex lecture, is it? Mom, I can't talk about this with Jesse sitting right here!"

"Excuse me?" she said. "If you are planning to be intimate with one another, why would you be embarrassed to talk about doing it safely?"

"Because you're my mother!" he cried. "And Jesse is my boyfriend!" Suddenly the room was quiet, and it dawned on Phillip what he'd just said. He turned to Jesse and looked him in the eye. Now it was Phillip who was on the verge of tears. "You're my boyfriend," he repeated softly.

"Yes," Jesse whispered as he nodded. "I really like the sound of that." Phillip thought for a second that Jesse was going to lean in and kiss him, right there in front of his mother. Instead Jesse shifted his gaze to look over at Mrs. Covington once more. "I promise you, I will never do anything to put your son at risk. We will be safe. And don't worry, it's not even an issue yet."

"Good!" Sarah said confidently. "That's all I wanted to hear." She stood up and stepped briskly over to the sofa, leaning in to kiss her son squarely on the forehead. "I love you with all my heart, and I'm so happy for you." She then leaned in to kiss Jesse on the cheek. "Welcome to the family ... officially."

Phillip stood up and embraced his mom, pulling her into himself with a firm bear hug. "Oh God, Mom," he cried. "You're the best! You're the best mom in the world! I love you so much." They were both crying when they finally drew back.

****

"I have an idea," Phillip said to Jesse after dinner. "When I was sick and couldn't really get out of the house, sometimes you'd come over and keep me company. We used to play a lot of board games, and I always kicked your butt in Scrabble."

"Oh?" Jesse said, and then he laughed.

"Don't you think that would be a good game to play now? I mean it involves memory, right?"

"So you're saying you want to kick my butt again?"

"No! I'm saying it might be fun ... or we can do something else. It's cool. We can walk down to the store where my dad works. The more things like that you see, the better your chances of sparking memories, don't ya think?"

"Whatever you want to do is fine," Jesse said.

"We could go swimming," he suggested.

"I'd love to, but don't you think I'd look a bit conspicuous wearing a shower cap?"

"We'll go buy you a real swimming cap. In fact, I bet you already have one. You used to swim at school."

"Let's play Scrabble, like you suggested to begin with. I already got to see you all wet and naked once today."

"Oh I see how you are. Once was more than enough, huh?" Phillip said with a teasing laugh.

"Yeah, because I doubt I could keep my hands off you if I saw you like that a second time."

"Well, you didn't keep your hands off me the first time."

"My point exactly!" Jesse exclaimed.

Phillip smiled at him and then suddenly became serious. "Jesse, I'm not sure you should spend the night here tonight. My room is right next to my parents'. I'm afraid they might hear us."

"You can stay at my house again then."

Phillip thought about the way they'd snuggled together in the twin bed. "I wonder, though … What's my mom gonna say about us always sleeping together now that she knows?"

"Phillip, you're eighteen, and your mom already told us that she approves of our relationship. She probably won't say anything. And if you want me to stay here tonight, that's fine too. We can sleep together without doing anything … ya know."

"But I *want* to do 'ya know'!" Phillip whispered.

"Go get the game. We'll decide where we sleep later," Jesse said.

As the game started, Phillip was surprised when Jesse used all of his tiles for a bingo on his second turn. He spelled the word "obdurate."

"That *is* a word, isn't it?" Phillip asked. "You know there are strict penalties for cheating."

Jesse scowled at him in mock indignation. "Of course it's a word. It means stubborn … like someone sitting at this table."

"Hey, your mom's the one who said you were stubborn today."

Two turns later Jesse again used all his tiles for a second bingo.

"Alacrity?" Phillip stared at the board. "Where are you

coming up with these words?" he asked suspiciously.

"It's a word!" Jesse insisted. "It means 'with enthusiasm or cheerfulness.' "

As the game continued, Phillip was astounded over and again by Jesse's newfound command of the English language. "I don't get it!" he said sincerely. "Don't get me wrong. I'm not being a sore loser; it just surprises me. Look at those words you came up with." The board was covered with impressively complex, polysyllabic words, most of which Phillip had never heard of.

"So I guess it's safe to say I didn't previously play this well?" Jesse asked.

"Uh, no." Phillip laughed. "Like I said, I used to kick your butt. Hey, are you sure they didn't give you a brain transplant when they did that surgery?" Phillip was still laughing but when the anger on Jesse's face registered, he immediately hedged. "Jesse, I'm just kidding. I'm so sorry!"

"Please don't say things like that," Jesse spat out. "I didn't have a brain *transplant*!" His tone was defensive, almost hostile.

"I didn't mean anything by it. Oh Jesse … please." Phillip's eyes were filling with tears. "I was only making a joke, but it was really … it was mean, and I'm sorry."

When Jesse turned back to look into Phillip's eyes, his expression had softened. "No, you're right. Of course it was a joke, and I totally overreacted." He grabbed hold of Phillip's hands, holding them between his own. "This is a stupid game, and it doesn't prove anything. I'm not sure why I remembered all those big words. Nobody uses language like that … I don't even know how I came up with them. Most of them … probably aren't real words at all … or they're misspelled."

"Jesse …" Phillip was ashamed of the high pitched, whiny quality of his own voice. He tried to push down his emotion as he continued. "It's not about the game. It's about the fact that … well, I'm an idiot sometimes. You just had a major surgery, and you almost died. Here I am making some lame joke about it. Will you … will you forgive me … please?"

Phillip couldn't believe his own callousness. He'd always expected that Jesse would be the strong one who didn't let small things bother him, but that was an unfair assumption. Anyone would be sensitive about a joke like that if they'd gone through all that Jesse had. Phillip should have been praising and encouraging him for how well he'd done, but instead he'd offended him. He'd insulted the single person he admired most.

Jesse released Phillip's hands and stood up, quickly stepping around the table to embrace him. "Phillip, you didn't say anything wrong. I … I wish I could explain. I don't know why I could suddenly remember all those things. It's like yesterday when I was talking about baseball. Whatever they did to my brain stimulated certain parts of my memory—technical things, details. But when it comes to people and experiences from my past … there's nothing there. I guess I'm just frustrated, and I took it out on you."

Phillip buried his head into Jesse's shoulder and hugged him tightly. "I understand why you feel that way. I should have realized how frustrating it was for you. I shouldn't have said such a stupid—"

"Phillip, shh. Not one more word, please. I overreacted, that's all. You are such a kind person. I know you'd never say anything on purpose to offend me, or to hurt me."

"I honestly wouldn't, Jesse," he whispered.

"Hey, do you like ice cream?"

Phillip backed away slightly to look into his eyes. Jesse reached down and gently wiped the tear streaks from his cheeks. Phillip nodded. "Sure." He smiled up at Jesse.

"Take me to your favorite ice cream place, and I'll get us both a huge sundae. Everyone feels better with ice cream, right?"

"Okay." Phillip grinned at him. "There's a House of Flavors a few blocks from here."

"Perfect," Jesse said, and they kissed.

Twelve

The following day Jesse came upon the obituary of Harold Wainwright.

Jesse and Phillip had spent the morning together. They'd gone for another run and afterword they'd spent some time outdoors watering the multitude of flowerbeds that surrounded the house. Phillip was wielding the hose and on a whim decided it would be funny to spray his friend. Jesse stood there momentarily in shock, wiping the water from his drenched face.

"Oh, you little shit. You are going to *die*!"

At this point it became a full-scale water war. Jesse, larger and stronger, had the advantage, and after wrestling with his attacker for a few tenuous moments, he finally seized the weapon of mass destruction. Holding the squirming Phillip in place, he positioned the nozzle of the hose in the waistband of the boy's shorts and power-blasted him.

"Stop! Oh God, it's cold!" Phillip protested as he began to dance around frantically. Jesse was right there with him every step of the way, mercilessly holding the nozzle in place.

Finally they lay tangled in each other's arms on the ground, both drenched. Soon their cries of laughter turned into gasps and moans of passion.

When Jesse finally looked up, he saw a pair of feet standing next to them and instantly pulled himself off the love-struck Phillip who'd been pinned beneath him. "Mrs. Covington!" Jesse gasped in surprise.

She was smiling as she stared down at them, shaking her head. "You've made a swimming pool of my back yard," she scolded.

Jesse's first instinct was to apologize and offer to buy her a new yard, but then he remembered he had no money. "I'm sorry …" he said instead. "Um … *we're* sorry!"

Phillip was laughing again. "I nailed him!" he boasted. "Mom, you should have seen the look on Jesse's face when I sprayed him with the hose. It was so funny!"

She shook her head, stifling laughter of her own. "Well, I suppose the grass really did need watering. Are you sure you want the neighbors to … well, you know—"

"We got carried away, Mrs. Covington," Jesse quickly confessed as he rose to his feet. "We really are sorry."

"Who's gonna see us anyway?" Phillip asked. "The only neighbor who can see into our back yard is Mrs. Huntington, and she is like almost eighty."

"Mrs. Huntington is seventy-eight—a very young seventy-eight," Sarah said reprovingly. "I doubt she'd care if she saw two boys kissing, but just the same, if you're worried about Jesse's parents finding out before you're ready to tell them, you have to think about discretion."

"A point well taken," Jesse said, nodding furiously. "Like I said, we got carried away, and we're very sorry."

"Oh lighten up," Phillip said, as he jumped to his feet and wrapped his arms around Jesse's waist. "I don't care who sees me kissing my boyfriend. I don't even care if *Dad* sees!"

"You don't care if Dad sees what?" The three of them turned to the voice behind them. It was Phillip's father, Kyle.

Jesse looked down at Phillip, who had released his grip on Jesse's waist. They stepped slightly apart as Phillip's jaw dropped open.

"Um," Phillip hesitated. "Dad, you're home!"

"Phillip and Jesse got into a water fight," Sarah said as she stepped over to her husband. "I was scolding them, and Phillip said he wasn't worried about what you'd say when you saw their mess."

Kyle stared at her, bewildered, then laughed. "Why would I care about a little water? It's ninety degrees out today. I could use a drenching myself."

"We can take care of that for you, Dad," Phillip said, lunging for the hose.

Kyle raised his hands in the air as if in a hold-up. "Whoa! Just kidding … I think I'll pass."

"Aww, come on!" Phillip said teasingly. "It's just a little water."

Later that afternoon, when Jesse finally went back home, he realized that this was the very first moment he'd been apart from Phillip. Ever since Phillip came over two days prior—the day that Jesse got home from the hospital—they'd been together constantly.

Jesse confessed that he didn't want to leave. He wanted to stay with Phillip forever, as silly as that might sound. But they both knew it wasn't practical for them to be together every single minute. Jesse finally decided that he'd spend the evening with his parents but would call Phillip before bed. He didn't want to sleep alone … not tonight nor any night from that point forward.

After chatting with his mom a few minutes, he decided to take a shower. Afterward, while in his bedroom getting dressed, he checked the news on the Internet. By force of habit, he scanned the stock market numbers. Then the business news and the sports. Finally he perused the front-page and headline news. On page three he discovered the small article, complete with a photo of the ailing seventy-eight-year-old Wainwright.

He gasped as he stared at his own death notice.

It was not a typical obituary. In fact it wasn't even listed in the section where all the other obits were published. It was a capsule of his former life, briefly stating that Wainwright had served for three decades as CEO of the world's largest insurance company, and that he had died a multibillionaire.

The startling thing about the article was that it had praised Wainwright for his philanthropy. It went on to say how he'd bequeathed all of his property and large sums of money to each member of his personal staff. This was a decision Wainwright had made during the last few days leading up to the transition. He'd given each of his employees one million dollars apiece and left each of his mansions to one of these "common" people.

As Jesse stared at the screen, looking into the sad eyes of the elderly man in the photo, he regretted that he had not done more. Even after all of this money had been doled out to all these people, even after the 300 million that had been paid to Drayton, even after the hefty sum that had been transferred into the secret account in the name of Jesse Warren, billions were still unspent. All that money would go to waste. It would be fought over by distant relatives and people who suddenly appeared out of nowhere. He knew the whole thing was sure to be a clusterfuck of the highest magnitude.

He remembered a quote he had once heard by some rich person. Was it Rockefeller or Hughes, or Warren Buffet? He couldn't quite recall, but it went like this, "A man who dies rich, dies in disgrace." So true. All those years he'd had so many opportunities to improve the world. He could easily have given away ninety percent of all his assets and still remained a multi-millionaire. Why had he been so selfish?

And now, as he stared at the computer screen, it moved him to tears seeing the way his former self had been lauded as a hero. Big fucking deal! He gave away a small fraction of his massive fortune upon his death, and the people who had received it were the same individuals who had worked for him for years, tolerating his arrogance.

The certified letter containing the access code to the Swiss bank account would be arriving soon. Maybe he couldn't tell his parents or Phillip about the account. Maybe he couldn't hand them over large amounts of cash or buy them gifts, but he was beginning to formulate a plan on how to help them. He could do it anonymously, so that they would never realize the true source of their newfound fortune.

His hands shook as he nervously logged into the email account of Harold Wainwright. It was time to send a letter.

****

The ringtone of Phillip's phone awakened him a little after eight the next morning. Barely conscious, he fumbled for his cell on the nightstand. He smiled when he saw it was Jesse calling, even though he'd spoken to him only a few hours earlier. They'd stayed up late, talking on the phone until Phillip started nodding off, a little past midnight.

"Good morning," he said groggily. He was still sleepy, yet happy. Jesse could have called him a dozen times or more at any time of the morning, and he would not have been upset. "Did you miss me?"

"You were the first thing I thought of when I woke up," Jesse confessed. "Let's not do this anymore. I can't stand not sleeping with you!"

"I know," Phillip said, laughing. "You should have called me. You could have come over and crawled into bed with me. I'd have let you in."

"I know." Jesse's voice sounded so sweet, so full of admiration and sincerity. Phillip wanted to tell him he loved him, but he wanted to say it while looking him in the eyes. "Do you know what today is?" Jesse went on.

"Saturday?" Phillip guessed.

Jesse laughed. "Yeah … and it's 'free food' day."

"What?" Phillip asked, now laughing himself.

"Get your butt out of bed. We have work to do!"

"Jesse, you're not making any sense …"

"Get up, get dressed, and I'll be over there in twenty minutes. We can use my dad's car, but you've got to drive."

"Okay," Phillip said, "but where am I driving?"

"Tell you when I get there."

"Jesse, what's 'free food' day?" Phillip was already rubbing the sleep from his eyes.

"See you in a few!" The phone line went dead.

Phillip had no clue what Jesse was talking about, but in truth it didn't matter. All that mattered was spending time with Jess. He stumbled out of bed and marched out to the bathroom to shower and brush his teeth. He was fully dressed in a pair of jeans and tee shirt when the doorbell rang about a half-hour later.

Jesse stepped inside as Phillip opened the door, and before the door was even closed behind them they were locked in a passionate kiss. "Oh baby, I missed you last night," Jesse said.

"Mmm," Phillip said, as he tasted Jesse's minty breath. "Where are we going?" he asked.

"Well …" Jesse was smiling at him. "I volunteered us."

"You what? What do ya mean, 'volunteered us'?" Phillip was smiling broadly, his hands pressed against Jesse's chest as he looked up into his eyes.

"We're spending the morning down at the Breath of Life Ministries Food Pantry. We're going to help them organize their food donations and prepare care packages. Then we're going to work in the kitchen, making hot meals to serve to the homeless and hungry people who come to the shelter. Then this evening …" Jesse took a breath before continuing. "This evening, we're going to take meals out to the homeless people on the streets."

"Really?" Phillip asked. "Wow … that's cool, but why?"

"I just … um … I want to be doing something, ya know. I want to be involved in something, making a difference somehow."

"How did you hear about this place?" Phillip asked.

"Internet. Then I called them last night."

"How come you didn't tell me… I mean, when we were on the phone?"

Jesse kissed his forehead. "Well, to surprise you, I guess. I didn't want you to talk me out of it or anything."

Phillip was taken aback. "Jesse, why would I talk you out of it? I think it's great!"

"Really? I was hoping you'd say that."

"Really!" Phillip assured him. "Not only do we get to help other people, but we do it together. That's the part I like most. Are you sure you're not trying to do too much, too fast, though?"

"No … I want to do more, actually. Phillip, after what I've been through, I want to take advantage of every single second. I don't want to waste my life this time by being selfish!"

"This time?"

"I mean since the accident."

Phillip was astounded by Jesse's sudden commitment to community service, but he liked it. He liked it a lot. "Well, Jesse, you never were selfish—even before the accident. You've always been a generous person who was willing to help anyone in need."

"But this is different," Jesse said. "I don't want to help people because it will make me feel good about myself. I want to do it because it's what we all should be doing. I've been very blessed, and I want to give back a little."

"I'm the one who feels blessed," Phillip said as he wrapped his arms around Jesse's waist. "You know what? You're absolutely amazing!"

"You're not so bad yourself," Jesse said as he leaned in to kiss him.

****

When Phillip and Jesse arrived at the food kitchen that morning, they were greeted on the front porch by a middle-aged African American woman. "Well, what do we have here?" she said as she placed her hands on her hips. "I don't remember the probate court telling me they'd be sending over more juvies to do community service."

"We weren't sent from the court, Ma'am," Jesse said. "We're volunteers. I think I talked to you on the phone last night." He extended his hand to offer a handshake. "I'm Jesse Warren, and this is my friend, Phillip Covington."

"Ah, yes! I remember now, but I pictured you so much older. You know, you sound a lot more mature on the phone than what you look in person. I'm Morgan, Morgan Dennison. Well come on in, and let me show you around." They were still standing on the front porch, under the hand-painted, "Breath of Life Ministries: Feeding the Hungry" sign.

Phillip sensed immediately that Morgan was a sincere person. Her wide-eyed, honest expression inspired trust. He smiled at her sweetly as he shook her hand. The warmth of her handshake traveled straight to his heart. "Hi," he said. "Nice to meet you."

"So what brings you boys out here on a Saturday morning?" she asked as she unlocked the front door. She motioned for them to follow her inside. "Shouldn't you be out shooting hoops or chasing girls or somethin'?"

Jesse laughed obligingly. "Well, to be honest, Ms. Dennison—"

"Morgan," she corrected him with an insistent nod.

"Morgan, to be honest with you, Phillip and I both have had experiences … Well, let's just say we both realize how brief life is. Phillip had cancer, and I recently had brain surgery after a head injury."

"Bless your hearts," she said as she grabbed hold of Phillip's hand and squeezed it affectionately.

"Well, we're just so grateful for all the blessings we've been given. We both could have died, but we were given a second chance, and we want to make the best of it. We want to do some good with our lives."

"And you're both so young. Just babies!" She reached up and adjusted her glasses.

Morgan wore her hair in cornrows, and her glasses were

over-sized, with plastic frames. She had a youthful, trim physique and was dressed comfortably yet conservatively in a pair of Levis and plain knit pullover. Phillip instantly knew he was going to love her.

"And you," she said, directing her gaze at Phillip, "how are you now? Is the cancer gone?"

"My leukemia is in remission, Ma'am. Yes, it's gone."

"Wonderful! Praise God! And Jesse, how long ago was this surgery?"

"About a week ago," he said.

Morgan gasped and placed her hand over her mouth. "Merciful heavens!" she declared. "And already you're out-and-about? Shouldn't you be … well, ya know … in bed resting?"

Jesse laughed. "I did a five-mile run the day after I got home from the hospital. I feel great, and if my hair would just hurry up and grow back, I'd be completely back to normal."

"Well it's gettin' there. Just give it time … and you look great just the way you are. I like that little hat. It's very 'in,' you know."

"Really?" he said.

"Oh yeah! Very 'in.' I'm a school teacher—teach ninth grade English. I know all about what's in and what's not. You should get yourself one of those do-rags."

Phillip cracked up. "I'm sorry, but I am visualizing it!"

Jesse reached over and playfully slugged Phillip on the shoulder. "You making fun of me?"

Phillip's laugher instantly faded and his expression sobered. "No! I'm … uh …"

"I'm just kidding, guy," Jesse said.

Morgan looked at the couple before her, gazing first at Jesse then at Phillip. "Okay," she said with a decisive tone. "I see there's a little more than friendship going on here. No?"

Phillip turned to look at her, saying nothing, but merely nodding.

"Well good!" she said confidently. "Lord knows the world can use a little more love. Come on, I'll show you the pantry."

As Morgan was giving the boys a tour of the facility, another volunteer arrived. Murphy was a portly gentleman in his late fifties, and when Morgan introduced him to Jesse and Phillip he assessed them skeptically. As was the case with Morgan when she first saw the boys, Murphy assumed they'd been assigned community service by judicial order.

"Murphy," she explained, "Jesse and Phillip are actual volunteers ... of their own free will and everything! They came to help."

"Well, I'll be," he said, scratching his head. He reached out and shook the boys' hands. When the old gent finally released it, Phillip thought for a second his hand might be broken.

"Nice to meet you, sir," he said.

"Well, here's the situation," Morgan explained. "Usually we have one more person who helps. Her name is Elizabeth. She and I go to the same church. But Elizabeth is not well today, so Murphy and I thought it'd just be the two of us.

"Murphy is our driver. He has a van, and he goes around to stores and businesses to get donations. We have donation boxes in all the supermarkets, and some of the bakeries and small stores usually make donations of day-old products or canned and packaged goods. Murphy spends most of the morning running his route while Elizabeth and I stay here and do the cooking."

"You do all this by yourself?" Phillip asked.

"Well, like I said earlier, sometimes we get 'volunteers,' but usually they are people sent to us from the court who have to complete a community service requirement as part of their sentence. I'm not sure we've ever had a true volunteer. Have we, Murphy?"

"Can't say as we have," he said, shaking his head.

"Morgan, how many people do you usually feed every Saturday?" Phillip inquired.

"Oh, last week I think we served about a hundred forty hot meals here at the food pantry. But after we're done serving here, we take whatever is left over and drive around in the van looking for homeless people who might be hungry."

"Here in Dayton?" Phillip asked.

"Oh yes, hon. You'd be surprised. Last week we served another sixty meals that way."

"So you're saying that there are just three of you, and you served two hundred meals?" Jesse asked.

"Plus we give away the care packages. Some don't necessarily come for the hot meal, but they come to get the groceries. We don't turn anyone away … long as there are supplies available, that is."

Jesse shook his head as he looked at the couple before him. "I sense there's a little more than friendship going on here." He repeated the same phrase she'd used earlier. "I see that you two are really angels."

Morgan laughed as she grabbed hold of the elderly gentleman's arm. "Well bless your heart," she said to Jesse. "Are you ready to get to work?"

"You know it!" Phillip chimed in.

Phillip agreed to stay and help Morgan at the food pantry, while Jesse left with Murphy to run the donation route. It wasn't exactly what Phillip had hoped would happen—he'd envisioned himself spending the day with Jesse—but since he'd taken such an instant liking to Morgan, it suited him fine.

While they were working in the kitchen together, Morgan began asking Phillip questions about his relationship with Jesse. He explained to her how they'd always been best friends and how terrified he had been when Jesse was in the accident. Her eyes filled with tears of empathy as he described Jesse's injuries and the surgery that had saved him.

"It was a miracle, for sure," she said, raising her hands in the air. "Praise the Lord Almighty!"

Phillip was sitting on a tall stool next to the sink peeling potatoes. A red apron was cinched snugly around his lithe frame. "You're just the cutest little thing, sittin' there like that," Morgan observed. "That young man of yours must be crazy about you."

Phillip, worried that his face was turning as red as his apron, smiled shyly. "Thanks," he said quietly. "I think we're pretty crazy about each other, actually."

"So how did you figure out you were the way you are?" she asked.

"Gay?"

"Yes. It must be hard to accept when you're different than most other people. I've always believed that God chooses the most special souls to be gay or lesbian. He picks the strongest among us, and he blesses them with the most precious gifts. All the gay people I've known have been sensitive and sweet and compassionate. God's angels."

"Well, maybe not all of them are so angelic, and in all honesty, Morgan … I'm no angel."

"Well, no one's perfect, my dear, but I can tell already you're not a typical teenager. Believe me, I know all about teens. I teach ninth grade."

"Oh my gosh," Phillip said, careful not to take the Lord's name in vain, "I think that'd be the hardest job in the world."

She nodded and smiled. "Yeah, it's challenging at times, but not without rewards. In that sense, it's similar to what we do here. It's so easy to be discouraged, but the gratitude of the people we help makes it all worthwhile."

****

Jesse was exhilarated by his excursion with Murphy. Granted, it had been a lot of physical work, but Jesse now had a young, vital body, which made it easy to heft the heavy

142

crates and overstuffed boxes. In fact, seeing Murphy struggle—obviously short-of-breath as he attempted to load the van—spurred Jesse on to work all the harder. "Let me get that, sir," he said to Murphy as he bent over to pick up a box of canned goods. Beads of sweat glistened on Murphy's forehead, and he looked up to see Jesse standing beside him.

"Not as young as I used to be," he conceded. He stepped back and chuckled, patting his protruding stomach. "And I don't suppose this big ole gut helps much, either."

Jesse smiled at him and placed his hand on his shoulder. "It's crazy how our bodies change as we get older. It's like all of a sudden you look in the mirror and wonder ... what happened."

"Young man, you have no idea," Murphy said.

If you only knew, thought Jesse.

What startled Jesse most was witnessing firsthand how many food items were thrown out every single day. Nearly all the donations were items that would otherwise have gone straight into the dumpster. When he thought of all the hungry or homeless people in the country, he couldn't believe companies could be so wasteful.

Yet he was also pleased that some businesses were willing to help. Most of the food items they received looked perfectly fine to Jesse. Granted they were not necessarily the prime commodities a supermarket would want on display, but they were still edible and the produce was by no means rotten. For example, they had received two full cases of bananas from one grocer. The skins were starting to brown, but Murphy explained that they would use the best looking bunches for the care packages. Morgan would take the ripest bananas home to make banana bread, which would be included in next week's food boxes.

Jesse looked back upon his previous existence and wondered just how much food he had wasted. How many times had his kitchen staff prepared exquisite meals of which he'd merely eaten a small portion? What had happened to the remainder? He'd required his cooks to keep his pantries fully stocked so that he could request any food item on a whim. Surely this must have resulted in massive waste. He shook his head as he stared out the window of the van, allowing the regret to wash over him. Hopefully his staff had kept the leftovers for themselves and their families. Perhaps they had even donated some items to organizations such as this ministry. He knew it was unlikely, though. Most of his staff had known better than to risk the ire of the heartless Harold Wainwright.

When Murphy and Jesse finally arrived back at the food pantry and stepped out of the van, they were greeted by the sound of laughter. He turned to see Morgan with her arm around Phillip; they were both smiling broadly. Jesse nearly laughed himself upon seeing Phillip in his bright red apron. He looked absolutely adorable.

"What's so funny?" Jesse asked.

"Oh, Morgan is just telling me stories," Phillip said as he stepped closer to Jesse.

"I like your apron," Jesse whispered.

"Stop!" Phillip said, "or you'll make me blush."

"Too late. You already are." Jesse wanted to lean in and kiss him, but instead he grabbed hold of Phillip's elbow and began leading him toward the back of the van. "We got a lot of donations," he said. "You're not going to believe how much stuff these stores just throw away."

"Oh, I know," Morgan spoke up. "It makes me sick when we aren't able to make the rounds for pick-ups. I know that all that food is going straight out to the trash."

"Really?" Phillip said. "What's wrong with it?"

"Nothing, really," she said. "It's just that American consumers expect their purchases to be perfect. If a store sees that a piece of fruit is getting too ripe or has a bruise on it, out it goes. As for a lot of the other items like canned goods, these stores constantly are changing their floor layout. They discontinue items and then whatever stock they have on the shelf they just pitch."

"Seems like they'd wait and try to sell the rest of their inventory instead of just discarding it," Jesse said.

"That would make too much sense," Morgan laughed. "But hey, I'm not complaining. I'm just thankful they let us take it off their hands."

"Right," Jesse agreed. "So what do we do now?"

"I'm going to back the van up to the garage door. We'll unload it right in there and begin assembling the care packages."

"And when we're done, it will be time to serve lunch. Usually people start showing up by eleven o'clock."

"Guess we better get a move on then," Phillip said.

****

According to Morgan, it was a slow week. They'd only served a little over one hundred meals. She explained that spring and summer were always slower. The homeless people had a lot more options of places to go for food. When it snowed or the temperature dropped below freezing, things got busy.

"I can't believe people right here in our city are homeless like that ... in the winter."

"Oh baby, it's sad." She shook her head.

They had finished serving the meal and were in the kitchen cleaning up, using cardboard trays to package the remaining hot food. "We start with a set route, delivering hot meals to our regular shut-ins; then we go down to the plaza where most of the homeless people congregate and pass out the remaining meals."

"Who are these shut-ins?" Phillip asked.

"Elderly people, mostly. We have one younger gentleman who is in a wheelchair. He lives alone."

"Really? What does he do the rest of the week when you aren't delivering meals?"

"He has a chore service provider who looks in on him and runs errands," Morgan explained. "She doesn't visit him on weekends, so this works out perfect."

Jesse was outside chatting with Murphy while Phillip and Morgan worked in the kitchen. "Murphy had to quit smoking about a year ago," Morgan said, changing the subject. "Every week after we serve lunch, he goes outside and has one cigarette. That's all he smokes now. Goes the rest of the whole week without any."

"Wow, I wonder why he even tempts himself with that one," Phillip said. "I think it would be hard to smoke just one and then stop, I mean if he was really addicted."

"Oh he definitely was addicted. He smoked three or four packs a day. I guess I don't begrudge him that one minor indulgence. It's once a week and in moderation."

"He seems so nice."

"He's a sweet man. His wife passed a couple years ago. That's when he first started volunteering. He has not missed a single week."

"And what about Elizabeth?"

"Oh Lordy!" Morgan said. "Wait 'til you meet sweet Lizbeth. She's a sweetheart, but I swear that girl is a scatterbrain."

It took them about an hour to clean up the kitchen and prepare the food trays. Phillip was surprised when he began hauling them out to the van that all the care packages they'd made earlier were gone. It hadn't taken long for them to be dispersed.

That evening the four of them crowded together into the van. Jesse and Phillip sat in the back amidst the boxes containing the food trays and handed them up to Morgan and Murphy as needed. After they'd finished their rounds to the shut-ins, they drove downtown, and the four of them piled out. Some of the homeless people had seen the van when it pulled up and were already waiting. Phillip loved being able to hand the hot meals directly to the recipients. They seemed incredibly grateful, almost as if they'd won the lottery.

That was only their first stop, though, and they still had quite a few food trays left. Murphy drove down through the streets of the city, looking for needy people. Phillip stared out the side window of the van, himself on the lookout. "Wait!" he cried. "There are a couple people down there. It looks like they are lying on the pavement, right in front of the alley."

"Yeah, right over by that vent," Jesse said.

Morgan turned to look out her own window. "Oh Lordy," she sighed. "They're warming their feet on the vent."

Murphy stopped the van while Jesse and Phillip jumped out, each grabbing a meal. They went over to the two street people who were huddled together. The night air was already starting to get chilly. "Would you like a hot meal?" Phillip asked.

"Oh bless your heart," one of them replied. She looked to be merely a teenager, and her feet were bare. She was shivering. "Thank you so much."

The boy beside her was about her age. He did not say anything but took the food from Jesse and nodded.

"God bless you," Phillip said as he turned to head back to the van. Suddenly he stopped, though, realizing Jesse was not following. As he turned around, his heart caught in his throat. Jesse was removing his sneakers, handing them to the young man sitting there on the street.

Phillip looked down to see the girl's feet, realizing they were about the size of his own. He rushed back to her and slipped off his own shoes. Tears filled her eyes as she looked up at him. She had already begun devouring the food on her lap, but she quickly set the tray aside and stood up. She stepped over to Phillip and embraced him. "God bless you," she repeated back to him. "God bless you." Her voice was but a whisper in his ear.

Jesse and Phillip held hands and walked back to the van in their stocking feet.

Thirteen

During the entire course of his previous life—nearly eighty years—Jesse had never felt so alive. Yes, when he had said that he wanted to do the community service work because it was the right thing to do, he had been sincere. He was motivated by a genuine desire to make the world a better place, not just a need to feel better about who he had been. He *did* want to be his brother's keeper. He *did* want to live a better life his second time around.

The way it made him feel was a fringe benefit. And it was not the same feeling he had experienced in his previous life when once a year he wrote out a large check to some charity. During those times, he had been able tell himself that he was a really decent person. He'd been able to forget, momentarily anyway, all of the lives his decisions had adversely affected.

He thought about the young black boy lying on the street who now wore his shoes. How did such a beautiful young man end up on the street like that? Was he a runaway? Was he a drug addict or male prostitute? The girl beside him appeared to be just as young, but in her eyes there had been a look of maturity. Her words, "bless your heart," made him feel as if she were an old soul. And there they were, lying there without any shoes. Couldn't they have gone somewhere for help? Weren't there welfare programs to help kids like that? What about their families? What about school?

An entirely new vista was beginning to open to Jesse. He thought he had known all about the world. In his previous life he'd traveled extensively. He was unequivocally cosmopolitan. Now he realized just how blind he'd been. He

149

had never seen the loss, the pain, the desperation. He had been utterly oblivious to those in need.

Jesse was eager to shower love upon Phillip that evening. The boy was becoming everything to him. Although he'd known him for a matter of days, Jesse realized he had never loved anyone the way he loved that boy. The sincere goodness of his character, the compassion of his heart, the sensitivity of his soul—Phillip was everything Jesse could have hoped or dreamed to find in a lover and friend. Phillip had completely filled the void left by Jacob.

Beneath the surface of his new happiness, however, Jesse had started to experience twinges of anxiety. The cause was one word Phillip used too frequently and freely: remission. His cancer was in *remission*. Earlier that day he'd gone so far as to say that he was cured. Oh, if only this were true! Jesse prayed it was, but he feared otherwise. He knew from his years in the medical insurance industry that "in remission" did not mean cured.

What if the cancer came back? What if Phillip were to get sick again? What if he were to …? Jesse couldn't allow himself to think about these possibilities. After having lost Jacob, the love of his life, Jesse found the thought of losing Phillip, Jacob's virtual clone, unbearable.

There had to be a way to ensure this would not happen. Jesse had to begin thinking proactively. He needed to develop a contingency plan. He needed to find a way to save Phillip. He had lost the love of his first life because of his own greed and stupidity. This time around, however, he was not going to make the same mistakes. He would spare no cost to protect Phillip. He'd do anything to keep him alive and by his side.

Jesse kissed every inch of Phillip's nubile body that evening, and as he did so, the boy squirmed and moaned delightedly. Jesse already realized how he felt about Phillip.

He already knew he was in love.

"I love you, Phillip," he whispered, as they drifted off to sleep.

****

"I love you," Phillip whispered into Jesse's ear. They were alone in Phillip's bedroom. "And I want you to make love to me."

Ever since Jesse had confessed his love for him two nights earlier, Phillip's heart had soared. At last the boys were completely alone. The parents were gone. They had nothing scheduled that day. They'd already returned from their daily run, and now it was simply time to be together, to kiss and touch and demonstrate their passion for each other.

When Jesse first verbalized his love for Phillip, the boy had not immediately responded. It had taken a while for him to absorb the overwhelming reality that this young man who'd been the center of his universe for so long loved him in return.

When Phillip finally allowed himself to express his feelings aloud, they poured out of him with potency unlike anything he'd ever experienced. His eyes filled with tears, and his voice was barely a whisper. "I love you with all my heart."

With both gentleness and urgency, Jesse guided him toward the bed, repeatedly kissing Phillip's cherubic face. First his cheeks, then his forehead, and finally his lips—he showered the boy with affection. The sweet, tender kisses demonstrated the purity of Jesse's love. Phillip gasped as Jesse pressed his body against him. Opening their mouths, they tasted each other's tongues. Phillip closed his eyes as he felt Jesse's strength surround him. That embrace was so amazingly protective. He reached up to run his hands across Jesse's back, wrapping his fingers securely around the broad shoulders.

"Oh God, I love you," Jesse declared. "I love you so

much." The crush of their lips together was passionate and sensual. Phillip swooned within those strong and loving arms, and he relaxed as nimble fingers deftly grasped the hem of his tee shirt. Phillip raised his arms as Jesse pulled the shirt upward, neither of them wanting to separate long enough to remove the obstructive article of clothing. Once it had been discarded, their mouths reconnected, and Phillip began groping at Jesse's clothing.

Hurriedly Jesse stripped off his own shirt, and Phillip felt the press of Jesse's bare skin against his own. It was smooth and hot, and Phillip reached up to place his palms against the hard pectorals that pressed against him. Phillip stood on his tiptoes, straining to hold his mouth as firmly against Jesse's as possible, all the while grasping at Jesse's erect nipples. He eagerly pinched them between his thumbs and forefingers. Jesse moaned and drove his tongue deep into Phillip's hungry mouth.

Jesse was holding Phillip's head with both hands, cupping his face in the palm of his hands. Phillip felt himself being guided backwards, as Jesse walked him closer to the bed. When Phillip felt the back of his calves rub against the bed, he allowed himself to be eased down and lovingly yet assertively pressed into the mattress. Jesse slid atop him, pinning the bare-chested boy beneath him. Phillip moaned excitedly, grasping at his lover and kissing him passionately.

"Baby," Jesse whispered, "I want you so bad ..."

Phillip sighed, too excited to speak. His big brown eyes widened as he stared up at his blond, athletic lover. Jesse had pulled away from him and was reaching for the waistband of Phillip's running shorts. "Oh please," Phillip finally managed.

In one smooth movement, Jesse slid Phillip's running shorts down past his thighs. Phillip raised his legs as Jesse pulled the shorts and underwear off, discarding them carelessly behind him. Phillip then lay completely exposed, naked but for his ankle socks. As he looked up into Jesse's eyes, his heart beat a little faster. Jesse smiled down at him hungrily. He seemed to be scanning Phillip's luscious body, taking in every inch. Suddenly he dove back down onto the naked boy, burying his face in Phillip's neck as he grabbed hold of the erection that throbbed so enticingly against him.

The dual sensations of Jesse's passionate assault sent a shivering wave of pleasure through Phillip's body, and he moaned spontaneously. He felt the grip of Jesse's firm hand around his rigid shaft, and the heat of Jesse's expert tongue against the erogenous zone of his neck. When Jesse's free hand reached up to tweak Phillip's left nipple, the boy squirmed with delight. "Oh god, Jesse!" he cried.

"I want …" Jesse sputtered. "I want … you. I want to make love to you."

Phillip clawed at the back of Jesse's head, pulling him toward his mouth. Again they kissed as Jesse rubbed Phillip's chest and hard-on simultaneously.

"Please Jesse, take 'em off!" Phillip cried. He tried leaning forward to get his hands on the waistband of Jesse's shorts, but Jesse's body was pressed against him, holding him in place. Phillip sighed in exasperation and once again allowed himself to be ravaged by his dominant lover.

When Jesse pulled away from him again, Phillip hurriedly reached for Jesse's shorts, pulling them down to expose the evidence of his lover's arousal. As Jesse stood beside the bed, frantically undressing, Phillip slid down and took him in his mouth. Jesse moaned and clutched Phillip's shoulders to steady himself. The erection was hard yet smooth against Phillip's tongue, and he slickly surrounded it with his mouth, swallowing the entire shaft down to its root.

Jesse sighed and laughed at the same time as the pleasurable sensation momentarily became his primary focus. "Baby, don't make me cum," he whispered. "Not yet."

Phillip was gasping as he came up for air. "Want you …" he moaned.

Jesse bent forward and again kissed his boy, driving his tongue forcefully into the eager mouth. Phillip felt himself being guided once again to his former reclining position. On his back, he stared up at his naked lover. His heart was pounding in his chest. He knew he was ready for what was about to happen, but he was still nervous.

"Baby, what's wrong?" Jesse asked. "Are you afraid? You know I won't hurt you ..."

Phillip smiled at him and shook his head. "No, I'm just ... I'm a little nervous. It's my first time."

"Are you ready?" Jesse asked. "Are you sure? Because I can wait ..."

"No! I'm sure. Yes, I'm ready," Phillip said, practically pleading. "In the drawer ..." Phillip pointed to the bedside stand.

Jesse opened the drawer, removing a bottle of gel and a packet of condoms. *Extra Large.* Jesse smiled as he read the package. Phillip was a virgin, and for all he knew, Jesse was as well, yet neither of them could be certain. Jesse's broad grin told Phillip it was perfectly fine. The precaution of the prophylactics was acceptable. "Do you want to put one on me?" Jesse asked, handing the box to Phillip.

As Phillip clumsily fumbled with the package, he felt his legs being raised. The gentle pressure of Jesse's finger against his opening made him squirm just a bit. It was a unique feeling that sort of tickled. Jesse was sliding his lubed finger back and forth. Phillip sighed and relaxed, momentarily forgetting about the box of condoms he was holding.

"Oh Jesse," he moaned, "feels good ... "

Jesse grinned as he looked into Phillip's eyes. Slowly he inserted his finger.

"Aaahhh," Phillip whimpered, not allowing his gaze to stray from Jesse's sweet face. He'd never imagined the feeling would be so pleasurable. Jesse's movement inside of him was slow and measured, and Phillip felt a surge of excitement wash over him. His cock throbbed against his abdomen as his lover probed him. Gradually the finger thrusts quickened as Jesse eased more deeply into him, first with only one finger, then with more lube and a second finger. As Jesse began to rotate his digits, loosening the sphincter, Phillip writhed on the bed.

"Oh Jesse," he cried, "it feels so good." Jesse was smiling down at his face as he added a third finger.

"Open the box," he whispered, and Phillip refocused his concentration on the package in his hand. Quickly he tore it open and removed one of the foil packets. As he tore away the wrapper, he felt Jesse pull his fingers out, only to quickly re-enter, this time more forcefully with only one digit. He was driving his middle finger deeply into Phillip, probing him. As the finger tapped against Phillip's prostate, he moaned and clutched the bed sheets with his free hand. "Oh god! It's gonna make me cum!"

"Not yet," Jesse whispered, laughing just a little as he stared at his lover's face. He leaned in and kissed Phillip while continuing to drive his finger in and out of the tight hole. Phillip was so aroused that he knew he would go over the edge were he merely to touch his throbbing erection, so he wrapped both arms tightly around Jesse's torso as they kissed.

"Inside me," he gasped, "I need you inside me!"

Jesse pulled his finger out of Phillip and repositioned himself, sliding his groin close enough for Phillip to reach. Clumsily Phillip fumbled with the condom, attempting to position it as quickly as possible. He dropped it accidentally on the mattress, and in frustration was nearly tempted to abandon the safe-sex precaution altogether. When Jesse calmly picked it up and handed it back to Phillip, his hands were shaking. He wanted Jesse so badly it was all he could do to calm himself.

"Take your time," Jesse soothingly reassured him. Lovingly he carded his hands through Phillip's thick, dark hair.

Phillip smiled up at the handsome, athletic man who stood before him. That smooth, bronze chest, cleft so perfectly between two magnificent pecs, made Phillip's heart beat even more rapidly. Jesse's sparkling white teeth shone behind his slightly parted lips as Phillip eased the condom against the bulbous mushroom head of Jesse's cock. Slowly and deliberately he rolled it down, snugly sheathing the rigid shaft.

"Oh my God, are you sexy," Jesse confessed as he stared down at Phillip. "The way you look up at me with those eyes—those big, brown, beautiful eyes!"

Within an instant Jesse was atop the boy again, pinning him to the mattress beneath them. Phillip, once more on his back, enjoyed the feel of his lover as he bore down upon him, the weight of Jesse's body pressing him into the mattress. He squirmed beneath the hard chest that held him in place, futilely trying to get even closer to the man he loved, the man who was already wrapped around him.

Jesse's hot breath against Phillip's neck was like a flame. The fingers that gripped the sides of his lithe body were as tantalizing as feathers delightfully tickling his sensitive skin. This mixture of raw masculine power and delicate gentleness was an experience beyond Phillip's wildest dreams. The passion that rose within Phillip was so powerful it brought tears to his eyes.

As Jesse's lips again connected with Phillip's, he noticed the dampness on the boy's face. "Oh baby," he whispered, pulling away and staring into his eyes. "Why are you crying?"

"I'm sorry," Phillip responded, quickly shaking his head. "I'm just so … so happy. I want you so bad!"

Jesse kissed him once more, simultaneously driving his tongue deeply into Phillip's mouth and his finger into the tight channel between Phillip's legs. The dual entry was sudden and a bit shocking to Phillip, though not unwelcome. Phillip spread his legs wide and pulled his knees toward his chest. As Jesse eased his mouth off of Phillip's, his finger remained deep inside him. "I want to make love to you," Jesse whispered. "Want you so bad."

Jesse smoothly slid onto mattress, kneeling between Phillip's legs. With his free hand he reached for a pillow and placed it against the boy's butt-cheeks. "Lift up," he whispered, and then slid the pillow in place as Phillip eased himself onto the cushion. Jesse grabbed the bottle of gel and squeezed a stream onto his sheathed erection, dropping the tube carelessly beside him. His other hand was still busy fingering Phillip's tight hole.

As Jesse slowly fisted his erection, Phillip stared directly into his eyes. Jesse pumped his cock with one hand and thrust into Phillip with the other. Gradually he inched closer, and Phillip reached up to touch his chest. He was now so close that Phillip felt the heat of Jesse's groin against the tender flesh of his globes. He felt momentarily vacated when Jesse removed his finger, but the feeling was short-lived. Instantly it was replaced by the pressure of a swollen cockhead against his rosebud.

"I don't want to hurt you," Jesse confessed. "Please tell me ..."

"Please!" Phillip cried. "It's okay."

As Jesse began to enter him, Phillip stared directly into his eyes. The crown slowly penetrated him, and as Jesse eased into the tight hole, a wave of pain washed over Phillip. Fearfully and reflexively, Phillip contracted his sphincter, and the pain instantly overwhelmed him. "Ahhh!" he cried, grasping frantically at the bed sheets.

Jesse immediately withdrew. "Phillip! Are you okay?"

Phillip nodded his head vigorously. He could not believe the intensity of the pain, and as he continued to writhe on the bed, it only worsened.

"Relax," Jesse whispered. "Babe, relax and ride out the wave of pain. Let yourself go completely limp ..." He was leaning forward, positioning his mouth next to Phillip's ear.

Phillip felt as if someone had rammed a baseball bat inside him, and to his chagrin, tears streamed down his cheeks. He hated himself for being so wimpy.

"I'm sorry," Jesse said softly. "Oh baby, I don't want to hurt you."

Phillip shook his head and then quickly looked away. "No, I'm sorry." He felt a gentle hand under his chin, guiding his head to a position where he was again staring into Jesse's deep blue eyes.

"Shhh," Jesse said, "Relax … you've got to trust me. If you relax, the pain will stop."

Phillip sighed and let go of the sheets, allowing his body to completely let go. His legs were now stretched out flat against the mattress, and Jesse was gently rubbing his hands up and down Phillip's thighs. He was right; the pain was going away. The tidal wave of torment had only lasted a few seconds. The agony had reminded Phillip of being kicked in the nuts, only worse.

"It's okay," Phillip said, "I'm so sorry … it hurt so bad."

Jesse kissed him on the forehead, threading his fingers through Phillip's hair. "Shh … I told you to tell me if it hurt."

"Let's try again," Phillip said.

"Why don't we wait?" Jesse replied. "We have lots of time."

"No … please Jesse, I think it'll be okay. I was just so nervous."

Jesse slid back into position between Phillip's legs. He reached down and began to stroke Phillip, and within seconds he was rock hard again. Jesse then picked up the tube of gel and liberally applied a stream to his own sheathed cock.

"Okay, I'll try again. Relax as I enter, okay? And then bear down a little, like you're pushing back against me as I slide into you."

"Okay," Phillip said, his voice barely a squeak.

When Jesse entered him the second time, Phillip's impulse was to tense up, but he willed himself to remain calm. He did as Jesse had instructed and completely relaxed. He felt the heat of Jesse's groin pressing against him as the thick shaft stretched open his hole. Then, at the exact moment of entry, he bore down. There was no pain, none whatsoever.

Phillip smiled at Jesse as he looked into his eyes. Feeling his lover inside of him excited Phillip, and his cock throbbed against his abdomen. "Oh Jesse, it feels good. It doesn't hurt this time."

Jesse thrust deeper, and the entirety of his shaft was surrounded by Phillip's tight channel. He looked down at Phillip, almost as if to request permission. "Do it!" Phillip said. "Fuck me …" and Jesse began to pump himself back and forth, thrusting his hips as he drove his cock repeatedly into Phillip.

The sensation of Jesse's cock stabbing Phillip's prostate was exponentially more intense than the earlier finger thrusts, and Phillip very quickly realized he was edging toward orgasm. "Oh God!" Phillip cried, "Jesse, you're gonna make me cum!"

"Good," Jesse said. He was now panting, a sheen of sweat coating his forehead. "I wanna fuck the cum right out of you." Jesse proceeded to do precisely that.

"Oh, Oh," Phillip gasped. He moaned as Jesse's cock rammed deep within him. "Jesse!"

The exact moment that Phillip felt himself crossing the point of no return, Jesse thrust deep within him, burying himself balls-deep as he reached down to fist Phillip's throbbing erection. A rope of hot cum erupted from Phillip, and a shiver traveled through his entire body. He writhed on the mattress, clutching at Jesse's torso as the heat of Jesse's lips crushed against his own. Phillip wrapped his arms around his lover as they both panted, gasping for breath.

"Oh damn!" Jesse moaned, growling into Phillip's ear.

"Oh my God … holy fuck!" He was half-laughing, half-moaning.

"You came?" Phillip asked. Jesse was still inside him.

Jesse nodded as he leaned back and slowly pulled out. "At the exact moment you did." Phillip grabbed hold of Jesse and pushed him back on the mattress, climbing atop him. He drove his tongue deep into Jesse's mouth as he passionately Frenched him.

"I love you, Jesse Warren!" he cried. "I love you so damn much!"

Fourteen

Margo was in the kitchen on the phone when the boys entered the following morning. Jesse headed straight for the refrigerator, smiling affectionately at his mother as he brushed by her. He pulled out a carton of orange juice, twisting off the cap and raising the jug to his mouth. Frantically Margo waved her arms and pointed toward the kitchen cupboard, indicating to her son he needed to use a glass. Jesse shrugged and put the jug down on the counter. He took out two large glasses and poured juice for Phillip and him.

"Look," Margo said into the receiver, "this is some sort of mistake!" She was holding a document in her hand. "I just explained to the other operator, I tried making my mortgage payment this morning online and it wouldn't go through. The automated message told me the account was closed. They said my balance is zero." She laughed before continuing. "We just remortgaged our home a couple months ago, and we have thirty years of payments ahead of us. Can you get this fixed so I can make my payment?" She shook her head as she listened to the response. "I've already been on hold for the past twenty minutes ... okay, yes. I'll wait."

She placed her hand over the receiver and turned to Jesse. "Sorry, sweetie. Computer screw-up or something. You boys want some breakfast?"

"We just finished our run, and we gotta go back down to the food pantry today. We're gonna stop and eat on the way."

"You need money? I think I've got a ten in my purse ... Yes! Hello ..." She listened intently to the person on the other end of the line. "Wait! What are you saying? Some *charity* paid our mortgage off? The whole thing!" She moved toward the kitchen table, easing herself into a chair. "But … why?"

Jesse turned to look at Phillip, who was smiling broadly. "Oh my god!" Phillip whispered. "It's a miracle!"

"Are you sure?" Margo's voice was now nearly hysterical. "I … I just don't understand!" Tears streamed down her cheeks. "Why did they pick us?"

Quickly she mimed writing to indicate she needed a pen and paper. Jesse hurriedly stepped over and retrieved a notepad from the kitchen drawer. He handed it to his mother, along with a ball point pen. "Can you give me their number or address or something? I need to contact them and at the very least thank them!" She was trying to write while struggling to maintain some semblance of control over her emotions.

Phillip slid a box of tissue across the table toward her.

"And that's all you have, just a brief notation on the account: 'Paid in full by the New Beginnings Foundation'? There is no phone number or address or anything?"

She pulled a tissue from the box and wiped her eyes. "My husband—he's not gonna believe this! This is such a miracle. Oh, thank you! Thank you so much!"

When she hung up the phone, Jesse was staring down at her. "What happened?" he asked, pretending to be puzzled. "A charity paid off our mortgage?"

"Yes! Oh my God, yes! I don't know why, though. I don't know what we did to deserve this."

"Mom! That's fantastic. Don't look a gift horse … um, you know the saying. You *do* deserve it though. After all you've been through this year, I just think God's looking out for you."

"For all of us, Jesse. It truly is a miracle. I've got to call your father!"

"Why don't you join us for breakfast, Mrs. Warren?" Phillip offered. "To celebrate."

She looked up and smiled at him through her tears.

"Why yes! I think I will, and I'm buying. I can afford it now." She stood up and hugged her son excitedly. Then she turned to Phillip and hugged him as well.

"Give us a few minutes to get cleaned up and changed," Jesse said.

"Okay honey. Oh, and you got a letter. It came certified. Looks like it might have come from an attorney's office or something. I almost opened it, but it's addressed to you. It's over on the desk."

"Hmm, okay," he said. "I'll grab it on my way upstairs."

"Well, let me know what it is …" The boys were already headed up the stairwell.

"Okay, Mom," Jesse hollered back at her as he clutched the letter from Thomas and Associates firmly in his hand and bounded the steps.

While Phillip was in the shower, Jesse logged onto his computer to check Harold Wainwright's email. As expected, he found in his inbox a response to the email he'd sent a few days previously.

Mr. Wainwright,

As perplexing and startling as your email was, I've got to admit that I'm not entirely surprised that you'd pull a stunt such as this. Faking your own death is certainly a complex matter, but if there is anyone who could pull it off, it certainly would be you. Had you not stated the code phrase, I'd have been convinced the email was a fraud, especially since I witnessed the burial of what I thought was your body.

Curiously I traced the IP address of the original email to Dayton, Ohio. Seems an odd place to forge a new beginning. I simply hope you will be afforded the time and good health that you need to carry out your noble wishes before it is finally time for you to pass on. I'm quite impressed with the list you provided, and I will do everything within my power to ensure that your wishes are carried out.

You will be pleased to know that it was not too late for me to transfer the bulk of your funds into the hands of the charitable foundation we established. The remaining amount of your capital has been dispensed as you'd requested in your will, and all that now remains is a mere pittance of a couple million dollars. The legal fees and final expenses are sure to eat that up rather quickly. I was able to accomplish this by producing an addendum to your last will and testament. This, of course, was signed by you prior to your departure and was witnessed by two members of your household staff.

The Swiss account under the name Jesse Warren has been set up, and a certified letter has been mailed to the accountholder containing the pass code. Curiously, this also went to an address in Dayton, Ohio. Several of the charitable endowments also were awarded to recipients located in that city. I'm not certain as to why you have chosen this locale to do all of this long-overdue good work, but again I'm thoroughly impressed by your generosity.

On a personal note, I'd like to thank you for the generous bequest. I can assure you, sir, the money will be put to good use. Upon the completion of your directives, I plan to close up the firm and retire. I'd like to use the remainder of my years doing something positive—something that will make a difference. I thank you for making this possible.

My thoughts and prayers are with you, and I pray your remaining days are comfortable and satisfying. May you find the peace you have been seeking. God bless you.

Chris

Jesse smiled to himself and heaved a sigh of relief. When he had sent the email to Chris, he knew it might already be too late. There was only a slim chance that Chris would be able to access the accounts of Harold Wainwright and transfer the majority of the funds to the New Beginnings charity. He suspected that Chris may be able to finagle a way, because Chris was the executor of Wainwright's estate. Jesse was confident that Chris would abide by his wishes and see to it that the donations were made according to his instructions. The remainder of the money would be in the hands of the newly founded charity, which would be up to Chris to administrate.

Jesse was closing the email and logging off the computer when Phillip entered the bedroom, a towel around his waist. "Your turn," Phillip said.

"Come 'ere," Jesse said, motioning for him. "Wish I could have showered with you." His voice was a whisper, very seductive.

"Me, too." Phillip smiled just before leaning in to kiss Jesse. "You better hurry. Your mom's waiting."

"She can wait a few seconds longer while you kiss me," Jesse said. Seeing his boy in front of him, hair dripping and wearing nothing but a towel, was almost too much. He debated cancelling breakfast altogether. "I loved last night, babe. You were amazing."

Phillip grinned. "Go!" he urged. "If you ... um ...start something now, we'll really be late."

Quickly Jesse grabbed the end of the towel and pulled it away from Phillip's body, discarding it on the floor. "Jesse!" Phillip protested. "I ... we ... we can't do this now!"

Jesse laughed as he wrapped his fist around the rigid pole in front of him. "Can't do what?" he asked teasingly.

"Please!"

"Please what? You want me to stop?"

"No ... or I mean, yes!" Phillip pulled away from him and snatched the towel from the floor. "Get in the shower!" he commanded. "Get in there now, and behave!"

****

Twenty minutes later at the local diner the threesome sat together in a booth. Jesse couldn't believe how famished he was. He was amazed by how much food he had to consume to satisfy his hunger. It felt as if he could eat non-stop and never be full.

"Honey, I just can't believe how much your eating habits have changed," Margo observed. "You barely eat anything anymore."

Jesse looked up at her, surprised, as he shoveled a forkful of vegetarian omelet in his mouth. "Mother, how can you say that? I eat like a pig."

"Vegetarian omelets? Rye toast? It's very different, and that egg substitute ... yuck."

"Lots of things are different about the new Jesse, Mrs. Warren," Phillip interjected. "But I like the changes. I think he's matured a lot. It's like he has a little more class now or something."

Jesse laughed. "Would it make you happy if I ordered a big pound of bacon? Or maybe a side of greasy hashbrowns? It isn't that I'm trying to be a snob or anything. I just want to be healthy. I almost died, ya know, and I guess I have more of an appreciation for the fact that I've got to take care of my body."

"And maybe your tastes changed," Phillip suggested. "They say that as we age our tastes change naturally. Maybe that part of your brain was affected."

"Well I suppose it's a good thing you're eating healthier," Jesse's mom conceded. "I just want to make sure you're getting enough."

"Mother, trust me. I am. And Phillip, it wouldn't hurt you to try eating a little healthier yourself. That sausage thing you've been stuffing in your mouth is heart attack on a plate."

Phillip scowled at him in mock protest and then suddenly smiled. "But I *love* big juicy sausages."

"Jesse! Phillip!" an excited voice greeted them from behind. The boys turned to see Morgan approaching their table. "I can't believe I ran into you here. I was gonna call you on your cell phone. I have some amazing news!"

"Hi, Morgan," Jesse smiled. "We were on our way to the food pantry and decided to stop for breakfast. This is my mother, Margo Warren."

"I work with Jesse and Phillip at the food pantry," Morgan said, extending her hand to Mrs. Warren. "It's so nice to meet you."

"Won't you join us?" Margo asked, sliding over to make room for their guest.

"Oh I can't stay long, but thank you. The most amazing thing just happened. I got a phone call. It was from a charity I've never heard of—an organization called New Beginnings."

Margo's mouth dropped open.

"They've made a very generous donation to the outreach. Jesse, you're not gonna believe this! Five million dollars! They want us to build an entire new facility."

"Are you serious?" Phillip exclaimed. "Oh my goodness!"

"Praise the Lord!" Morgan said, raising her hands in the air. "I just can't believe it. I've never even heard of this group."

"Did you say 'New Beginnings' charity?" Margo asked.

"Yes, do you know who they are?"

"They just completely paid off our mortgage. I called my bank this morning and my account had been closed. They paid every cent."

"This is amazing … but why? Who's behind this?"

"What are the odds that you both would just suddenly—miraculously—get these huge gifts?" Phillip said. "And both by the same charity. You two don't even know each other!"

"It must be someone who knows us both. Someone had to give them our name."

Margo and Morgan stared at the boys then looked at each other.

"Phillip, did *you* give them our name?" Margo asked, her eyes again brimming with tears.

The boy sat there, looking back at them and smiling. He slowly shook his head. "I wish I had," he said, "but I never even heard of New Beginnings until an hour ago at your house."

"Jesse, what about you?" Morgan asked. "You and Phillip are the only two people who know both your mother and me."

Nervously, Jesse laughed. He hadn't anticipated that his mother would meet Morgan Dennison. He also had never considered that he'd be under a microscope, suspected of being responsible for the good deed. "I've been in the hospital, in a coma, for the past three months. How could I have given anyone your names? And I just met Morgan a few days ago."

Morgan studied him intently. "This is true," she nodded. "You really wouldn't have had time. Charities like this don't just pass out millions of dollars on a whim. They wouldn't even have had time to learn about Breath of Life Ministries."

"Well then, I guess it's got to be a coincidence," Jesse surmised.

"No, wait!" Margo said. "Why would this organization just give us all this money? We're just ordinary people. We're not a church or a ministry or anything. How do they even know us, and why would they pick us?"

"I bet they did it because of Jesse," Phillip said. "A lot of people know about his accident. It got a lot of press, and his recovery truly is a miracle. I bet someone who followed the story turned your name into this charity, and they decided to help you out because of all you'd been through."

Morgan was smiling. "It's true. That's got to be it. Or maybe it's God's way of bringing us together." Gently she placed her hand on Margo's.

"Like I said earlier, Mother," Jesse said lightheartedly, "don't look a gift horse in the mouth. I'm sure they gave you the money because they felt you deserved it. Look at all the sacrifices you've made. Why don't you quit worrying about why this has happened and just enjoy the fact that it has?"

"Oh baby, I *do* enjoy it, and I appreciate it more than I can say. It just doesn't seem real. It's like winning the lottery or something."

"Well, I personally think it's about time these huge organizations started doing nice things for individuals. It'd be nice if some of these big businesses would do the same. It's high time they gave back a little instead of expending all their efforts on finding tax loopholes and conniving to swindle anyone and everyone out of every little cent they possibly can to fatten their profits. It's absolutely *criminal*, disgusting, and it makes me sick."

The three of them stared at Jesse in disbelief. His face was red with fury.

"Jesse, where'd that come from?" Phillip gently touched his arm. "I had no idea you were this passionate."

Morgan smiled at the boys sweetly. "Oh I knew how passionate he was. I knew it immediately when I met you two last Saturday.

"Jesse, you're so young, and you're out to change the world. I admire you. I love your idealism, and I hope you remain true to your principles as you get older. You mark my words, one of these days you're gonna hold a high political office. You're gonna be one of those people who goes places ..."

Jesse shook his head. "No! You're missing the point. This is not about me!"

"Oh baby, I know," Morgan quickly responded. "You have a beautiful soul. I know you believe every word you're saying, and you don't mean any of it selfishly. But we need people like you. We need people who are passionate."

"Well, whoever did this, I am so thankful," Margo said. "I don't think anything was owed to me—to us. It's the most generous thing anyone's done for our family."

"Whoever is responsible," Phillip said, "must be a saint."

Or maybe a devil. Maybe a selfish old man who squandered every opportunity he had to do good but who has now, miraculously, been given a second chance. Maybe he just wanted to do the right thing for once—finally.

Jesse looked straight in Phillip's brown eyes. "I doubt it," he said softly.

Fifteen

Jesse paced the floor nervously as he contemplated his error. He'd moved too quickly and tried to do too much. It would be a matter of days—perhaps hours—before Phillip's family received the news that their financial prayers had been answered, and Jesse knew that the timing of the windfall was going to be far too obvious. There was no way anyone would believe it was a coincidence.

Certainly there was no danger that anyone would figure out the truth about his real identity. The truth was basically unimaginable. It wasn't as if Margo would wake up one morning and demand an answer to the question, "Who are you, and what have you done with my son Jesse?"

Jesse feared, however, that his loved ones would begin to figure out he was involved in these unbelievably generous monetary bequests. They would begin searching, trying to trace the source of the money. What if they ultimately discovered it all had come from Wainwright's estate?

But was there really anything to fear? Wainwright was dead. His body was cold, buried six feet underground. There was no real danger that his identity would be exposed.

Jesse's main concern was not exposure. What he really feared was that his efforts toward redemption would be tarnished. If the recipients of his generosity discovered he was in some way responsible, how could this actually be atonement? He didn't want recognition. He didn't want praise and gratitude. He just wanted to level the playing field. He wanted to pay for the evils of his previous existence.

It all felt wrong. Shouldn't seeing the flow of cash from his multi-billion dollar estate into the hands of the truly needy feel more gratifying? Shouldn't there be at least a tiny abatement of the guilt that overwhelmed him? There was not. He did not feel any better about himself now than he did before the money had been transferred.

He knew the age-old saying, "You can't take it with you." Amazingly, though, he'd gamed the system. He had in fact taken it with him, almost all of it. Originally he'd planned to give it all up, but he'd cunningly managed to salvage almost the entirety of his estate, diverting the money into the hands of a fabricated charity. He'd planned to use every last cent of it to set things right, to use this blood money for good. To save lives rather than discard them. To heal instead of wound. To give instead of take.

But the allotments had not appeased his guilt. They had not taken away his regret. Could it be that genuine atonement could not be purchased? Could it be that forgiveness was not a commodity that could be sold to the highest bidder? Even a billion dollars was not enough to buy a clean conscience.

Jesse stopped and stared at his reflection in the full length mirror. Beautiful! The sight of the young man before his eyes was breathtaking. He was everything Harold Wainwright could have ever yearned to be. Jesse Warren embodied everything that was good. He was loyal, compassionate, idealistic, and remarkably determined. Jesse Warren was a man of astounding integrity. He was the antithesis of Harold Wainwright.

Jesse Warren did not exist, however, and the reflection in that mirror belonged to an imposter.

Slowly Jesse backed away from the mirror and turned toward his single bed. Falling against the mattress, he buried his face in the cheap polyester-blend pillow and wept.

****

"Are you all right, Sport?" Kyle Covington looked over at his son, sitting in the passenger seat next to him.

"Yeah, Dad, sure. Why?"

"You just look tired," Kyle said, smiling.

"Oh, I guess I am a bit pooped out," Phillip conceded. "This morning I went for a run with Jesse, and then we worked for a while at the food pantry. We were there for like four hours."

"That's pretty cool that you're doin' all that stuff. What made you guys decide to get involved like that?"

"It was Jesse's idea, and you're not gonna believe what happened today, Dad. Some charity gave the food pantry five million dollars!"

Kyle again glanced over at his son, a bit startled. "Really? That's incredible."

"I know. They're gonna build a whole new facility, and the lady who runs it has asked Jesse and me to become paid staff members. At first I said yes, of course, but Jesse told her we don't want to do it for money."

"Well, I can see his point," Kyle responded, "but there is nothing wrong with a charity like that having a paid staff. If they want someone to work for them full-time, they almost have to pay them. But are you sure you want to take a job right now, anyway?"

Phillip shrugged. "I dunno. I'm gonna work there no matter what, but I'm not sure if it'll be full-time. I like the volunteer stuff, and plus I get to spend more time with Jesse."

"You've been spendin' a lot of time with him since he came back …"

Phillip sighed and looked away, staring out the window. He paused for a moment before responding. "Dad, can I tell you something?"

"Sure," Kyle said, sensing the weightiness of his son's tone. He pulled the vehicle into a parking space and turned off the engine. "What's up?"

Phillip turned to his father, looking him straight in the eye. "Dad … Jesse and me …"

Kyle continued to stare into the big brown eyes of his only son, waiting expectantly.

"I love Jesse," Phillip finally said. "Well, no … it's not just that. I'm *in love* with Jesse." In spite of himself, the boy smiled nervously, but he did not look away from his father's gaze.

"You're saying you're gay?" his dad asked evenly.

Phillip nodded. "Yes, Dad. I'm gay, and I'm in love with Jesse Warren."

Kyle reached up and cupped his palm around the back of his son's head. "Thank you for telling me," he said in a whisper. There were tears in his eyes. "I love you son, and nothing can change that."

"I love you too, Dad," Phillip replied, his voice choking up. "I've wanted to tell you, but—"

"It's hard, I know," Kyle said. "And I've suspected. I was just waiting for you to tell me when you were ready."

"I didn't wanna disappoint you, but I can't change who I am."

"I don't ever want you to change, Phillip. You're my son, and I love you just the way you are. "He pulled the boy into his loving embrace.

****

Timothy Drayton walked briskly down the corridor at Ingenico Enterprises Research Facilities, heading toward his office. His thoughts were full of the recently successful transfer. Drayton had been tracking the progress of the subject, prepared to pull the plug at any time … if need be. But it seemed things were going far better than he'd anticipated.

Reports from Dr. Sheldon at the Dayton Memorial Hospital were extremely favorable. According to his associate, the Warren family was doing well. Young Jesse was experiencing a remarkable recovery, and many of his "memories" were coming back, in spite of the setback of his initial amnesia.

Drayton was also aware of the scandal that had erupted over the disposal of multi-billionaire Harold Wainwright's estate. Apparently the executor of his estate produced a document—an addendum to the late Wainwright's last will and testament—bequeathing nearly the entirety of his liquid assets to a single charity. Most remarkably, this charity had been chartered right around the time of Wainwright's "death."

Dr. Drayton was highly motivated to investigate this new charity and track the flow of money. He suspected it might be a straw man, a means of laundering the money and diverting it back into the hands of Wainwright—or, Jesse Warren, rather. Yet when Timothy Drayton began digging, he discovered such was not the case. Dozens of bestowments had been made benefitting what appeared to be reputable causes. The only discrepancies he had noted were the large sum that had gone to the mortgage company holding the Warrens' home loan, and the other large sum that had gone to a college fund for a Phillip Covington along with another bestowment of cash to pay off the boy's medical expenses.

Although Phillip Covington knew almost nothing about the doctor, Drayton knew everything about Phillip's life. He recalled, in vivid detail, the day Jacob had received the letter announcing the birth of his grand-nephew.

"Sarah had a baby!" Jacob exclaimed as he held the embossed card in the air, "and she's named him after me!"

Timothy smiled at his lover, pleased to see the joy again in his once-beautiful face. Sadly, it was not so beautiful any more, but rather emaciated. The plague had begun to take its toll, and time was running out.

"How touching," Timothy said, smiling obligingly.

"Yes, truly it is. It is so crazy, though, Tim … this baby picture. This boy, he looks exactly like—well, like the photo of me when I was born."

"A family resemblance, of course."

"No, I think it's more than that. He even has the same birthmark I used to have. See, right there on his left cheek. As I grew up, it faded and eventually disappeared, but it was exactly like that! A star."

"Hmm," Drayton cajoled his lover, humoring him. "An omen of sorts?"

"And … and he's the exact same length and weight as I was. I can't believe it! It's like … like he's my clone."

Drayton raised his eyebrows and laughed. "Ah, you and your imagination. I think the world is too small for more than one of you. One Jacob Klein is plenty."

As Drayton contemplated the irony of the current situation, he shuddered. What a bizarre coincidence that his subject, Jesse Warren, would now be involved with this boy who was related to his former lover. In fact, Jacob had been the lover of both Harold and Timothy, and now the boy who'd been created to become Jacob's donor was intimately involved with Harold Wainwright—or Jesse Warren, rather.

It was the perfect plan, and it would certainly have worked, had Jacob not discovered the truth.

"What is this?" Jacob demanded, thrusting a file into the hands of his partner. "Timothy, are you fucking crazy?"

Drayton glanced at the file and placed it on the desk beside him, stepping over to console his irate lover. "Jake, just calm down. I can explain." He reached out to place his hand on Jacob's shoulder, but his lover recoiled.

"You're a madman!" he cried. "You … you …you manufactured a clone!"

"It's not like that, Jacob. Just sit down. Let me explain … please."

Jacob shook his head, tears streaming down his cheeks. "And then what, Tim? What was to become of him—my nephew—when you transferred my brain into his body?"

"Not your brain, your consciousness. Your memories … the essence of who you are—"

"Answer my fucking question! What would become of my nephew?"

"Jacob, please. He's not really even your nephew. He's you! He's a copy of you, an exact replica. The procedure will merely transfer your memories into a newer version of your body, a version untainted by the virus ..."

"For the love of God, Tim! He's a tiny child, still a baby. You're going to transfer my memories into the body of a toddler?"

"Please sit. You're exhausting yourself," Drayton urged. "Please sit down and I'll explain everything. You must trust me ... please. I did it for you. For us."

"No," Jacob said adamantly, again shaking his head. "I won't be a part of this! I won't steal my niece's only child from her, not after all she's been through. And I won't steal the life of an innocent baby in order to extend my own!" Jacob turned quickly, as if to storm out of the room, but was suddenly overcome by a fit of coughing. Gasping for breath between merciless onslaughts of coughing, he doubled over.

Drayton rushed to his side, placing his arm around his shoulder and steadying him. He handed Jacob a tissue. By now his lover was hacking up blood. Drayton steered him toward the sofa and reached for the oxygen mask. "Here," he said in his most soothing voice. "Sit ... and breathe. Just calm down."

Jacob's eyes were wide as he looked up at his lover. He inhaled the oxygen greedily, trying to regain his composure. His body began to calm. Timothy sat beside him and held his hand, and Jacob looked over at him, his eyes full of tears. Slowly he shook his head back and forth, and as he did so he squeezed Timothy's hand.

****

Jesse stepped into the living room and stood there tentatively, waiting for his parents to notice. As his mother looked up at him, he held his arms wide and grinned. "Ta da!" he declared, pointing at his head.

"No hat!" Margo cried. "Oh Jesse, your hair is growing out so fast, and you can barely even see the scar."

"Whaddya think?" he asked. "Think I'm ready to ditch the cap for good?"

His father nodded. "Your mother's right, Jesse. You look great. Nobody'd even notice the incision unless they knew about it."

"It's still a little shaggy," Jesse admitted. "My hair looks like … like a porcupine or something, sticking straight up, but I'm so over the hat."

"No honey, trust me, it looks great. Give it another inch and you'll actually be able to start combing and styling it. And I'm just amazed at how quickly the incision has healed."

"God, I looked like Frankenstein."

His mother smiled affectionately; then she stepped over and embraced him. "You're beautiful … the most adorable Frankenstein I've ever seen."

"Stop," Jesse said, as he pulled his mom against his chest. "Do you know how much I love you? Both of you."

"We love you too, son," Paul responded in a serious tone, bordering on emotional.

"Listen, I … well, I have to talk to you. I need to talk to both of you about …" He sighed.

"What is it, honey?" his mom said, taking a step back.

"Can we sit down?"

Jesse took a seat on the sofa, sitting directly across from his parents. They looked both expectant and worried. He knew it was the moment of truth; he had to come clean.

"Son, what's wrong?" Paul asked.

"Dad … Mom …" Jesse faltered.

"What is it, baby?" Margo asked, leaning forward in her chair.

"I have to tell you something, and it might not be easy

for you to hear. It might even hurt you … and if so, I'm sorry."

"Jesse—" Margo started, but Jesse plunged forward.

"I'm gay."

Jesse's mom stared at him, mouth agape, then looked over at her husband. For a moment, neither of them spoke. Just as Paul was about to speak, Jesse continued, "I know what you're probably thinking. You … um … well you may think I'm just confused after the accident. You probably think I was disoriented and lonely and … well, maybe even dependent. And you might think that all my time spent with Phillip has caused me to feel a connection that I'm somehow mistaking for romantic love … but Mom … Dad … I swear, it's not like that. I really love Phillip. I love him with all my heart, and I have for years. You probably think this is a phase, that it's something I'll outgrow. You may think I just need to meet the right woman. You might even think it's your fault, that you made some kind of mis—"

"Jesse!" his mom finally interrupted. "We know! We've known for a long time."

"Uh … you have?"

His mom was smiling. "Yes, honey. We already had this conversation … before the accident."

"We did?"

"Yes!" she was laughing. "Although you never told us you were in love with Phillip. Does he …?"

Jesse was grinning ear-to-ear. He nodded. "Yeah, Phillip knows. He's gay too … and he told me about himself first."

"We didn't want to bring it up," Paul said. "We planned to wait and see. When you woke up from your coma, we decided we'd wait and let you discover your feelings on your own—whatever they may be. Son, we were fine with your … um … sexual preferences before the accident. Nothing's changed."

Jesse looked into his father's eyes and an overwhelming

sense of appreciation swept over him. The feeling was more than that, though, much more. It was a familial connection—something he'd never experienced. Had the world changed so much in the past four or five decades that a young man could now share a father-son bond with his dad, even when the son was homosexual?

And how could it be that Jesse was so fortunate? He certainly didn't deserve to be in this place at this time, certainly not in this body. He'd always been the type who rejected the idea of a second chance. Life was short, and you had to make the best of it. Choose wisely, make the right decisions the first time around, because there certainly would be no replays.

Yet here he was, reincarnated, experiencing life again, and this time it was so different. This time his life was not about his ambitions. It was not about success or failure. It was not about the acquisition of wealth and prestige. It was about … others.

It was about his beautiful Phillip. It was about Margo and Paul, about Morgan and Murphy and their ministry. Life was about people! All the money and prestige and status in the world did not begin to equal the value of these precious relationships.

A memory came to him, then, unbidden, from another lifetime ….

"You look very sharp."

The young man stood in front of the full length mirror gazing at his reflection. He glanced up to see his mother approaching him from behind as he adjusted his necktie.

"Hello, mother. Well of course, would you have me give my valedictorian speech looking like a derelict?" Harold had never really known how to accept a compliment.

"No dear, of course not," she responded, gently pressing her fingertips against the fabric of his blazer, smoothing out the shoulders. "I'm so proud of you."

Ignoring her, he pulled away and reached over to the dresser to retrieve a pair of cufflinks.

"Let me help you with those," she insisted.

"I'll manage, Mother … thank you."

She stepped back, staring at her son with a beatific smile. "I'm so proud of you …"

"Mother," he sighed, "thank you … but we don't have time for this. We need to leave in thirty minutes."

"We have plenty of time. Please, indulge me, would you? Just a little. It's not every day a mother gets to see her son graduate … and head of his class, no less."

"Please mother, don't!"

"I'm sorry," she said, her smile fading. "I'm embarrassing you."

Irritated, he scowled as he fumbled with his cufflink, concentrating.

"Your father and I, we're both proud of you, son. You'll be the first in our family to—"

"Mother! Will you please stop?"

"I'm sorry, dear," she said sheepishly. She looked down at the floor, wringing her hands nervously. "I'll just wait for you downstairs."

As she turned to exit the room, Harold called to her. "Mother, wait." She stopped and turned to look at him once more. "Do you really think it's necessary to accompany me?"

She looked at him, somewhat puzzled. "You're my son … *our* son. Of course we'll accompany you to your graduation."

He finally finished securing the cufflinks and looked up to meet her gaze. "Perhaps you'd be more comfortable—"

"You're asking us not to attend your graduation ceremony?"

"I'm merely suggesting—"

"That we stay home, so as not to embarrass you."

"I didn't say that, Mother." But it was true. His parents

never knew when to keep their mouths shut, how to conduct themselves in public. It was humiliating at times, and he didn't want anything to ruin this day.

"Now dear, don't you fret. You won't even know we're there … we'll sit quietly and observe."

He rolled his eyes in disgust and heaved a sigh. "Very well. I just don't want any distractions. My future is it stake. There'll be important people in attendance—"

"Yes, of course," she said somberly. "I understand, and I assure you, Harold, your father and I will not humiliate you."

"Good," he said. "I'll be down momentarily."

It had been Harold's last conversation with his mother. Olivia Wainwright passed away that evening after suffering an unexpected heart attack. He'd been right. She had somehow found a way to ruin his big day.

Sixteen

It all seemed too good to be true. Everything Phillip had ever dreamed of was coming to fruition. Jesse had not only awakened from his coma, but he had emerged as a new man. He was even more heroic than before. In fact, it was unbelievable the way Jesse had matured. What was even more difficult to believe was that Jesse loved him.

For so many years Phillip had fantasized about such a relationship. In the back of his mind he feared that all of his feelings would remain unrequited, that Jesse would never know the depth of his love and admiration, yet suddenly everything had changed. Jesse now knew that Phillip was deeply in love with him, and the feeling was mutual.

This new Jesse was even more perfect than the pre-accident Jesse. He'd always been passionate about the things he loved—sports, music, fitness, cars—but now that same passion seemed to be newly focused on humanitarian rather than personal goals. Jesse's new sense of morality and honesty transcended the struggles of day-to-day living.

Phillip had heard of such things. The effects of a near-death experience were often life-altering. And perhaps Phillip's own brush with death provided just one more connection between Jesse and himself.

As he watched the bright red mixture of his blood and saliva wash down the drain, he feared that perhaps it was all just a cruel joke. His gums were bleeding again. He wondered how long he could hide his symptoms from Jesse. The fatigue. The bruising. The bleeding.

God had given them a miracle once. Was it too much to hope for another? Would God be so cruel as to offer him a second chance and then immediately snatch it away? No, he couldn't look at it like that. He couldn't allow himself to lose hope and faith. His love for Jesse was stronger than that. He had believed before, and his dream came true. This was only a test … and he wasn't going to fail. He wasn't going to stop believing, no matter what.

****

"Can we just skip the run today?" Phillip said as he wrapped his arms around Jesse's waist. Phillip was standing behind him, pressing his cheek against the center of Jesse's back.

Jesse turned and embraced his boyfriend, staring down into his eyes. "Why, Babe? What's wrong?"

"Nothing … nothin's wrong. I just think I'd rather stay in and curl up together … and ya know …"

Jesse smiled lovingly. "And you suddenly don't think it's important for us to stay fit? You want your boyfriend to get all lazy and fat? You think that's sexy?"

Phillip nodded eagerly. "Yeah … I bet you'd be cute even if you did get a little pudgy. I think we should do what we used to. Pig out on cheeseburgers." He laughed as he visualized the possibility. "And then after I fatten you up, I'll have love handles to grab hold of."

Jesse laughed along with him. "I don't think so. Are you okay?" He took a step back, holding Phillip by the shoulders. "Are you … are you feeling all right?"

"Yeah, sure."

"Phillip! You don't look … you don't look like you're feeling all right. Are you tired?"

"Well," Phillip sighed as he broke from Jesse's gaze, "I guess I am a little tired. Yesterday kind of wore me out. I just need a day off, to skip the run, just for today."

"Okay. Of course, oh my God. I've been pushing you too hard, expecting too much!"

"No, no!" Phillip insisted. "I'm just a wimp sometimes. I

want to be pushed, believe me. I love every minute of it ... I don't know. I just am a little tired. Let's not make a big deal of it, okay?"

Jesse looked at him seriously. "I'm talking to your mom. I think you should go see your doctor."

Phillip shook his head adamantly. "No, please Jesse. I have an appointment next week ... don't worry my mother."

Jesse framed Phillip's face with his palms, holding his head firmly to force him to meet his gaze. "I won't talk to your mom, but you have to promise me. Promise that you'll tell the doctor about feeling tired."

"I will," Phillip whispered. "I promise. Now kiss me."

****

It was 6:30 the following morning when Phillip was awakened by his cell phone. "Jesse," he said groggily as he stifled a yawn, "it's only Thursday. We don't have food pantry 'til Saturday."

"Wake up, Sunshine," Jesse said cheerfully, "and pack your bags! I'm taking you away."

Thirty minutes later they were on Highway 75, cruising north in the Ford Fusion.

"Are you gonna tell me where you're taking me?" Phillip asked, as he smiled at his boyfriend.

"Nope," Jesse said sternly.

"Well," Phillip huffed, "then I'm going back to sleep!" He leaned his head against the passenger door and closed his eyes.

"Good ..." Jesse said softly as he reached over to grasp Phillip's hand. "We've been going non-stop since I got home from the hospital, and you just need to rest. I'm taking you somewhere you can do exactly that."

"I don't wanna rest," Phillip protested without opening his eyes. He yawned. "I just wanna ... be ... with you." He was sound asleep.

JEFF ERNO

Jesse smiled and squeezed his hand. "Ditto," he whispered.

It was nearly four hours later that Phillip awakened again, and this time it was to the sound of classical music. "Where are we?" he asked, yawning.

Jesse reached over to turn down the volume on the stereo. "Are you hungry, babe?" he asked.

Phillip smiled, "Yeah, a little, and I have to go to the bathroom. Where are we?" he repeated.

"Saginaw. We're in Michigan."

"Really?" Phillip asked. "I've never been to Michigan. Are we close to Ann Arbor?"

Jesse shook his head. "Not really. That's southwest of here."

"I thought of going to the U of M. We talked about it before ... you and me."

"Oh really? I was gonna go there, too?"

Phillip shrugged. "You hadn't decided."

"Seriously, I think I need a year. You too. We both have to recover first before we head off to school somewhere. It's kinda like being a whole new person, like experiencing my family for the first time. I just wanna spend some time with Paul and Margo, I mean, my mom and dad ... and you."

"Jesse, I wanna go wherever you go." Phillip was suddenly crestfallen, interpreting Jesse's words as a hint that they might have to separate when they went away to college.

"I know," Jesse said reassuringly. "Of course I want to be with you, but if your life path requires you to go away to a different school, that isn't gonna change anything for us. I will still love you, and I'll wait for you."

"No!" Phillip insisted. "We've already been separated way too much. I don't care about my 'life path.' I care about you, and about us being together."

Jesse reached down to take Phillip's hand. "No matter, it's a long time away. We've got a year to decide. We should

start looking for schools that offer both of us what we need."
He pulled the car into the parking space at Burger King.

"You're taking us to Burger King?" Phillip observed, laughing. "My old Jesse really is back!"

Jesse sighed. "Well, I'm sure I can find something tolerable on the menu, and I know you like it."

"I just can't get over it," Phillip said, "the way your taste in food changed so drastically. And by the way, what the heck is that horrible music?" He unbuckled his seat belt and reached for the door handle.

"Bach," Jesse said. "You know, a little sophistication might do us both some good."

Phillip rolled his eyes disgustedly. "No thanks. I'll pass."

"Just close your eyes, listen—"

"If I don't get inside fast, there's gonna be a puddle on your seat."

"Go!" Jesse said, exasperatedly, "I'll meet ya inside."

****

It was fifteen minutes later when Phillip finally emerged from the restroom. Jesse had started to worry. Phillip looked so tired, in spite of his four-hour nap.

"Are you all right?" Jesse asked.

"Yeah, sure. Guess I'm just having a lazy day."

"Got you a Whopper," Jesse said, smiling.

"Really?" Phillip said cheekily. "I've had your whopper already ... and I like it."

"Oh?' Jesse grinned.

"Is that your salad? You want me to toss it for you?"

Jesse stared at his boyfriend, confused. He then laughed. "Am I missing something?"

Phillip's face was reddening. "Oh, sorry ... it's um ... well, I take it you're not familiar with that term—tossing your salad."

"Uhh ... no."

Phillip had sat down in the booth opposite his lover. He leaned forward to whisper, explaining the slang term to Jesse. It was now Jesse's turn to blush.

"So, where you takin' me?" Phillip asked.

"You really want me to spoil the surprise, don't you?"

Phillip nodded. "Well, just the fact you've kidnapped me in the wee hours of the morning and whisked me away is enough of a surprise. I think it's safe at this point for you to come clean. It won't ruin anything."

"All right," Jesse said, reaching across the table to take hold of Phillip's hand. "We're going to a northern Michigan resort. It's called Boyne Mountain."

"Really?" Phillip exclaimed. "I've heard of it. Isn't it a ski resort?"

"Yeah, but it's a summer resort too. Really beautiful up there, all kinds of lakes—and they have a big indoor water park. Golf. Tennis. Hiking. We'll be just a few miles from the lake … and the river. We can go swimming, water skiing, canoeing—"

"Wow." Phillip's eyes lit up. "How long we gonna be there?"

"I'll have you back in time for your doctor's appointment."

"But we have the food pantry this weekend."

"Food pantry's covered," Jesse assured him, "I talked to Morgan last night."

"I don't know what to say," Phillip said tearfully. "You're amazing, but how are you paying for all this?"

"Money's not so tight. Now that my parents' mortgage is paid off, they have a lot more money. They offered to pay for our weekend."

"Oh my God," Phillip said. "That is so sweet. I've got to call your mom and thank her." He pulled his phone from his pocket.

"No … don't bother. She's not really going to want to

talk on the phone. Um ... well, I think the reason they got rid of me is because they wanted some alone time ... if ya know what I mean."

Phillip twisted his face into an expression of revulsion. "Ew," he said, "I don't wanna picture it. Older people doing the ... ya know ... nasty!"

Jesse laughed. "Hey, they're not that old."

"Jesse, they're your parents! Doesn't it kinda gross you out to think about them going at it?"

Jesse shrugged. "I guess I see them now from a whole new perspective."

"Oh Jesse," Phillip said, "I was just joking. Of course I didn't mean—"

"Yeah, I know. You're right. It's disturbing to think of your own parents making love. It's not something any of us want to visualize."

"Disturbing?" Phillip asked. "It just amazes me ... blows me away sometimes ... the way you've changed. You talk so different now, and you have such good taste. Even the way you dress. It's so ... *stylish*."

"Well you've got good taste in clothes yourself, babe. I just have to get you to eat better and improve your musical preferences."

"We used to love all the same music," Phillip protested, and it used to be that I was the one with style when it came to my wardrobe. You were the jeans and tee shirt kinda guy—either that or athletic gear. Now you like classical music, and you're like a vegetarian or something."

"Maybe that thump on my head knocked some sophistication into me."

"Well, I like you both ways," Phillip confessed. "I mean I was crazy about you before, but even more so now. That doesn't mean I'm ready to completely change myself right now though. I still want to enjoy my cheeseburgers."

"Maybe it's like you said. Maybe I just grew up—matured or something. You'll get there someday yourself."

Phillip cocked his head to one side. "Yeah, you sure have grown up. Sometimes I feel like I can't keep up with you. None of that matters, though. You're still the man of my dreams, and I feel like I should pinch myself. I fantasized about you for so long. And now the reality of who you are is ten times better than the fantasy."

"You're just saying that cause I now can be seen in public without a hat. Now that my hair's grown back, I don't look quite like Frankenstein anymore."

"You're the hottest Frankenstein I ever laid eyes on."

"Your monster."

"My freak show, created in the laboratory of a mad scientist." Phillip laughed out loud, but Jesse's expression sobered. Instantly Phillip reacted in kind. "I'm sorry, Jesse … I … It was a joke."

Jesse's smile was warm and loving. "Yes, I know. But you're right. I am kinda freaky, with my scar and everything."

"No! That's not what I meant. Jesse."

Jesse leaned across the table, cupped Phillip's head in his hands and kissed him squarely on the lips. "Shh," he said. "I know what you meant, and I know you were kidding. I love you."

"Oh Jesse, I love you too."

****

Phillip stayed awake the remaining three hours of their trip. Holding Jesse's hand and stealing frequent glances, Phillip was overwhelmed by a sense of wonder. During his illness, when he'd all but abandoned hope, he'd dreamed of a future with Jesse. It was only a dream then, but now it had miraculously become reality.

He'd thought Jesse was lost, gone forever. It was the cruelest of ironies, the way Phillip had survived his own near death experience only to discover the one he loved most was going to die. By the grace of God, though, Jesse hadn't died, but had emerged from his coma a new man. The new Jesse was all Phillip had ever yearned for, and now they were forging ahead to build their perfect future.

But he was so tired, so very weak, and the bruising had returned. His gums were bleeding again. In his heart he knew what it all meant. Back in Saginaw at the Burger King, he'd nearly passed out in the restroom. He had no choice but to dismiss the symptoms, for to acknowledge them would be to admit defeat. Phillip was not about to allow this demon back into his life. He was not going to succumb to the beast and let the cancer take hold again. He had far too much to live for.

"It's so beautiful!" Phillip exclaimed. He was taking in the scenery of northern Michigan. "The hills … the trees …"

"I know," Jesse said, smiling as he squeezed Phillip's hand. "Wait'll you see the lake."

"I can't wait to see the bed," Phillip said, grinning back.

"Still tired, babe?"

"Who said anything about being tired?" Phillip asked. "I just can't wait to get *you* in it."

It was Jesse's turn to grin. He pressed harder on the accelerator. "We're almost there!"

And indeed the room was magnificent, including the bed. Within sixty seconds of their arrival Phillip had his lover pinned beneath him on the plush, king-sized mattress. Overcome by passion and lust, Phillip undressed his jock hero, kissing and fondling, caressing and tasting every inch of his torso. His neck, biceps, pectorals, and abdominals. His calves, shins, thighs, and buttocks. Even his gorgeous size-fourteen soles. When he finally took Jesse into his mouth, it was with hunger and eagerness, and most of all love.

Still panting and gasping for breath, Jesse was all but in tears. "Oh God," he moaned, "Phillip, I love you so much!"

Phillip gazed up into his eyes, sliding atop his spent lover, pressing his own bare chest against Jesse's. "Shh," Phillip cooed. "Just kiss me." His voice was sultry and dripping with sensuality, and as he spoke he felt Jesse beneath him, still throbbing. "Just kiss me, and let me feel you inside me."

For three hours they made passionate love, forgetting the world around them. After their third climax, both were finally spent. Exhausted and sweaty, they fell asleep in each other's arms. It was dinnertime when they finally awakened.

During their shower, Phillip nuzzled his back against Jesse's torso. "Babe, how'd you get this bruise?" Jesse asked, whispering in his ear.

Phillip turned, rubbing his soapy palms across Jesse's chest. "I don't remember," he said dismissively as he stood on tiptoe to kiss Jesse squarely on the lips. His fingertips glided down Jesse's body until they found their target. Phillip grasped the rigid pole and began to stroke. As he'd hoped, Jesse's concern about the bruising was almost immediately forgotten.

Seventeen

It was dark in the room when he awakened to the sound of his lover's voice. Confused, he looked around, waiting for his eyes to adjust to the dimness.

"Where am I?" he whispered, surprised at the clarity of his own voice.

"You're with me, and you're safe," the voice reassured him.

He turned toward the source of the reassurance and stared into that familiar face. His lover seemed so much older now. The lines around his eyes had a tale to tell, yet the face was as beautiful as he'd always remembered.

"Timothy," he said sweetly, smiling. "I ... I don't know what's happened to me ..."

"Jacob, you've been asleep. You've been sleeping for a long, long time now. Twelve long, lonely years."

Jacob gasped. "Twelve years? What year is it?"

"It doesn't matter," Timothy said, gently brushing his fingertips across the cheek of Jacob's smooth, young face.

"Wait!" Jacob cried, suddenly remembering. "What did you do? Timothy, please tell me—"

"Shh," Drayton tried to calm him. "You're fine now. Everything's fine. You're healthy again, and we have many, many years ahead of us."

"You did it! You did it when I begged you not to! You ... you—Timothy, get me a mirror!" Jacob flailed against the mattress, trying to free himself from his restraints.

"No, please Jacob, calm down," Timothy said, once again touching him, brushing the locks of jet black hair from his forehead. "I did not harm your nephew. We did not use him, as you'd requested ... demanded."

"Then how? Get me a fucking mirror! Let me up, Timothy! I need to get out of this damn bed."

Timothy sighed and stepped backward, away from his hostile lover. "Jacob, please don't force me to sedate you again. Please accept that I've done this for you—for *us*."

"What did you do?" He could feel the hot tears against his cheeks. "Tell me!"

"It was another," Timothy explained resignedly. "Another clone."

"Another innocent boy! You stole the life—the body—of an innocent boy." He felt nauseous. How did this happen? How'd he awaken into such a nightmare?

"A clone, Jacob. A body created from you, for you. A young, healthy body borne into existence so that you could live."

"No!" he cried, jerking frantically, trying to free his arms. "What happened to the boy? What happened to him when you stole his body?"

"I'm going to give you something to calm your nerves," Timothy said evenly. He retrieved a syringe from the counter.

Jacob shook his head frantically. "No!" he cried again. "Please Timothy, no."

"Shh," the doctor said once more. "Perhaps you're not quite ready."

"Timothy, for the love of God! Don't do this!"

"I love you so much, Angel. Why can't you see? Why can't you understand that I will go to any length to save you? There is nothing I will not do."

Within seconds blackness surrounded Jacob as he slipped once more into unconsciousness.

****

It was dark in the room when he awakened to the sound of his lover's voice. Confused, he looked around, waiting for his eyes to adjust to the dimness.

"Where am I?" he whispered, surprised at the clarity of his own voice.

"We're on vacation, babe. Remember? In Michigan."

"Oh yeah." Phillip smiled, remembering the events of the previous evening.

They'd driven into Boyne City, a small town about six miles from the resort, where they had dinner and strolled the beach. Too young to gain entry to the Sportsman's bar, they sat curbside on the street and listened to rock legend Bob Seger give a live, impromptu performance. A local, he regularly graced the small-town crowd with unannounced and unplanned visits.

It had been a beautiful night, and Phillip wanted to pinch himself, thinking he must have died and gone to heaven. The atmosphere was just so perfect for Jesse and him.

"I want to live here," Phillip said. He felt Jesse's touch, his lips gently pressing against his neck, his hands caressing his shoulders. "You didn't get enough of me last night?" Phillip teased.

"No," Jesse said, moaning.

Phillip laughed, brushing off the advances of his frisky lover. "What do we have planned for today?" he asked. As Jesse's hand made its way down Phillip's naked body and found his morning arousal, Philip squirmed on the mattress. "Hey!" he protested. Then again, "Hey!" in a much more welcoming voice. Within seconds the warmth of Jesse's mouth surrounded him.

Phillip sighed as he reached over and literally pinched his own arm. Yes, this indeed was heaven.

****

"I've never been golfing," Phillip admitted. "I mean, besides miniature golf."

"Well, I'm not sure how well I'll do myself," Jesse confessed. "It's been awhile, and I doubt I'll be able to concentrate with you looking like that."

Phillip stared at himself in the full length mirror. They were in the resort gift shop, and Jesse had just purchased him golf shoes, shorts, a polo shirt, and a visor. He was assessing his appearance in the fitting room mirror.

His laugh was giddy. "These shorts … I don't know."

"Mmm," Jesse said.

"Mmm?" Phillip repeated.

"Mmm, as in 'Mmm, mmm, good!'"

He felt Jesse's hand brush across his ass. "What do you take me for?" Phillip exclaimed in mock protest. "We're in public, ya know."

"Sorry, I can't help myself." He leaned in to whisper in Phillip's ear. "You do look adorable … hot as fuck!"

"Jesse, you *don't* wanna get me hard here. We'll have to go back to the room and then we'll never make it to the golf course. And you promised you'd teach me to golf."

"I'll show you how to hold your club, and what to do with your balls."

"And how to get a hole-in-one?"

"Now you're the one making *me* hard."

Phillip swatted Jesse's hand away from his rear and turned to face him. "I see how you are," he said. "I'm just a sex toy to you." He smiled broadly as he ran his eyes over Jesse's beautiful face, in spite of his pathetic attempt to play coy.

"Yes, you're right," Jesse admitted. "I wanna do you morning, noon, and night, and several times in between."

"Oh, okay," Phillip said cheerfully. "But right now we're going golfing." He turned and briskly strolled through the gift shop toward the front door.

Jesse quickly followed.

****

Drayton had himself struggled with ethical issues after first enlisting in the Rebirthing Project. As he sat alone in his

Ingenico office, he couldn't help but recall that first meeting with General Dawson at the Pentagon.

"Have a seat," Dawson instructed and took a seat as well, behind the big oak desk. "Dr. Drayton, it's a pleasure to meet you ... finally. I've heard remarkable things about your research."

"Thank you, sir," he responded humbly. He was trying desperately to conceal his nervousness.

"I've been reviewing your case studies. Some amazing stuff, and it's quite consistent with our goals here at the Rebirthing Project."

"The Rebirthing Project?"

"The Rebirthing Project has been years in the making, beginning back in the 1970's as a mere concept. To be honest, I never truly dreamed the day would come when it would be a reality. Until I heard of a doctor named Timothy Drayton and his incredible research."

"Thank you, sir," Drayton said, gulping a breath of air before continuing. "What is the mission of the project? What's it about? Neuron transmission?"

Dawson folded his hands together on the desk and nodded. "Partially," he said, "but more specifically, the Rebirthing Project's mission is to capitalize upon our scientific advancement to sustain and preserve life, precisely the lives of our most gifted, influential, and valuable members of society—"

"Presidents, world leaders?"

Dawson's face became more animated as he could no longer contain his enthusiasm. "And artists, scientists, teachers, doctors ..."

"Please sir, tell me more."

"Well, honestly, I think I should be asking you the questions. You're the brains behind the technology."

"Thank you, General, but all I have developed is a transmitter. In theory it can be implanted into the brain of a dying patient, transferring their consciousness into the mind of a donor. The big question, though, is where will we get these donor bodies? Who is going to sacrifice the body of a brain-dead loved one so that another can live?"

"Good question," the general replied, "but don't you think that some would consider it an honor to donate their loved one's body so that a President or world leader might live?"

Drayton stared at him skeptically and nodded hesitantly. "Perhaps, sir."

"Or …" the general said, smiling, "we could create replica bodies of the donors themselves."

"Clones?" Drayton gasped.

"Certainly you're aware of the scientific possibility, doctor. We've been cloning sheep and other lower life forms for years. Why not humans?"

"But, sir," Drayton protested, "the moral issues … the ethical dilemma …"

The general grew serious, swiveling in his chair to stare out the window. When he spoke, it was more to himself than to the doctor. "Survival of the fittest. In order for a species to survive, the fittest among them must be preserved. This never comes without sacrifice. Is it arrogant? Self-serving? Calculated and possibly even cruel?" He nodded to himself. "Of course it is. It's all of those things, but it is also necessary.

"Certainly the clones we've created will not come without their own consciousness. They will have intellect, emotions, and awareness. But then again, can't we say the same for the cattle we raise and butcher en masse every year? Can't we argue that humans have been sacrificing the consciousness of other, lesser species since the dawn of time? We even use the stem cells of aborted human fetuses to save lives …"

"Sir, it's not the same," Drayton protested quietly.

"No, of course it's not the same, but there's a parallel.

The point is, scientific advancement does not come without a price. There must be sacrifices."

"Sir … I don't know."

The general turned in his chair to look the doctor in the eye once more. "We can save him. We can save your Jacob."

So they knew. Of course they knew. They knew everything about him. They were the U.S. government. They probably even knew the color and size of his underwear. Drayton stared back at the general with a look of wide-eyed astonishment.

"We can clone Jacob Klein, and you as well. His disease does not have to be a death sentence. Drayton, think of the possibilities. Think of what this means! No longer is it true that we only live once. You can do it over and over again … if you'll just agree to sign onto the project."

"And if I don't?"

The general's gaze was cold and penetrating. "If you don't, we will attain the technology on our own, one way or another. Do the right thing, Timothy. Do it for you and Jacob, and for humanity."

Drayton reached up and rubbed his palms across his face, shaking his head in frustration. "How, sir?" he asked. "How do we transfer the consciousness into the body of a clone, when they already possess a consciousness of their own?"

"Delethium synapsonol."

"Drugs? You use drugs to render the clone brain dead?"

"DSL, as we prefer to call it. We do not kill the patient. We render him unconscious."

"You strip them of their consciousness, which is essentially killing them!" Drayton countered.

"They were created for this very purpose. They were created by us to be used to preserve an existing life."

"Sir, what of the lives of these clones? Who's to say they might not be the next world leader or Nobel Prize winner?

Who's to say what would become of them if you didn't kill them?"

"Listen to me, doctor. Listen carefully. We are a military operation. Our job is not to make ethical or moral decisions. Our job is to carry out missions. The Rebirthing Project has been commissioned by the Oval Office to use our research and technology to preserve the greatest human minds, and we will go forward with this. With or without you. Am I clear?"

Drayton sat there, still as a statue.

"Am I clear?" the general repeated, louder.

Timothy nodded. "Yes sir."

"Are you in?"

"When, sir? When can we start? When can we begin the process of saving Jacob? We don't have much time."

"The process has already started." He smiled ruefully. "Three years ago we obtained Jacob Klein's DNA, and a clone already exists. We will likely create a second clone, though."

It made sense to the doctor. He already knew why they'd want an additional clone, if not several. "Yes," Timothy said. "Clones are far more susceptible to disease. They can develop cancer, autoimmune diseases, and other illnesses at a far higher rate than their donors."

"Indeed," the general agreed. "Imagine cultivating a clone, raising it to the age of puberty and then discovering it had a heart defect, or leukemia or something. We need more than one."

"Where is this clone? Where do you have him … or it?"

"It is being raised by a family in Washington state and goes by the name Noah Kauffman. It is two years old. The second clone will be implanted in a relative of Jacob who lives in Dayton, Ohio. The young couple thinks they are receiving in vitro fertilization."

"What relative?" Drayton asked, alarmed.

"Klein's neice, Sarah Covington."

"No! Jacob would never …"

"Jacob will not know … unless you tell him. The parents will assume it's a matter of family resemblance, genetics."

"I hope the first child … or I mean the first clone … works."

"I hope so, too. This is our test case. After our first success, we will do others. Eventually you will be cloned, Dr. Drayton. I cannot imagine a young man like the new Jacob will be interested in remaining with an old man such as yourself. Plus we will need you for years to come."

"Very well," he said. "Then let's get started."

That was the beginning, how it all started. So much had happened since that initial meeting with General Dawson. So much had changed. The cloning had been a success. The initial transfers had worked, and now it was all coming together. Soon Timothy would undergo the surgical procedure to have the transmitter implanted in his brain, and he would assume the host body of Jesse Warren. The body currently preserved and utilized by Harold Wainwright.

Eighteen

"Who were those two guys?" Phillip asked.

"Who?" Jesse responded, suspecting Phillip was talking about the men he'd spoken to on the golf course.

"Those older guys … those men on the golf field."

"Golf course," Jesse corrected him. "The green."

"Whatever. They seemed …um … like snobs or something."

"They were. Insurance executives. Vultures. Leeches."

Phillip laughed. "Oh dear, you're not gonna start that again, are you?"

"It's true! Do you know how much money they've made off the backs of people like you and your parents? Do you know how many people have died because of their greed and love of the almighty dollar?"

"I could tell you didn't like them," Phillip said. They were waiting to be seated in the resort café. "What'd you say to them?"

"I told 'em what I thought of them. I told them to go to hell."

"Jesse, you didn't!"

"In a manner of speaking," he grinned. "I just did a little name-dropping?"

"Huh?" Phillip said. "What names—"

"Two today?" the hostess greeted them.

They followed her to their table and took their seats. After placing their drink order, Jesse patted Phillip's hand. "You did really well for your first time."

Phillip laughed. "I sucked."

"Well … maybe golf's not your game."

"Ya think? God, I was a laughing stock."

"You were so cute," Jesse said with a laugh.

"Ya know, I don't ever remember you golfing, Jesse. How'd you get so good at it?"

"You're asking me?" Jesse said. "I don't remember anything from before. I should be asking you."

"I know. That's what's weird, because I could swear you never played golf. In fact, I think I remember you telling me you didn't want to. When it came on TV you changed the channel. Said it was like watching paint dry."

Jesse laughed. "I said that?"

"Yeah, and I've got to say, I agreed with you."

"Oh babe … okay, I promise you, no more golf. But you have to promise me you'll at least wear the golf uniform for me."

"I do look kinda preppy," Phillip admitted. "I could be a rich snob myself, by the looks of me."

"We don't have to be rich to be happy," Jesse said. "And you'll never be a snob."

"Aww," Phillip said, taking Jesse's hand. "Let's go swimming next."

Jesse smiled. "That means we've got to go back to the room first … and change."

"I know," Phillip said, grinning devilishly.

After lunch they did head to their room to change … and to do a couple other things … before they drove into town. Lake Charlevoix was breathtaking, and Jesse was pleased with himself for choosing this vacation destination. The water was so clean that it appeared bright blue from the sun's luminescent reflection.

The clear, sunny day made for an idyllic encounter, and in spite of the many locals and tourists surrounding them, they were in their own world. Jesse had everything he'd ever wanted. All it had taken was a lifetime of searching.

Their afternoon was occupied with building sandcastles, applying sunscreen, and doing cannonballs from the docks at Whiting's Park. That evening they dined on hotdogs and potato chips from the park canteen. Jesse laughed as he wiped a dab of ketchup from the corner of Phillip's stuffed mouth.

"I knew I'd get you to eat meat again," Phillip said, mouth still full.

Jesse shrugged. "It wasn't bad."

"No, it was delicious. Hotdogs from the grill … Omigod! Yum."

"I don't even remember the last time I ate meat," Jesse confessed.

"Well, I'd say it was probably about five months ago, right before the accident."

Jesse nodded. "Yeah, right."

"That bruise on your arm, let me see it. I think it's getting worse." Jesse was concerned. It seemed darker, almost a deep purple color.

Phillip jumped up, grabbed his tee shirt and pulled it on. "It's nothing," he said.

"Phillip, it's not nothing!"

"Bet you can't beat me at tether ball—"

"Stop changing the subject."

"You think 'cause you're so much taller than me, I can't kick your butt," Phillip said. He put his hands on his hips and glared at Jesse, who remained seated on the grass.

"I don't wanna play tether ball."

"What then? Another swim?"

"I want you to tell me what's going on. Phillip, please. I don't want you getting sick again."

Phillip looked away and was silent for a moment before turning back to face Jesse. The tears in his eyes nearly broke Jesse's heart. "Ya know, if I am sick again, there's nothing I can do about it. I've done all there is to do."

Jesse stood up, embracing his boy. "No, Phillip. That's not true. We'll fight it together … like we did before."

"I'm tired of fighting. I'm tired of losing my hair, throwing up all the time. I'm tired of being so weak I can't even stand up. You have no idea what it's like, Jesse. The chemo … it's torture."

"But it saved you! If you hadn't fought so hard the first time, we'd never have had this. We would never have had the chance to be together like we are now. If we don't keep fighting, there will be no us. There'll be no future."

"Jesse," Phillip said, a sob escaping his throat, "you just don't understand. I'm tired of dying! I just want to *live*! I might not have much time left, even if I am lucky enough to have another remission. Eventually … eventually it will get me. If I spend every minute fighting, how can I even enjoy life?"

"Baby, no … no, it's not like that!"

"It is. Jesse it is like that! If I have a year left, five years … ten … who knows, and I spend every second worrying about treatments and pills and blood counts, then I'm not fucking living! I love you, goddamn it! I love you so much, and I want to fucking *live*!"

Phillip's body convulsed with sobs as Jesse held him in his arms. Jesse was crying now himself. "Baby, let's live," he said. "Let's live together. Let's make the best of every single second. No more tears! No more … no more needles and tests and toxic chemicals. Let's do it together, make the best of every second!"

"Yes," Phillip cried. "Oh Jesse, yes!"

Jesse knew what the bruise meant. He knew about the severity of Phillip's symptoms, and he knew in his heart that continuing to deny it would not save Phillip. All his years in the insurance industry had taught him about cancer. Saving Phillip was going to take far more than prayers and another round of chemo. It was going to take a miracle, and Jesse knew exactly who could deliver it.

****

"Boys, we have wonderful news!" Sarah exclaimed excitedly.

The three were seated in the Covington living room, just as they had when Jesse and Phillip had confessed their love. The only difference was that this time Phillip's father had joined them.

"We have news for you, too," Phillip said, smiling.

Mr. Covington spoke. "We'll go first." He smiled affectionately at his son. "Phillip, we received news today that all your medical bills have been paid, and that you now have a trust fund that will pay for your entire college education."

"I know," Phillip said casually. "I know all about it."

Sarah stared at her son in disbelief. "How? We just found out this afternoon."

"Mrs. Covington," Jesse said, "please let me explain."

Sarah and Kyle glanced at each other and then back at Jesse.

Jesse eyed them nervously before continuing, "Well, do you remember when I got out of the hospital after my surgery? Remember how the newspaper and television station ran an article about me?"

"Yes, of course," Sarah recalled. "You were quite the celebrity."

"Well it seems that this may have been more the case than I had actually realized. Apparently an older, wealthy gentleman happened to hear about my story, a man who was on his deathbed."

"He left Jesse a ton of money!" Phillip blurted out, then looked apologetically at his boyfriend.

"It's true," Jesse said. "He passed away only days after

hearing about my accident, and he bequeathed me the majority of his estate."

"Are you serious?" Kyle said. "Your parents … they must be shocked."

"They don't know," Jesse explained.

Now Kyle and Sarah really did seem confused. "Your mom and dad don't know about all this money, and yet you're telling us? How much money are you talking about?"

"Millions," Phillip said. "Jesse is the one responsible for the charity paying off his parent's house, and he doesn't want them to know."

"Oh Jesse!" Sarah gasped.

"And he's the one who donated the money to the food pantry and set up the trust fund for me and paid all our bills."

Jesse shook his head. "It's not like that." He sighed. "It was money that was given to me, and the charity is one hundred percent legitimate. I transferred most of the money to New Beginnings, and I simply suggested a few worthy causes to them. I honestly have nothing to do with the actual operation of the charity itself."

"But Jesse," Kyle said, "why haven't you told your mom and dad?"

"I just wanted them to experience a random act of kindness," he said, "and I wanted it to be anonymous. I still have a lot of money left, and I assure you, they'll benefit."

"Your father could quit his job. They could travel, never worry about money again for the rest of their lives," Sarah speculated.

"I know," Jesse said, and I want to do that for them. In fact, it is already in progress—they will get more money than they've ever dreamed of—but please keep our secret. Please, I don't want them to know it's from me."

"Jesse," Kyle said skeptically, "why are you telling this to us?"

"Phillip is relapsing," Jesse said sternly. "His symptoms are nearly full-blown."

Immediately Sarah was out of her chair and on her feet, stepping over to embrace her son. He held his hand up.

"Please, Mom—"

"We'll fight it," she cried. "We'll fight the cancer like we did before."

Phillip reached over and grabbed hold of Jesse's hand. He smiled warmly at his lover, and then turned back to look into his mother's eyes. "Mom, I'm going to Switzerland with Jesse."

"No!" Sarah cried. "I'm calling the doctor right now. I'm calling 911!"

"Mom, listen! I'm going to Switzerland … and I'm going to see a doctor there."

Kyle and Sarah looked at each other in shocked disbelief.

****

After the conversation on the beach, Jesse knew that only one course of action could save Phillip. Chemotherapy, radiation, bone-marrow transplants, they all were futile. Phillip was dying, and if he did not act fast, it would be too late.

Timothy Drayton had saved him when he was dying, and he could save Phillip. It was the only way.

Of course Jesse could not tell Phillip the entire truth. He couldn't tell Phillip that he was really a cancer-ridden old man on his deathbed who had stolen the body of eighteen-year-old Jesse Warren. It was so much more than that. Harold Wainwright no longer existed. Jesse Warren was his identity now, and Wainwright was merely a distant memory—one best forgotten.

It had been necessary for Jesse to tell Phillip about the money, and the explanation had to be believable, one his parent's would accept. So that evening, after their candid conversation on the beach, Jesse had another heart-to-heart with Phillip.

"I want to give you life, like you said. Whether it is for a year or ten years ... a week or just one hour. I want to make every second count. Phillip, come with me to Europe. Let me take you to places you've always dreamed of seeing ... and those you've never even heard of!"

"But how?" Phillip asked, smiling sweetly at his lover. "How do you propose to do that? Rob a bank?"

That was when Jesse told him about the money. He explained that he'd inherited a huge sum from a man he didn't even know. Then to prove himself, he logged into his bank account, using the numeric code that had been mailed to him by certified letter. Phillip sat there staring at the screen in shocked disbelief.

"Holy crap!" he said in a startled whisper. "Holy effin crap ..."

Phillip's eyes lit up, as if a light bulb had been turned on in his head. "So you *are* the common denominator. You're the one who paid off your parent's mortgage. You're the one who gave Morgan the money for the shelter ..."

"Well, sort of. I didn't do it directly. I had some of the money transferred into the hands of this charity. They are actually legit. They are 501(c), non-profit and all that. I did offer some suggestions for what to do with the endowment."

"You're amazing," Phillip said.

"So will you go with me? Will you let me give you the experience you deserve? And will you let this doctor examine you? I think he can save you. I think he can give us hope that no one else can."

"But how, Jesse? If he has a cure for cancer, why doesn't the whole world know about it? Why didn't the old man who left you all this money just go to Switzerland himself?"

Jesse shrugged. "He probably didn't know about it. I never met the old guy. He died right after I woke up from my coma."

"And what makes you think this doctor can save me?"

"He saved me!"

"Baby, that was different. You weren't dying of cancer."

"But Phillip, please trust me! I know that he's capable of saving you. They have a whole team of specialists there working on cures for all kinds of illnesses. He saved me from a brain injury … from being a permanent vegetable.

"Please let's just try! Please—"

"Yes. Yes of course, Jesse … of course I'll go with you. If I'm cured, we'll have many years together. If not, at least I'll have had the most amazing experience … along with the one I love more than life itself."

Jesse embraced him, knowing that the hope he would be offering Phillip did not actually include a future for the two of them.

However, it was the promise of life … for the one who deserved it most.

Nineteen

Everything began to fall apart for Drayton when the Administration changed. As quickly as it had all begun, it was likewise terminated. In a strange turn of events, Drayton found himself in that same Pentagon office arguing the case for the project to continue. The funding must not be eliminated.

Ironically it was Drayton who defended the project when ethical questions were raised. The new department chief, another General, was the one who stared at the doctor aghast. Cloning, delithium synapsonal, neuron transmission? It was preposterous, he said. Unethical and reprehensible.

The new administration's promises of transparency and openness seemed hollow to Drayton as they swept everything under the rug. The possibility that this project might be discovered by the media was unthinkable. Files were burned, documents shredded, and medical records expunged.

After they were done cleaning house, not much was left. Timothy still had his clinic in Switzerland. He still had Jacob, sleeping soundly in a coma, and another clone wandered around somewhere back in the U.S. Creating a clone of himself was now out of the question. He had to find another means to keep the project going. He had to shift focus.

Initially it was not as difficult as he'd imagined it to be. He applied for grants through the bureaucracies and was approved. The sheer lunacy of this reality was baffling to him. The Pentagon had shut down the project on "ethical" grounds, and yet with very little effort he was able to find available research dollars from other government agencies.

Those early days had been the most productive. They acquired equipment, built a worldwide network, and inched their way closer and closer to the day when the transmission of human consciousness from the mind of a dying patient to a donor's became reality. The months turned into years, and Drayton remained focused. Checking on Jacob's body daily, he watched his lover grow. He watched the body evolve from a six-year-old boy into a teenager, and then a young man. Soon it would be time to wake him. Soon, but not too soon.

When Timothy discovered that the grant monies had dried up, he had no choice but to seek out private funding. Ingenico Enterprises had operated for many years under the ruse of marketing anti-aging products. There was some revenue generated from these marketing tactics, but not nearly enough. They would have to sell an awful lot of wrinkle cream to make up for the income previously provided by the grants.

All of the research and testing had proven that the neuron transmitter had been successful. Firstly, the experiments with the chimps indicated that the transfer attempts had worked. Secondly, Jacob's consciousness had been transferred into the brain of a clone. But the unanswered question was, "Will the transfer be effective with a live donor?" Transferring to a clone may be entirely different than transferring into the mind of a donor who genetically differed from the patient. There had been several failures in the beginning with the chimps, and he feared humans might experience the same issues. As with all transplants, there was always the possibility of rejection.

If he used himself as the test case, the results could be disastrous. If the transmission failed, his consciousness could be lost. He'd be dead, and no one would remain to continue with the project. No one would be there to attend to Jacob—to feed, bathe, and care for his body. And most importantly, no one would be there to awaken him when the time was right.

Timothy was in Jacob's company, sitting peacefully

alongside his bed, when the thought came to him. *Wainwright!* Jacob had talked about him. He'd talked about their unrequited love, how he'd cared so deeply for Harold but that the man had chosen his career over romance. Jacob had recalled—not with bitterness, but with genuine warmth and fondness—how they'd been so happy together, albeit for a short time. Jacob mainly wondered how Harold had fared in life, if he'd found satisfaction and happiness in acquiring great wealth.

The doctor looked at the youthful body of his lover. It was fascinating to watch it grow and mature before his very eyes. The child had been six, barely school age, when Timothy had transferred his aging and dying partner's consciousness into the body. He knew at the time that Jacob would consider such an act an atrocity. Jacob would never have agreed to have his essence transferred into the body of a child; that would have been too much to bear.

For over a decade he had kept the new Jacob in storage as the body matured. The bubble that encased him protected his body, fed him intravenously, hydrated him, massaged his muscles, cleaned him, and even evacuated his bodily waste. Timothy grew impatient, wanting several times to awaken him, but he knew it would be a mistake to do it too soon.

Harold Wainwright was the answer. He was one of the wealthiest men alive, and if Drayton could convince him to invest in Ingenico, the project could be saved. If Drayton could appeal to the billionaire's greed or vanity, perhaps he would part with some of his money.

When Drayton began to investigate Wainwright, he discovered that the elderly insurance mogul was all but a recluse and reportedly dying. The doctor knew that Wainwright would have no interest in making an investment in any project. His life was all but over, and to approach the ailing man while on his deathbed would be pointless. Drayton would have to offer him something, some kind of hope.

That hope was life. Drayton could give Harold Wainwright a second chance at life, a new body, an opportunity to once again experience youth. If Harold agreed, it would solve all of Timothy's financial woes, and he would be the perfect test case. Of course, Drayton would have to monitor everything closely. He'd have to be prepared to pull the plug at any moment if need be. And, of course, when it came time to awaken Jacob, Wainwright would have to be terminated.

****

Phillip sat quietly in his seat at the airport terminal, resting his hand gently against Jesse's forearm. His life had become one fantastic event after another. Here they were in Pennsylvania, at the Philadelphia International Airport, awaiting their connecting flight to Rome, Italy.

"You have the passports?" Phillip whispered.

Jesse turned to him and smiled. "Stop fretting, baby. Of course I have the passports." He shifted in his seat and grasped Phillip's hand. "Did you take your meds?"

Phillip's scowl soon became a smile. "I need water. I have to take the pills with a full glass."

Jesse was instantly on his feet, "I'll be right back."

Phillip sighed and shook his head. They'd delayed their trip for nearly six weeks upon the request of Phillip's parents. He would have said no. He wanted more than anything to simply refuse treatment. It was Jesse who'd convinced him otherwise.

Phillip recalled how Jesse had remained at his side the entire time, starting from the moment the bad news was delivered. It was no surprise to him really. He'd known for quite a while. He also was not surprised that the hematologist had insisted upon rapid and aggressive treatment—another series of chemotherapy sessions.

"No," Phillip had stated calmly. "No more of those toxic

drugs." He'd turned to look into Jesse's eyes. "Remember, you promised."

They brought in the oncologist, who explained to Phillip in the most direct yet compassionate terms that he was correct—the chemo was not likely to save him. It would, however, sustain him. Without the treatment, he would decline rapidly, have a few weeks at most. "Please," she urged him, "consider another series."

"It could give us a few months," Jesse said, tears streaming down his cheeks. "It could give you the strength you'll need for our trip."

"But I can receive treatment there—in Switzerland."

"Baby, we have to get there first."

And so Phillip had capitulated. He'd agreed, and the chemotherapy began immediately. As expected, there were many side effects. The coughing fits and bloody mucus, the vomiting, diarrhea, and intense cramping, the utter fatigue— they would all have been unbearable if not for Jesse. And of course, Phillip had lost his hair.

When Phillip began his regimen of Imatinib, he found himself unable to sleep. He'd lie in bed for hours, hoping to doze off, tossing and turning. Jesse was always there, massaging his back, humming to him, holding him, gently caressing him. There were nights when Phillip would feign sleep simply to give Jesse a reprieve. Then as Jesse lay there finally slumbering beside him, Phillip would stare at his beautiful face. Jesse had become his guardian angel. His hero.

"Thanks," Phillip said, as Jesse handed him a bottle of Evian. "These pills ... ughh ... sometimes I can hardly swallow them." He removed a packet from his carry-on and popped out two four-hundred-milligram tablets. "It'll be okay. We just ate." He was supposed to take the medication with a full glass of water and a meal.

"Do you have your sleeping pills?" Jesse asked.

"I don't wanna sleep," Phillip countered.

"Babe, the flight is over eleven hours. You need to sleep, and when you awaken, we'll be there."

"In Italy!" Phillip beamed. "I can't believe we're going to Rome."

"And France ... and Germany ... and Switzerland."

"And then, who knows where? Then we'll have a lifetime together, after my treatment."

"Then you'll go on to lead a long, healthy life." Jesse squeezed his hand.

"With you ..."

****

Phillip's health deteriorated daily. He grew thinner and lost all his hair, yet his face was still the most beautiful thing Jesse had ever seen. His eyes, though tired and deep-set, still lit up when he looked at Jesse.

Sweet, innocent Phillip had no idea what Jesse had experienced in his former life. He was ignorant of the evil and greed and guilt that had blackened Jesse's soul ... before he was Jesse. As Phillip dozed in the first-class seat next to him, Jesse had but one regret. After this was over, Phillip would know. He'd know the truth about everything. He'd know that the real Jesse had died two months after the accident and that an imposter had taken his place. All that he and Phillip had shared together would be tainted.

Jesse prayed that this European vacation and his final sacrifice would be atonement enough. One day, years from now, when Phillip looked back on it all, maybe he could find a way to forgive him.

The fourteen thousand dollars Jesse had laid out for the two first-class, round-trip tickets to Rome was a bit of a waste, in that only one passenger would return. Yet Jesse considered the money well spent. It was critical that Phillip remain hopeful and continue to believe in their future together. Jesse feared that after the transfer Phillip would suffer agonizing grief. Not only would he mourn the loss of the real Jesse, but the loss of his former life. He would not be able to return to Ohio as himself. He would be the new Jesse.

It was all so complex, so very twisted. The body of Jesse Warren had already been inhabited by two souls, each dramatically different. The first had been filled with idealism, drive, and unfailing optimism. Snatched away by a horrendous accident, this bright young thing had been supplanted by a greedy, selfish old man. And now, this handsome shell would host the consciousness of Phillip, the deserving one. This final transfer would honor the memory of the real Jesse Warren while providing a second chance for a boy who'd barely had time to experience a first one.

Phillip shifted slightly in his seat, right before his body began to spasm. His eyes opened as the coughing took over. Jesse held one tissue after another over his boy's mouth. Wrapping his arm around Phillip's shoulder, he pulled him close as his frail body seized. When the coughing fit subsided, Phillip gasped, hungrily sucking in the air. "I'm sorry, Jesse," he whispered, his voice barely a croak.

"Are you okay?" Jesse signaled for the flight attendant. "He needs water."

"Thank you," Phillip said. "Where are we?"

"Still on the plane, but we're almost there. One hour more."

****

When the plane landed, Phillip felt a rush of adrenaline course through his veins, energizing him. He couldn't believe he was actually in Italy. Already he felt a thousand times better, and he assured himself that he and Jesse were going to make the best of their time together. Regardless of the final outcome, he was determined to make this vacation about living, not dying.

The hand of his partner rested against the small of his

back, gently guiding him through customs. To his astonishment, Jesse engaged the border police in Italian, promptly handing over both passports for inspection. Of course Phillip had no idea what Jesse was saying, but whatever it was, it seemed to work. Within seconds they had completed the process and were on their way to an airport shuttle.

Phillip stared out the window of the shuttle bus, taking in the structures of this ancient city. Again he felt Jesse's hand gently squeezing his own. "I love you," Phillip whispered. "Thank you for this."

They soon arrived at De La Ville Roma, a luxury hotel in the center of the city. Phillip had been impressed with the nice room they'd shared while vacationing in Michigan, but its amenities did not begin to compare to those offered in their Roman suite.

After Jesse tipped the hotel attendant and dismissed him, Phillip stood in the center of the main room, arms spread wide. "Jesse, I can't believe it! We have our own living room … and kitchen … and bath …"

"And mini bar," Jesse added.

"And mini bar!" Phillip ran over to his lover, embracing him. "I never expected this, never in a million years."

"Well, don't get too excited," Jesse teased. "We're going to stay in a variety of places, some not so luxurious."

"As long as we're together."

"Why don't you let me draw you a bath," Jesse suggested, nuzzling his nose into Phillip's neck.

"Why don't you draw *us* a bath?" Phillip countered.

"Mmm, even better. And then we can snuggle while we sleep off our jet lag."

"Sleep? No way, I'm not gonna sleep through my European vacation!" Phillip protested, stifling a yawn.

"Baby, I promise you as much time as you want. We're going to be in Italy at least three weeks."

"And then …?"

"France, Germany, Switzerland …"

"Are you sure we shouldn't go to Switzerland first and see the doctor? Maybe we should at least see what he has to say."

"We can do that," Jesse said soberly, pulling away slightly. "But he will probably want to begin treatment immediately."

Phillip stared at him, wide-eyed. "Oh Jesse, you're right. Let's wait. Let's enjoy our vacation together, every minute of it. We can go to the doctor at the end."

Jesse nodded. "But if you start to get real sick, or if you're too weak to go on, we're going to Drayton straightway."

"Don't worry, Jesse. You give me strength."

Jesse kissed him, tenderly yet with passion. "I'll start the bath."

They didn't leave their suite that night. The soothing sensation of the water jets in the tub relaxed Phillip as he leaned back against his lover's chest. He felt the strength of the arms that surrounded him.

"You're already getting your hair back," Jesse whispered.

Phillip giggled. "It's my turn to look like the skinhead."

He felt Jesse's arousal against his back. Closing his eyes, he allowed himself to relax completely, though his heart was beating rapidly. Then he felt it—Jesse's hand wrapping around him, gripping his shaft. He, too, was wildly aroused. Quietly he moaned as Jesse began to methodically stroke him. As Jesse's slippery palm caressed the sensitive underside of Phillip's erection, his free arm wrapped around Phillip's chest. His breath quickened, but he didn't open his eyes. "Jesse," he whispered, "it feels so good."

"I love you," Jesse said, his voice urgent. "I love you so much … with all my heart." He continued to stroke. "I'll do anything for you. *Any*thing!"

"Jesse!" Phillip cried.

"Please believe me … please understand …"

"Yes, Jesse. Yes!"

"Oh, God! You're everything to me. Phillip … my Phillip!"

Phillip cried out one more time, just as his body tensed. Involuntarily he thrust his pelvis completely out of the water as the semen erupted. Copious ropes burst from him, splashing against his abdomen and chest.

"Ohhh, ohhh!" He trembled as Jesse continued to hold him fiercely. "I love you, too. Oh, Jesse!"

As Phillip's orgasm gradually subsided, he grabbed hold of Jesse's wrist and gently pulled his arm away so that he might face his lover. The tears streaming down Jesse's cheeks startled him, and without hesitation he pressed his lips against those of his hero and protector. "Jesse, oh please don't cry."

Jesse smiled, shaking his head.

"We'll face this together. Oh Jesse, I know we will. We're strong enough. Everything's going to be fine. I won't leave you, I can't! I can't leave you yet."

Jesse nodded, wiping the tears from his cheeks. "I'm sorry," he whispered.

"No, I'm sorry. I'm sorry for what this is doing to you."

"It's not like that," Jesse assured him. "I just got a little emotional. I just … I was swept up in the moment."

Phillip knew it was more than that. He sensed Jesse's fear. "Jesse, baby …" Phillip started, "everything's going to be okay. Don't you remember our conversation on the beach, when we were in Michigan? We can't spend our time together living in fear of death. If we allow ourselves to worry so much about dying, we're not going to remember to live."

"I know," Jesse said, "and that's why we're here. We're here to live."

"Yes. So no more tears."

"No more tears," Jesse assured him.

"Promise?"

Jesse nodded. "Yes." And once again they kissed.

They had to shower after their bath, and then they wrapped each other in the luxurious blanket towels provided by the hotel. Jesse carried Phillip to the bedroom and gently placed him on the bed. After discarding the towels on the floor they curled up together, spooning. Phillip quickly drifted to sleep in the arms of his lover ... and awakened to a whole new day in Italy.

Twenty

It was time. Timothy had waited all these years, knowing full well that Jacob could not be awakened too soon. At the very least, the clone body must have attained the age of maturity. This was necessary for both physiological and psychological reasons. The clones were so susceptible to disease, especially during developmental years, a fact confirmed by the other clone—the Covington boy. Keeping this particular clone body encased and shrouded by the protection of the sealed bubble had given it time to fully develop before being exposed to bacteria and viruses. Timothy had also given it special vaccines to protect it from all the threats science had identified. Cancers like leukemia were caused by genetic defects, which he hoped were not present in this clone.

Even if no physical threats existed, Jacob would not have been ready psychologically.

The first attempt to awaken Jacob two years previously had not proven successful. He'd reacted violently. Rather than embracing a second chance at life, he'd bitterly accused Drayton of murder. He was angry and clearly in denial.

This time had to be different. The doctor had to convince his partner that he had done the right thing, that his new existence was part of a larger plan, a vision of a never-ending future for the two of them.

And frankly, Timothy was tired. He was exhausted from the struggle, the constant worrying. His existence was lonely, and his visits to the bedside of his now-youthful lover were hollow and disappointing. Sitting beside the bubble and staring at his beautiful face were not enough. He needed to hear Jacob's laugh. He needed to feel his touch.

Eventually it would all work out. After he'd found his own donor and had completed a transfer of his consciousness, the two of them could truly begin life anew. In the meantime, though, Jacob must at least be awakened.

This time he did not secure the restraints around the boy's wrists and ankles. He did not prepare a syringe, in case he had to once again sedate the patient. Drayton would allow Jacob to awaken fully, to express his feelings, whatever they might be. They'd simply go from there. He'd considered it all very carefully. He knew Jacob well enough to realize that although he might be emotional, he was also intelligent enough to think things through. He'd understand Drayton's motivations. He'd ultimately come to accept that what had been done could not be reversed. The two of them could then focus on their future together.

"Jacob," he whispered, "Jacob, it's time to wake up."

Jacob's eyes, large brown saucers, opened and stared up into the doctor's face. "Timothy," he whispered, "I love you."

****

Jesse recalled the warmth of those big brown eyes. There were times when he stared into the beautiful face of Phillip and was instantly transported back to a previous existence, one where an identical pair of eyes gazed lovingly upon him. Holding Phillip that night, their first night together in Italy, Jesse could feel the shallow intake and outtake of the boy's breaths.

"Mmm, I love holding you this way, feeling you breathe," Harold whispered.

"I love you," Jacob sighed, his eyes closed as he snuggled against his lover, his back spooned against Harold's chest.

Harold couldn't bring himself to say it, to verbalize those three all-important words. Instead he merely squeezed Jacob's body a little more tightly.

"You know, I've been thinking ..." Jacob finally spoke

after a brief pause. "We should get away somewhere, go on vacation."

Harold sighed as he felt the softness of Jacob's hair against his cheek. "Maybe ... perhaps in a few months. Right now I'm so busy with work."

"Harold, you haven't had a vacation since we met."

"True," Harold confessed, "but I told you from the beginning, my career is very important to me. Right now I'm at the top of my game, and if I don't seize the opportunity and strike while the iron is still hot, I may miss my chance—"

"Your chance? My God, Harold, you're a millionaire already."

"It's not only about money. One day I'll own the company. I'll control all of it ... as CEO."

"Even CEOs take vacations," Phillip countered lightheartedly. "If anyone deserves one, it's you."

"Well ... I'll think about it. Where do you want to go on vacation?"

"Anywhere. In fact, we don't even have to leave. We can have a vacation right here together."

"In that case, consider this my vacation ... right now, in bed with you."

Jacob laughed. "You know what I mean."

"Tell me, then, where do you want to go? If you could choose anywhere in the world ... where?"

"Hmm," Jacob considered. Squirming, he freed himself from Harold's protective embrace. Harold felt the boy's hand brush against his chest as he looked into his eyes. "Italy!" Jacob said. "I want to go to Italy."

"Really? Why?"

Dreamily Jacob closed his eyes as if imagining it. "The Vatican, Rome, the Tower of Pisa ..." he sighed. "Venice! Florence ... all of it. I've always wanted to go there."

The boy's excitement was infectious, and Harold smiled in spite of himself. "Okay ... I'll consider it. I'll see what I can do."

They never made it to Italy. The vacation never came.

Now here he was, although in a different body, finally in Rome with his lover. Phillip's warm flesh pressed against him. "Are you awake?" Jesse whispered.

"Mm hmm," Phillip responded, still not moving.

"Are you ready to see Rome?"

"Uh uh," Phillip groaned.

"Uh uh?"

"No ... I just want to stay here in this bed with you ... forever."

Jesse laughed. "That's fine. We can see the Pantheon another day. Vatican City can wait ... and the basilicas, the piazzas, and the Colosseum. We don't have to see all the ancient cathedrals, the Roman Forum, the Baths of Caracalla. There is no hurry to explore the catacombs, to visit the Spanish Steps—"

"Okay, okay! You're right ... but give me a minute to wake up."

Jesse kissed his neck lovingly. "Breakfast in bed, lover?"

"No." Phillip shrugged his shoulders in response to the tickling sensation of Jesse's whiskers. "You need to shave," he complained. "You're giving me whisker burn."

Jesse rubbed his cheek teasingly against Phillip's.

"Ouch!"

"I love you, Phillip. Even when you're grouchy."

"I'm not grouchy," Phillip whined. "I'm just ..." He laughed. "I'm grouchy, aren't I?"

He'd turned to face Jesse. "Grouchy and cute."

"Make love to me," Phillip said decisively. "Before breakfast."

"Even with my scratchy whiskers and my morning breath?"

"And your messed up hair and smelly armpits."

"Smelly armpits?" Jesse said, lifting his arm as if to inspect, then sniffing. "We just took a shower before bed."

"It doesn't matter. Make love to me. Make love to me as you are ... right now!"

"You want it bad, don't you?"

"I need you. I need you so bad!"

"Then take it back," Jesse teased. "Take back what you said about my armpits ... and my hair."

"I love your hair. I love your armpit hair, too. I love all of you, every inch!"

"Phillip ... I love you too."

They made love urgently, responding to each other's passion. When they both were finally spent, panting and gasping for air, Jesse looked into Phillip's smiling face.

"I guess you were right. I was a little grouchy."

"And now?"

"You've set my world aright ... again."

****

They spent two days seeing all the sites Jesse had mentioned: the Piazza del Campidoglio and the bronze statue of Emperor Aurelius, the Piazza Navona and the baroque wishing fountain, the Piazza di Spagna, the Piazza Rotundo and the Pantheon. The ancient city walls and triumphal arches were breathtaking. The churches and palaces, forums and basilicas with the amazing architecture and historic sculptures were like nothing Phillip had ever seen.

They traveled the city via bus. Jesse had bought them each a two-day pass, and the bus route included all the major points of interest within the city. A double-decker bus arrived at each stop every fifteen minutes, giving tourists the ability to create their own itineraries.

It was not until their third day in Rome that Phillip experienced the highlight of his Roman holiday. He and Jesse spent the entire day at Vatican City, and he saw with his own eyes the ceiling of the Sistine Chapel. Michelangelo's magnificent frescoes astonished him. Nothing he had seen in a book or on television could even begin to convey the heart-stopping impact of this work of art.

Rome was just the beginning. The weeks that followed included a three-day stay in a Tuscan villa, bicycle riding in the country, a full day at a huge water park in Cecina, a visit to Pisa—where Jesse photographed Phillip holding up the Leaning Tower—and a weekend in Venice.

Phillip was only beginning to fall in love with Italy when Jesse took him by rail to France. In Paris they dined on the Rue Mouffetard, visited the Louvre and the Eifel Tower and shopped at Les Galeries Layfayette. Their stay at Le Grand Hôtel Français was quaint yet romantic, and Phillip thought he would burst from consuming too much fine French food and wine.

They stayed in Paris for several days before traveling to the Andalucia region of Spain to enjoy the spectacular beaches and bask in the sun. They were impressed by the hospitality of the Spanish people, and Phillip was excited to finally get a chance to use the Spanish he'd learned in school. They also visited Madrid and Barcelona.

After Barcelona, the couple flew to London and then spent the better part of three weeks in the United Kingdom. They spent time in each of the four countries, but what Phillip enjoyed most was the two days they visited Alton Towers theme park. He was feeling better than he had in weeks and was excited by the fact that his hair was growing back.

By the time he and Jesse flew to Berlin, Phillip was nearly back to his old self. Jesse had been right. The trip had completely rejuvenated him, and he was starting to forget the reason they were on vacation in the first place. It was another remission, and Phillip couldn't help but wonder if this time it would last. Maybe he should suggest to Jesse that they forget about the doctor in Switzerland in case the chemotherapy had worked.

To Phillip's delight, Germany was celebrating Christopher Street Day during their stay in Berlin. For the first time Jesse took him to a gay bar, where Phillip was thrilled to express his feelings openly and publicly. They held hands and kissed and danced shirtless amidst the throng of young gay couples.

"Thank you for everything," Phillip whispered. They were standing on the balcony of their hotel suite in the early hours of the morning. "This has been the most amazing vacation of my life."

"No," Jesse responded, wrapping his arms around the smaller boy, "thank *you* for giving my life meaning. Thank you for showing me what life is all about."

Phillip smiled as he looked out to watch the sunrise. "Jesse, it's like ... when you woke up from that coma, you became an entirely new person. Don't get me wrong, you were just as wonderful before the accident, but now ... well, you're so much more serious. You're so mature, so unselfish. And honestly ... at times I wonder what I did to deserve you."

"Don't say that, baby," Jesse said, pulling the boy against his chest. "You deserve so much more than me. You know I'd give you anything. I'd give you the whole world if I could."

"Jesse, you have already."

They kissed. Phillip felt himself being swept away by the power of his emotions. He was here now, in the arms of his prince, his savior, his hero and protector. This was his fairy tale, his dream-come-true, and he didn't want it ever to end. He was determined to stay here in the arms of the man he loved.

****

"You can't keep me in this prison forever," Jacob complained.

"It's only for awhile longer," Timothy assured him. "Soon we'll be able to start over, to begin life anew."

"Do you want to explain to me exactly what that means? Tim, this is so crazy. It's like something out of a horror movie, and, well, I'm afraid to even imagine what else you have planned."

Drayton sighed, rubbing his temples with his fingertips. He was seated at his desk chair and Jacob sat opposite him on a sofa, staring out the plate glass window that overlooked the hilly Switzerland landscape.

"There is a boy, now nineteen, from Ohio. He died in an automobile accident. Or I should say, he's brain dead."

"So he's in a coma? And you're going to steal his body? Timothy, this is insane!"

"No, he's not in a coma. He's gone, completely."

"This makes no sense." Jacob stood up, pacing in front of the window.

"We transferred the consciousness of another dying patient into his brain … temporarily."

Jacob turned and stared at him incredulously. "You *what*?"

"It was a test case. If the transfer proved successful—which it seems to have—then we planned to proceed and use the host body for my own transfer."

"Oh my God! And where will you transfer the other … patient?"

"Jacob, the man was dying anyway. We gave him a few more months of life. We gave him a second chance at youth …"

"And now you are going to take it from him. Why do you do this? Why do you think it is perfectly okay to play God?"

"I'm tired of arguing with you," the doctor said in exasperation. "If you cannot see that I did all of this for you—for *us*—then I don't know what else to say to you. Look at you! Look at your body! You're twenty-two years old again, and all you can do is bitch."

"This isn't me, Timothy! This isn't my fucking body. This body belongs to someone entirely different, someone who was designed to resemble me, but with his own soul. Some child sacrificed his life so that I could selfishly go on living, and you seem to have no problem with that. What is wrong with you?" Jacob had stepped over to the desk, staring his aging lover in the eyes. He slammed his fist down violently to emphasize his point. "This has got to stop!"

Startled, the doctor leaned back in his chair, distancing himself. "Jacob, will you calm down?"

"No! No, this is so wrong. This is wrong on every level!"

"Listen to me," Drayton said, his voice quavering, "the clones, they never would have lived. They never would have survived independently. They're susceptible to disease—a thousand times more susceptible than other humans."

"And yet here I am!"

"Because I kept the body sealed in a protective bubble for over fifteen years. You have already developed. I gave you special treatments, vaccines. Your immune system is thriving. But, had we not done what we did, this body would already be dead."

"And the other one? The other clone ... my nephew. What became of him? Is he dead?"

"He's dying."

"I want to see him," Jacob insisted. He placed his palms flat on the desk and leaned in. "Timothy, I must see him. I'm begging you!"

Drayton shook his head. "I don't think that's a good idea ... not now."

"Why? He is a part of me. He came from me ... and I've got to see him before ... before it's too late."

Again the doctor sighed and shook his head. His phone rang, and he realized the call was from Ingenico Enterprises. "Sylvia?" he said as he picked up the receiver. He listened to the receptionist as Jacob continued to stare at him. "Very well, schedule an appointment for next week ... Yes, that's fine."

Drayton hung up the phone and stared into the face of his young lover. "Seems your request may be granted after all. Phillip Covington will be here next Wednesday."

Twenty-One

"What is that sound?" Phillip asked. "It's a dinging or something."

"Cows," Jesse said.

"Cows?"

They were at a train station in northern Switzerland, awaiting the departure of their train to Neuchatel. Phillip looked out over the meadows that surrounded them and saw that indeed there were cows, perhaps hundreds of them. All were brown, and all wearing bells around their necks.

"The cows all have bells," Jesse explained. "And that's what you're hearing—the constant ding-dong as they roam about, grazing."

Phillip smiled at Jesse, wondering how his boyfriend had acquired so much knowledge, become so wise. Over the course of their vacation, Jesse had surprised him many, many times. He'd spoken in Italian and French, had seemed to know the geography and points of interest almost instinctively. It was hard to believe he hadn't been to Europe before.

As if sensing what Phillip was thinking, Jesse explained, "It's just that I had already noticed them. I heard the sound and saw the cows in the meadow."

"Jesse, I've been thinking … maybe we should just skip our visit with this doctor."

Jesse shook his head. "Just because you've been feeling better for a while doesn't mean you've been cured. We've come this far. We have to at least hear what he has to say—see if he can help."

Phillip sighed. "I know … I know you're right, but I just have a weird feeling about this."

"What do you mean?"

"I don't know," Phillip said, again staring out at the meadow. He paused, then turned to face Jesse. "It's just that our trip has been so perfect. These past few weeks have been the absolute best of my life, and maybe I just am not ready for it to end yet. I'm not ready to go back to the needles and blood tests and all that stuff. I want this time together to go on."

"Phillip," Jesse said determinedly, "no matter what, you will always have these memories. You always will be able to carry this time within your heart and know that we shared it together ... and that I love you."

"You make it sound like you're the one who's dying," Phillip said.

Jesse shook his head as he reached out to take hold of Phillip's hand. "No, and don't say it like that. You're not going to die, either."

"Jesse, I love you so much, but I *am* dying. Unless this doctor gives me a miracle, we both know what is going to happen."

"He is going to give you a miracle, and you're going to live many more years. I promise you! I swear to you, Phillip. Please trust me."

Phillip embraced him.

"We have to board the train," Jesse said, pulling away.

Phillip reached up and gently wiped the tears from Jesse's cheeks. "Let's go get our miracle," he said, smiling through his own tears.

They boarded the train together, the train that would lead them to their ultimate destiny.

****

It had been five days since the transmitter had been implanted. Timothy's head was still bandaged, the incision not yet even close to being healed, yet he was up and about, performing all his duties. He had no choice. Jesse Warren would be arriving soon—the next day.

It would not be difficult. The worst of it was already complete. The donor brain already contained a receiver chip. What an amazing stroke of luck it was that the Warren boy had come of his own volition. The fact that he was coming here to the laboratory, where everything was located, seemed proof positive that the plan was destined to succeed.

Now it was merely a matter of sedating him, administering the drug to erase his consciousness, and making the transfer. Harold Wainwright would be gone forever, and Drayton would inhabit the youthful body of Jesse Warren. Supported by Wainwright's money, he and Jacob could go on to begin a new life together. The possibilities were limitless.

He had the other boy with him, though. The Covington boy—the clone. Drayton marveled that the young man had managed to stay alive. It did not matter though, not really. Soon enough he'd be gone, too, and Drayton doubted that the boy actually knew anything anyway. Even if his friend had told him any of it, he would not have believed.

"Can you explain it to me?" Jacob's voice startled him.

"Jacob," he said, "I didn't know you were here."

"Show me how it works. I want to know."

Timothy stared at him for a moment, then relaxed. "Very well. It begins with this." He opened a drawer and removed a small chip, not larger than a nickel. "This chip functions as either a transmitter or receiver, and it is implanted in the brain."

"Okay … and then?"

"After it has been implanted, we are able to communicate with it. We can gather data. Actually, it is not data to begin with. It is human consciousness. It is uploaded to our computer and then converted to data. The process takes no more than two or three minutes.

"We then transfer the data to the receiver chip that has been implanted in the donor brain. There it is converted from data back to consciousness. The donor awakens with the consciousness that has been transmitted."

"What becomes of the donor's original consciousness?" Jacob asked nonchalantly.

"The transfer will not work if there is an existing consciousness. A transfer can only be made into the mind of a brain-dead donor."

"So you somehow delete their consciousness prior to the transfer?"

"With a drug, administered intravenously. Delithium synopsonal."

"And this is what you plan to do with the boy?"

Drayton sighed. It was tiring to repeat this so many times, and he really didn't want to argue any more. "No Jacob, he's not really a boy." His tone was edgy, irritable. "I told you this already. Jesse Warren was killed months ago and his body is temporarily being inhabited by the consciousness of an elderly man—a man who should himself have died around the same time the boy had his accident."

"Please humor me, Timothy. I just want to understand."

The doctor rolled his eyes. "Very well."

"So you have to administer this drug and delete the consciousness of this elderly man. Then you can transfer your own consciousness into the body?"

"Correct."

"And you will be able to do this while you are awake?"

"I will have to be sedated. I can either have my assistant perform the transfer or program it to execute at a specific time."

"I'd think it wiser if you used an assistant."

"I don't know ..." Drayton stared off, looking over Jacob's head, thinking. "I don't want to disclose the transfer to anyone, not even my assistant. I want us to start life anew together, undetected. I want us to simply get away … get the fuck away from here. We'll go as far as we need to. We'll begin a new life and leave all this behind. We'll have years and years together, and this time we'll do it right. We won't make the same mistakes."

"Our second chance."

"Yes," Timothy whispered. "Second chances for both of us."

"So I guess all we can do at this point is wait … "

Drayton nodded.

Jacob turned to leave the room. "Oh, and please … remember you promised me I'd get to see the boy—my nephew."

"Of course," Drayton said. "I'll inform you as soon as he arrives."

****

It seemed so sterile and eerily quiet. They were the only ones in the waiting room and, other than the receptionist, presumably in the entire building. Even as they'd entered and made their way down the long corridor that led to the receptionist's window, Jesse had seen no signs of life. After ringing the bell, they waited at least a full minute before a face appeared. As if expecting them, she buzzed them in and they took a seat in the lounge.

There was no coffee or water cooler. No periodicals to read. It felt almost like a library with no books, and as the boys sat there, it was as if they knew instinctively that silence was expected. Finally after at least twenty minutes, the door opened, and the receptionist invited Jesse in.

"Shouldn't I come with you?" Phillip asked.

Jesse squeezed his hand. "It's okay. The doctor probably wants to see me first and examine me. This is the first he's seen me since my operation."

Phillip nodded. "Oh yeah, that's right."

"I'll come back for you."

Phillip smiled. "Okay."

Jesse recognized the receptionist, who was not really a receptionist at all. He recognized her as Dr. Russell, the anesthesiologist who had assisted Drayton with his surgery several months previously. He wondered if she knew who he really was. If so, she offered no signs. Jesse followed her, easily keeping pace with her brisk steps as she led him down another long corridor. Stopping in front of an archway, she removed a card from the pocket of her blazer and swiped it through a reader. The door buzzed, and she turned the knob and pushed it open, ushering Jesse inside.

The office was stately, furnished with solid oak cabinetry and a huge desk. It seemed almost Presidential. Dr. Russell motioned for Jesse to take a seat on the leather sofa, and he did so. He heard the door close behind him, and as he turned toward the sound, he noticed that the doctor was already gone.

As Jesse perused the room, he noticed the framed diplomas, awards, and licenses of Doctor Timothy Drayton. There was a desktop computer on the far side of the desk and a smaller laptop on the opposite end. Papers were neatly stacked on the desk blotter, and just as Jesse was starting to feel tempted to stand up and inspect them more closely, he again heard the door behind him.

Drayton entered. His head was bandaged in the same way Jesse's had been after surgery. Jesse stood and extended his hand, but the doctor ignored him and stepped behind the monolithic desk to take a seat.

"What brings you here?" Drayton got right to the point.

"I'm doing fine, and thanks for asking," Jesse said sarcastically.

The doctor stared at him. "You do realize the risk you've taken, coming here to my office?"

Jesse scowled at him, then gradually his expression

changed to a smile. "Drayton, you came to my home town, to my hospital room, performed a major surgery on my brain, which drew enormous media attention, and you're worried about the risk my visit to you here would pose?"

"It was neither your town nor your hospital room. It was Jesse Warren's. And the details of the surgery were and remain classified. Harold, cut to the chase. What the fuck do you want?"

"I want you to save Phillip," Jesse said flatly.

The doctor stared at him quizzically. "What are you talking about? You mean the boy you have with you? The Covington boy?"

"He's dying … terminal leukemia."

"I'm aware of his condition," Drayton said dryly, "and there's unfortunately nothing I can do for him. Neither hematology nor oncology are my specialties."

Jesse's expression was stone sober when he delivered his next statement. "I want you to give him my body."

The doctor, who had been looking down at the stack of papers on his desk, suddenly looked up, raising his eyebrows. "Come again?"

"I've lived my life … and then some. I had my chance, and then a second chance. There is nothing that can be done to save Phillip. He is terminal. Bone marrow transplant, chemotherapy, radiation, medication … it's all too late. In a matter of weeks he will be gone, and there is nothing anyone can do to stop it … other than you."

"I don't do charity work," Drayton said.

"I'll pay you—"

"You'll be dead," Drayton said. "Don't you realize what you're asking? I cannot transfer Phillip's consciousness into your—or Jesse Warren's—body without first exterminating you."

"Of course I realize this. I will give you everything I have … which is still millions."

"I knew you were a fucking liar. You told me you'd given it all up, but I should have known you'd find a way to take it with you." Drayton pushed his chair back and stood up.

"I had the money transferred to my account in an attempt to right my wrongs. I've used as much of it as possible to do some good—"

"Built a food pantry, paid off a couple mortgages. Wow, you really fucking changed the world, Harold. Do you honestly think these meager attempts to atone will undo all the damage you did in the eighty years of your previous life?"

Jesse hung his head, feeling the weight of the doctor's words. "I know," he whispered. "God how I know."

"Let the boy die with dignity. I can't save him, and frankly I don't understand why you even give a shit." The doctor headed for the door, stepping briskly past the sofa. "Let yourself out," he said dramatically.

"I love him!" Jesse screamed.

Timothy stopped, his hand on the doorknob. He turned to look at Jesse's tear-streaked face. "You love him? Oh that's rich! That's really fucking rich. Do you love him the same way you loved Jacob?"

"I love him the way I wish I'd loved Jacob," Jesse confessed.

"Well, Jacob is gone! You can't redeem yourself with this boy. You can't have a second chance!"

"Please …" Jesse cried. "Please, I'm begging you. Let him live. No matter what you say, no matter how angry and bitter you are toward me, it is not the boy's fault. Phillip is so pure. He's so innocent, so full of potential. He's so … so very much like Jacob.

"Please do it for him. Do it for Jacob's memory … You , you do know who he is? You do know he's Jacob's nephew?"

Drayton stepped toward the sofa. "There will be no way to explain it to him. He would awaken in that body …" The doctor used an open-handed gesture to point toward Jesse.

"He'd have an entirely new identity, and it would place our entire project at risk."

"But he'd have life, and he'd … he'd get used to his new body. He'd find a way to reconnect with his family eventually. He could always go back to Ohio as Jesse Warren, and he'd still be next door to his own family. They could be told that Phillip had died … here, and the body could be returned—"

"You've thought this through."

"Yes, it's the only way."

Drayton sighed, reaching up to rub his forehead and then wincing slightly at his own touch. The incision was still tender. "This evening," he said decisively. "We'll need to do it right away."

"Can't I have one more night?"

"Now or never."

"I want to spend the afternoon with him, be with him as he prepares for surgery."

Drayton nodded.

"And he mustn't know. He'd never agree to it. He cannot know what is going to happen."

"I know how to handle the boy," Drayton said. "I want the money transferred into my account today, before we begin."

Jesse nodded. "Of course."

****

Phillip heard the buzz of the door and looked up, hoping Jesse had returned. What walked through the archway, however, was the most startling sight he'd ever seen. He sat there momentarily, mouth agape, as he stared at the mirror image of himself.

"Phillip?" the young man said. "I'm Jacob."

Unable to speak, he stared wide-eyed.

"I know … I know it's a bit disturbing. I'm sorry."

"Who are you? Are you my … um … twin?" This was

240

insane. How was it possible? They say that every person has a twin somewhere, but this was more than just a resemblance.

"Actually, I'm your uncle."

Phillip shook his head. "No ... you can't be. My Uncle Jacob is dead. He died years ago when I was a baby, and he's much older than you."

"I did not die," Jacob said reassuringly. "Phillip, do you know what place this is? Do you know what they do here?"

He shook his head.

"They are geneticists, and these laboratories ... well, they have invented what you might call the fountain of youth. And ... that's what you're here for, isn't it?"

Phillip again began to stammer. "Um ... uh ... No, I'm here to see the doctor. My friend Jesse, he said the doctor could maybe cure me ... I have cancer."

"Like you, I was dying when I came here." He stepped closer and motioned toward the empty chair beside Phillip. "May I sit down?"

Phillip nodded.

"I was dying of a terminal disease, and the doctor saved me."

"But why? How come everyone thinks you're dead? My mom even said you'd died. We have one of your paintings in our living room."

Jacob smiled. "You do? Which one?"

"I don't know ... that's not the point. This is crazy!"

"Phillip, I wanted to see you." He gently placed his hand on the boy's wrist. "And I'm so glad I did."

"Why do you look so much like me? You look exactly—"

"When you were born, you even had the same birthmark as me. I don't know why. It's genetics, I guess."

Phillip wondered if Jesse knew about all this. He remembered how Jesse had accidentally called him by the wrong name. He'd called him Jacob, but it really made no sense. How would Jesse even know Jacob? And Jesse had recognized the painting!

"Please don't be afraid," Jacob said. "I promise you, we want to help you."

"Where is Jesse now?" Phillip demanded.

"He's with the doctor, and he'll be back soon. Would you like anything? Are you thirsty or hungry?"

He shook his head. "This is just so strange. I … um … I need to see him."

"He's very close to you," Jacob observed. "You care very much for him, don't you?"

"I love him."

"You're *in* love with him."

Phillip nodded. "Yes … I'm gay."

"I should have known," Jacob said, smiling. "I'm also homosexual."

"I'm sorry, but this all just seems like a dream or something. I … can't believe it." Phillip stood up, backing away from Jacob. "I need to see Jesse! I need to see him now!"

"Shh," Jacob said, trying to calm him. "Everything's going to be all right."

Phillip felt as if the room were spinning. He was lightheaded. "Stay away from me! I want Jesse! I need to see Jesse now!" His legs felt like jelly, and he reached out to grab hold of the back of a chair. The room continued to spin. He felt even fainter. Suddenly the roar of an ocean filled his ears, and his world turned to blackness. He collapsed on the floor, gasping for breath as he succumbed to unconsciousness.

****

"You must give him my body!" Jacob demanded.

"Calm yourself, and listen to what you're saying! Are you insane?" Drayton stared at his lover in shocked disbelief. "I'm not going to kill you in order to allow your clone to live."

"He's a young boy! He's a young, beautiful boy with his whole life ahead of him. I've already lived my life, Timothy. I've lived my life with no regrets, and … and I shouldn't even be here."

"Jacob, please … stop this nonsense. Take a sleeping pill and go lie down. You're … you're talking like a mad man."

"There isn't much time," Jacob insisted. "He is dying."

"Jacob, sit down and listen to me. I have this under control. Of course the clone is dying. As I told you already, it's a miracle he's lived this long. I promise you, he will not suffer. He'll go quickly."

"No!" he screamed hysterically.

Drayton threw up his arms in exasperation. "What is it about this kid? First Wainwright and now you? Why is everyone so hell-bent on saving this damn clone?" He knew instantly by the expression on Jacob's face that he'd made a terrible slip of the tongue.

"Wainwright? … Harold?"

The doctor shook his head, immediately trying to deny it.

"He's the one! He's the old man. He's the one you transferred into the boy!"

"Jacob! Listen to me."

"You're a fucking monster!" They were in the laboratory, and Jacob had been pacing back and forth. He'd stopped dead in his tracks to confront the doctor he now recognized as a mad scientist. "What have you become? What have you turned into? What gives you the right to wield such power, to play God?"

The doctor had stepped away, inching his way to another counter, where a syringe lay ready for his use. "It's not like that," he said calmly. "We needed Wainwright. We needed his money … and we needed him as a test case."

"You transferred Harold into the body of that boy, knowing all the while that eventually you'd kill him and steal the body for yourself! And now … now you expect me to just accept this? You think I'll go on and start a new life with you after you've killed him?"

"Jacob," the doctor said soothingly, "you're upset. I

understand. Really I do. It's a lot to comprehend, and you've always been so emotional."

"I loved him! You knew how much I loved him."

"Yes, indeed I did know. For all those years I tolerated your carrying a torch for that one unrequited love. That love that kept you from me—kept you from giving yourself fully to me. Kept you from trusting me and loving me the way I loved you."

"You don't love me, and you never did! You love the power. You love the control and the … the … the way I needed you so desperately!" Angry tears were streaming down his cheeks.

"And you still need me. You will always need me. As we build our new lives together, you'll need me even more. But baby, isn't this how it's supposed to be? Isn't this what you've always wanted?"

"No! Oh my God, no! Tim, please, this has got to stop. You've got to let me go … you don't own me."

The rage in the doctor's eyes was terrifying, and Jacob instinctively took a step backward, realizing that he was suddenly pressed against the counter.

"Baby," the doctor said, his voice deep and sinister, "you don't know what you're saying. It's your emotions again. It's those damned, uncontrollable emotions."

"No!" Jacob cried, just as he felt the sting of the needle. "Timothy, no!" His world turned to black.

Twenty-two

Jesse sat next to the bedside, quietly holding Phillip's hand. The boy was unconscious, his head bandaged after the brain surgery he'd just undergone. God how Jesse loved him. Memories of the previous months flooded his mind, and as the hot tears streamed down his cheeks he realized he had no regrets. For seventy-eight years he'd lived a life full of horrific regrets, but these past months had been the most meaningful of his existence.

"I know you probably can't hear me," Jesse began, "but I have to try. I have to try to make you hear. I have to tell you, in case you don't know it for sure … that I absolutely love you. I love every little thing about you.

"Phillip … oh God, my Phillip! I love that adorable smile of yours. It's mischievous, ya know. Devilish and angelic at the same time. And those big brown eyes. They had me from the start."

Jesse sighed and gently squeezed his boy's hand. "But it's not about your looks. It's your heart—the most beautiful thing about you. You're so full of love. You're the most generous, forgiving, trusting, and caring soul I've ever known.

"There's so much you could complain about. You've suffered so much—been through so many trials. You're not like that, though. You have such strength—strength I can only imagine. And all of it has been so terribly unfair. You, of all people, never deserved such pain.

"You gave me hope. You gave my life purpose. You fulfilled me!" His voice was beginning to crack.

"And now … now I have only one thing to give you in return. I love you … always."

The boy's eyes never opened. He didn't respond by

squeezing Jesse's hand, and Jesse realized sadly that his words had most likely fallen upon deaf ears. But they were necessary nonetheless. He had to say his final goodbyes.

****

Drayton looked down at the young man on the gurney, remembering the last time he'd prepared to operate on the same body. He recalled how they had administered the delithium, wiping the boy's mind of any trace of consciousness prior to transferring the wretched soul of Harold Wainwright into the youthful body.

And now, finally, it was time to rid the world once and for all of this blight upon humanity.

It would be such poetic justice. Drayton smiled to himself, imagining his satisfaction when Harold realized what had occurred. He was going to transfer Harold's consciousness from the body of Jesse Warren into the dying clone body.

Harold was going to get the agonizing death he deserved!

Drayton fantasized about how delicious it would be to see the look of horror in his eyes when he realized that the boy he loved so much was already gone. Even better, he couldn't wait to inform Harold that the body of Jesse Warren was going to host the mind of the man who did this to him. It was going to be such sweet revenge.

"It's very admirable, what you're doing," Drayton said.

Jesse looked up at and responded sincerely. "Thank you."

"Do you have any last words?"

Jesse paused momentarily. "Please … please tell Phillip— when he awakens in this body—please tell him how much I love him. Tell him not to feel any guilt. Tell him to consider it my gift to him … his second chance at life."

"Of course," Drayton said reassuringly. "Of course, I'll tell him all of that.

"Now shall we begin?" Jesse nodded soberly.

"We will at first administer the sedative. You will lose consciousness prior to the injection of delithium. It will be like falling asleep, utterly painless."

Again he nodded.

"Now close your eyes and begin counting backwards from one hundred."

"One hundred …" Jesse whispered.

"Ninety-nine …" I love you Phillip.

"Ninety-eight …" We'll be together again someday.

"Ninety-seven …" He was so sleepy, so drowsy.

"Ninety …"

The tunnel was again before him. The bright light. He stepped toward it, hearing the blips of the heart monitor in the distant background. The light grew brighter as he approached.

****

He awakened with a start. Where was he?

As he opened his eyes, it took a few moments for them to adjust to the darkness. He was home, in his bedroom. Jacob threw back the covers and shifted on the bed, dragging his legs out as he attempted to stand. He felt so woozy, and suddenly had to grab hold of the nightstand to steady himself.

Dear God, he thought. Am I too late?

The house was three miles from the laboratory, and he didn't have the strength to make it on foot. He hadn't driven in years, though. He had to try. He had to get there as soon as possible. Retrieving the spare set of keys from the rack beside the door, he headed toward the garage. Heaving the door open, he stepped into the garage, only to realize that both vehicles were gone.

He'd never make it on foot.

Panicked, he quickly looked around and saw, in the corner, his bicycle. He raced toward it. *Please don't let me be too late!* He pulled the bike out and straddled it. It wobbled as he began to pedal, but within seconds he steadied himself. Pedaling as fast as he could, he shot down the driveway and headed toward Ingenico Labratories.

Jacob hadn't ridden a bicycle in years and didn't realize what a trek a three mile jaunt could be. By the time he sprinted up the steps and swiped his identification badge through the reader, he was winded and gasping for breath.

As he raced down the hall, one thought kept racing through his mind. *I've got to save Phillip!*

As Jacob entered, the doctor was holding a syringe and poised to inject its content into the boy's IV tube. "Stop!" Jacob cried.

Startled, Drayton turned to face him. "Jacob!"

"Please, Timothy, don't do it!"

"I'm doing it for us," Drayton said. "Can't you see?"

Jacob shook his head. "Timothy, no. There is no more us."

"You don't know what you're saying," Drayton said, his expression wild and wide-eyed.

"I don't love you! I don't want to spend another single moment with you."

"Please," Timothy cried, "Please don't say that!"

"It's true. I hate you, Timothy Drayton. I hate who you've become." He took another step toward the doctor.

"No!" Drayton screamed. "You ... you don't mean it!"

"I mean every fucking word. You fucking psycho!"

In shock and rage the doctor lifted his arm above his head and rushed toward Jacob. Jacob grabbed the older man's wrist. Drayton was wielding the syringe like a weapon. As they wrestled, the stronger and younger Jacob easily overpowered the doctor. He pushed the madman backward against the wall.

Slowly Jacob guided the doctor's arm downward toward his own neck, and then with a final, powerful thrust, he jabbed the needle into his flesh. The doctor spasmed as Jacob slammed the doctor repeatedly into the wall, driving the plunger inward and injecting the delithium synopsonal into his jugular.

Drayton was dead.

Jacob gasped. Although a few sobs escaped him, he soon regained control of his emotions. He shook his head, as if to clear his mind. Timothy had accused him of being too emotional, and in this case his advice was sound. He needed to stay calm. He needed to act methodically.

Jacob made his way to the computer. He stared at it briefly, and then looked over at the boy one last time. After typing in a series of commands, he pushed his chair back.

With calm resolve Jacob opened the drawer and removed another syringe. He inserted the syringe into the bottle of medication and drew in the lethal drug. Then he walked over to the dying boy.

"Good night, sweet prince," he whispered, and leaned in to kiss his identical twin on the forehead.

Jacob pulled the curtain around the boy and made his way to the other gurney, a few feet away. He lay down as he glanced at his watch. *Sixty seconds.* He took a deep breath and uttered his last words. "For you, Phillip"; then he thrust the syringe into his own jugular.

****

When Jesse awakened he instantly realized he'd been duped. He was not dead, and Phillip had not been transferred into his body. "No!" he screamed, sobbing, as the horrible truth washed over him. "Drayton!" he cried. "What have you done?"

He looked down at his body in shock and wondered momentarily if this was part of a dream. Perhaps he really had died. Perhaps he was now ...

He jumped down from the gurney and grabbed hold of

the table beside him, steadying himself. He ripped off the oxygen tube from his face and carelessly pulled the IV from his arm. He was oblivious to the bleeding. He had to find Phillip!

As he stumbled out of the room and into the hallway, he glanced over to the room on the opposite side of the corridor. Through the glass he saw the pulled curtain, and instinctively he knew. Phillip was in there. Phillip was behind the curtain.

He had to grab hold of the door frame to keep from falling. His hospital gown was soaked with blood. Stumbling, he lurched forward, grabbing hold of the curtain and frantically ripping it apart. There before him lay his worst nightmare—truly the most horrific thing he could have imagined.

"Phillip!" he cried. His own voice startled him. His cry was primal, urgent, and laden with grief and agony. "Oh my Phillip!" he said to the lifeless body of the one he loved more than life itself. "I'm so sorry," he wept. "I'm so very sorry. It was supposed to be me! It was supposed to be me!"

He lost track of time as he remained kneeling beside Phillip, sobbing, clinging desperately to the lifeless hand of his lover. Finally his voice grew quiet, as silent tears continued to flow. "My darling," he whispered, "I love you … I love you … I love you …"

When he stood up at last, he leaned in to kiss his sweet Phillip one final time. As he pressed his lips against the still-warm lips of his departed lover, he slowly drew the sheet up and over the beautiful, peaceful face. "Goodbye," he whispered, and turned to leave.

As Jesse stepped outside the curtain, he gasped and pressed a hand against his heart. "Phillip!" he cried.

"Jesse! Oh my God, you're bleeding!" Phillip rushed toward him and embraced him. "Are you all right?"

Jesse clasped the boy tightly to his chest. "Where were you?" he cried.

"I don't know. I woke up a few moments ago and I heard crying. And … um … my neck hurts."

Jesse held his boy by the shoulders and, jaw slack with amazement, ran his eyes over the now perfect body. He stared directly into the new Phillip's big brown eyes and said, "Phillip, you're fine. You're absolutely, perfectly fine! And … let's get the hell out of here!"

Epilogue

Jesse burst through the door to find Phillip and Morgan preparing several large trays of lasagna. They were making the evening meal for the homeless shelter, and Phillip again had his apron cinched tightly around his narrow waist. Jesse frantically waved a letter over his head.

Phillip looked up and smiled. "You passed?"

"I passed the bar!" he shouted.

"He passed the bar!" Phillip repeated, turning to Morgan and beaming from ear-to-ear.

Jesse wrapped his arms around the boy, lifting him off his feet. Phillip giggled in delight.

"Oh Jesse," Morgan chimed in, "congratulations!"

It had not been an easy road for either boy. When they returned from Switzerland, Jesse had to face the reality that he was now just like every other college-aged kid—penniless. His money was gone, tucked away in a Swiss bank account under the name of Timothy Drayton.

It didn't matter, though. The money had never mattered, and most of the time he was thankful not to face the temptations and entrapments of wealth. He had everything he wanted. He had Phillip. He had a family who loved and supported him. He had a purpose in life.

With his college degree and newly-acquired law degree, Jesse was determined to make a difference in the world. He and Phillip still volunteered every weekend at the homeless shelter. They became involved in numerous causes ranging from environmental stewardship to civil rights issues.

Phillip had gotten his first job as an elementary school art teacher the previous Fall, and they moved into their own apartment around Christmas-time. They adopted a Shih tzu puppy named Barnaby, a little pistol they both loved dearly.

Jesse was never able to answer all of Phillip's questions about what had happened in Switzerland, except to say that Ingenico Laboratories had indeed delivered a miracle cure. When the doctors back home examined his body, Phillip received a clean bill of health.

Phillip marveled that he no longer had the scar on his chest, that his ear showed no sign of ever being pierced, and that he suddenly had a full head of hair; however, he was so thrilled to be healthy again that those details seemed trivial.

Jesse was not likely to ever be a billionaire, not in this lifetime. He wasn't on the fast track to rise to the top of a Fortune 500 company, and he was never going to be famous. If the couple ever made it back to Europe it would be because they'd worked hard to save up for a grand vacation. Jesse continued to drive the Ford Fusion his parents had given him, though it now had over a hundred thousand miles on it, and Phillip relied primarily upon public transportation.

Life was perfect, and Jesse wouldn't change a single thing … not for all the money in the world.

Jeff Erno became a published author in 2009 with his first novel, *Dumb Jock*. His works now include a total of eight novels. He currently lives in Michigan and writes full-time.

You can find Jeff on the Web at www.jefferno.com.